GW01605841

William Corlett started his career as an actor but more recently he has turned novelist, his fourth book being *The Dark Side of the Moon*. He also writes television drama. He was awarded the 1981 Pye Television Award for the Best Children's Television Writer.

Judy Allen, the author of five teenage novels, has also written non-fiction for children. She has had two radio plays broadcast and her first adult novel is due to be published in 1982.

Barriers is directed by Bob Hird and Tony Kysh who have both won awards for their previous productions on television.

Barriers

based on the Tyne Tees Television Series by
William Corlett
from an idea by **Margaret Bottomley**

JUDY ALLEN

Hamish Hamilton/Rainbird

First published in Great Britain simultaneously by
Hamish Hamilton Children's Books and Sphere Books Ltd. 1981
in association with
The Rainbird Publishing Group Ltd.

British Library Cataloguing in Publication Data
Corlett, William
Barriers.
I. Title II. Allen, Judy
823'.914[J] PZ7
ISBN 0-241-10718-0

Printed in Great Britain

Prologue

The Austro-Hungarian border. 1963. Night-time and a blueish grey mist hanging in the trees, blurring the road, diffusing the lights from the Border Post. On the Hungarian side a black Mercedes nosing slowly along, showing no lights. The border, and its barrier, perhaps six hundred yards ahead. Quietness. Even the car engine muffled by the mist.

Suddenly, a roar of sound and speed. The car racing for the barrier, crashing through it, splinters flying high. Border guards leaping clear, recovering, firing. Bullets smashing the rear window, one shattering the offside back tyre. The car door opening and a man's figure half-falling, half-jumping out. Rolling. The car speeding ahead. Guards pursuing. The lone man crouching into the undergrowth, unseen. The car skidding, slewing sideways on its damaged wheel, exploding into an orange flower of flame, crashing head-on into a wall. The border guards approaching. The car burning vividly against the grey night.

The hidden man, well back from the road, watching. Then, still crouching low, limping away, unnoticed.

Chapter One

Far away in both time and place, in the Borders of Scotland seventeen years later, Billy Stanyon braced himself for the pole vault. He wasn't particularly interested in sports but athletics training was part of the curriculum at Hadrian's Academy and at seventeen he was tall, long-legged, healthy—he could usually acquit himself well enough. He was one of those boys sports masters regard as 'useful second-eleven material'. He began his run, trying to ignore the distracting movements of half the rest of his class who had been set to cover the hurdling track that encircled the jump. He ran, thudded the end of the pole against the ground, rose with some grace but insufficient height, and caught the bar. As he landed on the waiting mattress, the bar dropped behind him. Even before he had time to get up he heard the sports master's sarcastic voice, 'You're supposed to go over it, Stanyon, not through it.'

'Oh very funny,' said Billy, half-laughing. He rolled off the mattress and stood up. He didn't mind that he'd missed the jump, but neither did he mind when the whistle sounded for the end of the session. The class jogged back through the afternoon sunlight to the great Gothic pile that was the school and, perhaps more urgently, to the huge basement shower-room. It was such a safe environment, this public school, that few of the boys realized just how protected they were from the rest of the world, which was kept at bay by surrounding wall and railing and two pairs of huge iron gates. A wide drive, with groups of shallow steps at intervals, stretched from the main gates to the great gravelled forecourt with its solemn founder's statue. On either side of the drive lay tended lawns and shrubbery. The rest of the grounds, which spread so far behind the school that the perimeter could not be clearly made out from the building itself, had been expertly landscaped to include not only the athletics track, rugby and cricket pitches and tennis courts, but also some magnificent single trees, an elegant avenue, a small copse, more lawns, and a semi-wild shrubbery down by the smaller iron side-gate. The outside world came in delivery vans or else, on speech days and concert days, in the gleaming cars of parents.

Billy was content and, though he knew next summer would be his last at Hadrian's, he had barely considered what life might be like afterwards. It was not that he was especially academic, any more than he was especially sporty. In fact he had been advised to try for just two A levels, English and History, and there didn't seem much hope of a university place. But he enjoyed the routine of the life, the companionship, playing the flute in the school orchestra, setting the world to rights with his study mate, Spike. As he hurried with the rest in to the splendid turreted building, which stood like a minor fortress on its gentle hill, he had no way of knowing that in the world outside something had happened which meant that for him nothing would ever be the same again. Although in terms of his life the event had been a major one, its ripples had not quite reached him. Not quite, but almost.

In the communal shower he tipped his head back, letting the water plaster his thick blond hair to his head and stream down his face and body. Odd shouts and bursts of laughter echoed against the tiles, and the sprays from the shower heads gave out a continuous background hissing sound, so that when Spike, who was already dressed, came back to call to him over the half-wall, Billy couldn't hear his words.

'What?'

'I said, The Drip wants you in his study,' shouted Spike. 'When you're ready.'

'Now what?' said Billy, without much interest.

The headmaster, who remembered most of the names of his pupils, rarely sent for them individually unless displeased about something, but he was a mild-mannered man and his displeasure was never very distressing.

Billy dried and dressed and, with his still-wet hair uncharacteristically sleek, went up the stairs and down the long wide corridor to the Head's study above the front door, a large room which had a good view of the drive from its high windows. He knocked and then, because he had been sent for, opened the door and stepped just inside.

'It's Stanyon, sir,' he said. 'You wanted to see me?'

'Come in . . . er . . . William,' said the Headmaster. He was standing beside his large desk, resting his knuckles on its edge in rather an awkward fashion, as if temporarily unsure what to do with himself. There was another man in the room with him, tall, white-haired, still in his coat, standing with his back to the room, looking out of the window. He turned as the Headmaster spoke and Billy saw that he was Mr Whitaker, senior partner in the firm of Newcastle solicitors where his own father had worked for as long as he could remember. Billy, who barely knew him, gave him a faint uncertain smile and moved towards the desk, where confrontations in this room generally took place. Whitaker did not smile back, his face was grave.

'Here's Mr Whitaker come to see you,' said the Headmaster unnecessarily, and then, to Whitaker, 'Would you like to see him alone—or would you like me to be here?'

'I don't suppose there are rules over these things,' said Whitaker unhappily, crossing the room towards Billy who stood glancing from one to the other. 'We solicitors like rules.' He stood facing the boy. 'Hallo, Billy,' he said. 'Hallo, sir' said Billy, rather uncertainly.

'Billy, I have some... bad news for you. I don't know any way of softening this kind of blow so I must simply tell you. Your parents have had a sailing accident—out from the Lizard. They ran into unexpectedly bad weather.' He shifted uncomfortably where he stood and then went on. 'The lifeboat... well... I'm sorry, Billy. They were both drowned.'

Billy stood. Quite still.

Whitaker drew a deep sigh. 'Under the terms of the will,' he said, in his quiet solicitor's voice, 'I am your legal guardian. I've come to drive you down to Newcastle. You can stay at my house. The—the funeral is tomorrow.'

The Headmaster moved up on Billy from the other side and laid a hand on his shoulder. 'I can't tell you how sorry I am, Stanyon,' he said. 'I've arranged for matron to pack a bag for you. You may leave at once.'

'Thank you,' said Billy.

Unnerved by his stillness, the Headmaster talked on. 'Mr Whitaker assures me you will be able to continue your studies here,' he said. 'So we look forward to seeing you back as soon as possible.' He made an attempt to sound bracing. 'It's early in the term—and A levels are ahead.'

'Yes sir,' said Billy.

On the drive through the quiet border country and into the noise and grime of Newcastle he was silent. Whitaker drove the twenty-year-old Rover at the steady, rather stately pace which suited the car's and his own character, and did not speak either.

'After the funeral,' said Billy at last, 'I'd like to go to the holiday cottage, at Bamburgh.'

'That can be arranged,' said Whitaker.

'We had nice times there,' said Billy, 'but it was just for weekends and things. Not—a proper home.' He glanced quickly at Whitaker's impassive profile, and added, 'It won't seem quite so empty of them as the Newcastle house.'

Whitaker negotiated a roundabout with meticulous attention, and then nodded. 'I understand,' he said. 'I'll drive us up there directly afterwards. We can stay the night.'

'Thank you,' said Billy.

His first tears did not come until the curtains of the crematorium opened and the two coffins began to move out of sight. His mother's was noticeably smaller. Coffins can look impersonal. Because of the discrepancy in sizes, these did not. Ashes to ashes. Dust to dust. In the sure and certain hope of the resurrection to eternal life. Billy stood alone in the front pew. The others, Whitaker and a few friends and business associates of his parents, saw only his back, not the tears.

Bamburgh was for holidays, retreats, escapes. On the wide flat glistening sands Billy kept his back to Whitaker, walking ahead, fists in the pockets of his windcheater, pacing beside the sea. Whitaker, who walked with a stick though he gave no impression of limping, called from behind, 'You go too fast for me.'

Billy stood, staring out at the vast sea and sky. 'Do you believe all that rubbish?' he said. 'About the resurrection to eternal life?'

Whitaker caught up and stood beside him, leaning on the stick, squinting up at the wheeling gulls. 'Awfully hard to prove,' he said. 'One way or another.'

'Will I have to sell the cottage?'

'Here in Bamburgh? Not if you want to keep it.'

'Just the Newcastle house?'

Whitaker was beginning to feel the cold. It was a grey autumn day and the steady sea breeze carried intimations of winter. 'You won't *have* to sell anything,' he said. 'But what would you want with a house and a cottage? We will have to make certain plans, young man.'

'Yes,' said Billy. The tears were welling up again. He turned away and continued to walk. The great, curved beach was immense. From his viewpoint it looked as though it would be possible to walk north by the sea forever.

'You're expected back at school at the beginning of next week,' said Whitaker behind him. 'You have A levels.' He raised his voice as the distance between them widened. 'You hear me? We will have to talk.'

Billy stood still again. 'So you don't think there's this "life after death" either, then,' he said, without looking round.

'I didn't say one way or the other,' said Whitaker. 'A long training in law has left me cautious on all matters of supposition.'

Billy moved away again. Just two paces. 'They were sailing to the Scillies,' he said. 'They'd been looking forward to it for...' He kicked viciously at the sand.

'When my wife died,' said Whitaker, 'I found it best just to... go on as normal.' Then added, more to himself than to Billy, 'Of course, I was older.'

Billy turned suddenly to face him, almost accusingly. 'I wish they'd had other children,' he said. 'That I had brothers and sisters.'

Whitaker looked at him, a slight puzzled frown on his face. Then, 'I'm going back to the cottage,' he said curtly. 'This wind is cold.'

It was just a two-up two-down fisherman's cottage, with a bathroom built on to the back where the old outside lavatory had been, and pleasant, comfortable furniture, the kind that doesn't react badly to damp clothes and sand-filled shoes. It could be made welcoming at a moment's notice with its well-stocked deep-freeze and back-yard coal bunker.

Billy lit the fire and after supper they sat by it. Whitaker had brought a bottle of whisky. He offered a glass to Billy, who shook his head, then poured himself a generous nightcap and held it up, watching the flames through the glowing amber liquid.

'I want you to sell the house and everything in it,' said Billy suddenly. 'But I don't want you to sell this cottage.'

Whitaker watched him, where he sat on the floor by the hearth. 'I see,' he said.

'I have to live somewhere,' said Billy defensively. 'During the holidays.'

Whitaker took a drink of whisky and set the glass down on the table at his elbow. 'You can't live on your own,' he said. 'You're under age.'

'But we don't know each other,' said Billy almost angrily. 'I can't just move in with you.'

Whitaker sighed. 'It's what your parents wanted.'

Billy stared into the fire. 'They didn't ask me.'

'They hardly asked me. We never thought this would happen, obviously. How old are you?'

'Eighteen,' said Billy firmly, and then, more softly, 'next May.'

'You'll be of age then. You can go where you please.'

Billy looked round at him doubtfully. 'We might not get on.'

'I don't suppose for a minute that we shall,' said Whitaker impassively. 'I don't like children. But as you have seen, my house is large. With any luck we'll hardly meet.' He swilled the whisky round and round in the glass. 'I'm sorry, Billy, I don't know you well enough to know what to say to you. I think I expected you to cry... public schools make a chap so... I shall of course deal with all the legal and practical matters. That's a function I do understand. There is a will. It's very straightforward. You are sole beneficiary...' He shifted uncomfortably in his chair. 'However, we can't discuss business here.'

'Why not?'

'I'm not on home ground.'

'Does that matter?'

'These things are easier in an office. It's less personal, with the clatter of the typewriter next door.'

'But we're both here now,' said Billy. 'If it's so straightforward, can't we get it over with?'

Whitaker rose. 'In the office,' he said firmly. 'I'm going to bed. We must start early tomorrow—fifty miles is a long journey for an old man and an old car.' He drained his glass and set it down. 'Seven o'clock start,' he said, making for the door. 'I must be in the office by nine.' He was looking very tired, Billy noticed.

At the door he turned. 'The bed will be damp,' he said crossly. He moved back into the room and picked up the whisky bottle and the glass. 'I shall take this up,' he said irritably, 'for warmth.'

Whitaker's house and his office stood side by side, two early Georgian buildings in a quiet terrace. On the opposite side of the road there was nothing but the peaceful greenery of a row of small, fenced gardens, one for each house. Outside the front door to the office a brass plate read 'Whitaker, Belton, Stanyon: Solicitors'. Outside the front door to the house a similar plate read simply 'Whitaker: Private'. Although there was a study in the house which was not at all unlike Whitaker's office on the other side of the wall, he refused to discuss anything with Billy until he had changed from his casual Bamburgh clothes into his dark suit and could face him across the office desk in the time-honoured manner of a family solicitor.

Billy sat quietly while Whitaker conducted the formal ritual of the reading of the will. The situation still seemed unreal to him. On the way up to Whitaker's first floor office he had passed the door of his father's office and for one brief second had considered opening it to say hallo. The instant realization that the room would be empty, which came before he had even reached out his hand, hit him with as much force as had Whitaker's words when the news had first been broken.

Whitaker finished reading and passed the document across the desk. 'You want to read it?' he asked.

Billy shook his head. It had been, as Whitaker had said, perfectly straightforward and he didn't want to see his parents' signatures. He began to get up. 'That's it then,' he said flatly.

'Not quite,' said Whitaker, who was looking uneasy again, rather as he had when refusing to discuss business in the cottage at Bamburgh. 'As principal executor,' he said, 'I have other duties to perform.' He took his glasses off, laid them on top of the will, and picked up an envelope beside it. 'They are laid out in this letter.' He held the letter but didn't look at it. The envelope had already been opened.

'I am requested to inform you,' said Whitaker, 'of something that frankly I thought you knew. Something you should have been told years ago. Alan and Marian Stanyon were... they were your adopted parents, Billy.'

Billy sat quite still and stared at him, his blue eyes very large. For a moment he looked much younger than his age.

Whitaker paused and then, getting no immediate response, hurried on. 'You came to them when you were a year old, I believe. Obviously this makes no difference whatsoever to anything that has happened. I personally was under the impression that they had told you. That is always considered the best course in these matters. In this letter, they inform me otherwise. They ask me to tell you and then—to hand you this letter.' He picked up a second envelope, sealed, from the desk in front of him and, leaning forward, placed it in front of Billy.

On the front of the envelope Billy saw his own name, in his mother's handwriting. He stared at it blankly.

'I'm sure they did what they did for the best,' Whitaker was saying.

Billy sat as he had sat throughout, upright on his chair, hands clasped between his knees. He made no move towards the envelope. In a way, he wished he hadn't recognized the writing. 'You read it, Mr Whitaker,' he said.

'No, Billy,' said Whitaker. 'It's a personal letter to you.'

Billy gripped his hands more tightly together. 'You read it to me,' he said.

Whitaker sighed, but he put his glasses on again, slit the envelope with his paperknife and took out a single sheet of paper. 'It's dated 8 May, 1970,' he said. 'The same date as the letter to me.' He looked over the top of his glasses. 'You're sure you want me to read it.'

Billy nodded.

Whitaker cleared his throat. 'My darling Billy,' he read. 'Today is your seventh birthday and since you went to bed your father and I have been talking so much about you. Of our hopes for you, our plans. One day we will tell you about how we came to get you, but not yet. Is it selfish not to want to lose you?' Abruptly Whitaker refolded the sheet and pushed it back into its envelope. 'This is a private letter,' he said. 'You're old enough to read it yourself.' He reached down beside his desk and picked up a black leather music case. He stood up and put it on the desk in front of Billy. 'I am also instructed to give you this,' he said. From his pocket he took a neatly labelled key and set it on top of the case. 'I have no idea what is inside,' he said. 'It has been in my custody since the will and the letter were lodged, ten years ago.'

Billy stood up. Slowly he took the key and put it in his pocket, then picked up the case by the handle. 'Thank you,' he said. 'Thank you, Mr Whitaker. It can't have been easy for you.'

'Oh, public school manners again,' said Whitaker, embarrassed. 'I'm sorry, Billy. It came as a complete surprise to me. I always assumed they had told you. Alan was a most meticulous man.'

'I think I'll go out for a little,' said Billy. 'I think I'll just... be on my own, you know?'

'Of course,' said Whitaker. 'I usually have a light lunch in the house at one. Don't be late.'

Billy nodded. Then he went out of the room, carrying the case, closing the door quietly behind him. Whitaker heard his steps going down the stairs, past Alan Stanyon's office, and out into the street. As the street door closed some of his formal, solicitor's manner left him. He stood up and hurried across to his own door calling, 'Pricey, Pricey.' He opened the door. In her adjoining office his secretary, Miss Price, was rising from her desk, gathering up a file. She had worked for Whitaker for just over thirty years and although she was nearly sixty, and Whitaker himself nearly seventy, neither of them had begun to contemplate retirement. Working together had become a way of life; neither approved of change.

'How did it go?' said Miss Price, walking into his office in her neat cardigan, her neat skirt.

'I don't know how it went. The young are a different breed. Oh, confound it! I could do with a whisky.'

'Well you're not getting one,' said Miss Price, unperturbed. She crossed his room to put the file on his desk. 'Mr Belton wanted you to go through this, you remember?'

Whitaker stood rather forlornly in the middle of his room. 'Can't I have a whisky?' he said. 'Just a little one?'

'You have a whisky at 12.30,' said Miss Price.

'I hope he's all right.'

'They're very tough, the young,' said Miss Price. 'They can take all manner of blows.' She turned abruptly and made for the door. 'Poor Mr Stanyon,' she said quietly, her back to Whitaker, 'We're going to miss him.'

'I thought he'd been told, do you see,' said Whitaker, rather desperately.

'He'll be all right,' said Miss Price more gently. 'He just needs—time—to adjust. We all adjust to circumstances. Eventually.'

Chapter Two

Lunchtime arrived, but Billy did not. Unsettled and irritable, Whitaker drank his soup alone; ate a sliver of cheese; sliced up an apple, ate one piece then pushed the rest around the plate. He had set the lunch table for two for the first time since his wife had died. He very rarely entertained guests for weekday lunches and seldom at any other time. Usually, he returned to the office promptly at two. Today, though he had looked at his watch several times, he sat where he was, watching the peeled apple slices turning brown and listening for the front door.

When the door did open it was not Billy who came through it but Miss Price, who had held a key to the house for almost as long as she had held a key to the office. 'It's only me,' she said, coming into the dining-room. 'I wondered where you'd got to.'

'It's 2.30,' said Whitaker. 'He should have been here long ago. I told him luncheon at one.'

Miss Price shrugged. 'The young don't live by the clock,' she said.

'They do in my house,' said Whitaker.

'If he comes back and you're not here, he can find you in the office, you know,' said Miss Price mildly. 'It is only next door.'

'He's gone back to Bamburgh,' said Whitaker, crunching his napkin in his hand and banging it onto the table beside his plate.

'How do you know?'

'I shall pack a bag and drive up there,' said Whitaker, pushing back his chair and standing up. 'I'm not doing that journey three times in one day. We must stay the night. Again.'

'But you can't be sure he's at Bamburgh,' said Miss Price. 'And Mr Belton needs to talk to you this afternoon about the Johnson land deal.'

'Go back to the office, Pricey,' said Whitaker. 'I'll be in tomorrow, at the usual time.'

The Bamburgh sky was greyer than before, the wind colder. The clouds that scudded in from the east were grey and fat. The sea, which only the day before had been calm and wide, was broken into angry waves which seemed to bring the horizon nearer. Billy walked slowly along the sands and over the occasional low, flat, blackly-wet rocks, his hands in the pockets of his coat, the ends of his scarf pulled by sudden gusts. A mixture of chill wind, sea spray and tears had left his face blotched, his nose red.

From Whitaker's office he had gone straight to his parents' house in Newcastle. He wasn't sure why. He still had his key and the moment he had let himself in he had known that he'd made a mistake. He hadn't known where in the house to go — into the kitchen where his mother wasn't, into the study where his father wasn't, into the empty living-room. They had left the house tidy when they set out for their two-week holiday. It looked neat and expectant, waiting to welcome them back. Billy had hurried out, locked it and left it to its waiting. He'd hitched a ride with a truck bound for Berwick, then in a private car that was bound for Bamburgh itself. Both drivers had found him a silent passenger.

He had lit the cottage fire, then opened the black leather music case and taken out the strange mixture of things he found inside. The main thing was the flute for which the case had been made — a good flute, better than his own. But someone had chosen to use the case as a kind of reliquary, and packed in around the flute were a neat packet of letters, three photographs, a silver locket, a fir-cone, a pebble and a small glass owl. He had stared for a long time at one of the photographs, of a young man and a girl, a pretty girl with long fair hair. He had a flower in his buttonhole, she carried a posy and looked up at him, smiling. Though they were not in conventional wedding clothes, it somehow had the look of a wedding photograph. His parents. Personal mementoes of two people he did not know — though they were his parents, his real mother and father.

Now he walked by the unfriendly sea, while the hidden sun crossed the sky and the grey light began to fail; a small figure on the vast empty beach.

Perhaps because the beach was so totally empty, he sensed that someone was approaching from the dunes behind him long before he heard the crunch of shoes on sand.

'Hallo, Mr Whitaker,' he said, without looking round.

Whitaker stood beside him, at the head of a long line of footprints which stretched back to the dunes and the road. They stood in silence for a moment, looking out across the sea. Then Whitaker tapped angrily with his walking stick on the surface of the sand, which glistened in the light filtering through clouds low down in the sky. 'My car does twenty-five miles to the gallon,' he said. 'I have today driven a hundred miles. The price of petrol is at a premium. It will of course feature in your account.'

Billy stood still, the wind whipping at his hair and making his eyes water. 'I wanted to be alone,' he said.

'Did it occur to you,' said Whitaker more gently, 'that I might be worried?'

'I don't know who I am,' said Billy, quite quietly. The wind took the words.

'What?' said Whitaker.

'I don't know who I am,' said Billy, almost shouting.

'Do any of us?' said Whitaker.

'Why did they tell me?' said Billy. 'Why? I don't know who I am any more. I was William Stanyon. I was in the sixth at Hadrian's Academy. I went there because Alan Stanyon went there. Like father like...son.' He spoke the words with exaggerated clarity. 'I—don't—know—who—I—am.'

'You're you,' said Whitaker.

'*Who?* When I knocked on the Head's door I said "It's Stanyon, Sir". But it wasn't, was it? It was someone without a name.'

'If it's the name that matters,' said Whitaker, 'Yours *is* Stanyon. You were legally adopted.' He took a letter from his pocket and held it towards Billy. 'You forgot the letter from your mother—your adopted mother. Be a man, Billy.'

Billy snatched the letter from his hand, tore it into pieces and cast the pieces into the sea. A wave broke over them and drew them out of reach. 'I don't know who I am,' he said desperately.

Whitaker reached out to put a hand on his shoulder. 'None of us do, Billy,' he said. 'None of us. I think you have a start over most of us. At least you realize.'

'I'm no one,' said Billy softly.

'You're you, Billy,' said Whitaker, 'and you will be what you make of yourself. Yes, you're alone. But so am I.' He closed the top of his coat against the wind from the sea. 'It's not a bad condition.'

Billy turned sharply and faced him for the first time. 'I'm going to find them,' he said.

'Them?'

'My parents. But not my mother and father...they were the ones who looked after me all these years. *They're* my mother and father. I'm going to find my parents.' He looked at Whitaker and saw him clearly for the first time, hunched in his coat, leaning on his stick, the trilby pressed down over his white hair, his face pinched in the east wind. 'You're cold,' he said. 'Come back to the cottage. I've lit the fire.'

Whitaker nodded with some relief. 'I know,' he said. 'I went inside to leave my case.' They turned and followed his tracks back up to the road. 'I shouldn't have torn the letter,' said Billy. 'Ah well,' said Whitaker. 'It's done now.'

In the cottage the fire was burning well. 'Did you bring your whisky with you?' said Billy as they took off their coats.

'I did. I shall have to consider leaving a bottle here if these emergency visits are to become a habit.'

'I'm sorry,'' said Billy.

Whitaker opened his small case, took out the bottle, glanced at his watch and nodded approvingly. 'Opening time,' he said quietly, and carried the bottle into the kitchen to find a glass. 'It's just that I would have appreciated your letting me know,' he said. 'I am responsible for you.'

'I've unpacked the music case,' said Billy rather shyly, following him. 'Would you like to see?'

The case and its contents were still spread out on the kitchen breakfast bar, where he had left them. Whitaker poured his whisky and sat down on one of the stools. Billy pulled up the other and they stared at the strange little collection.

'I've been through them so many times,' said Billy. 'But I don't really understand. Why a flute? It's so odd. I mean, that's my instrument.'

'Why did you choose the flute?' said Whitaker.

'I don't remember. I think... yes, I think I wanted to learn an instrument, and Mother suggested the flute.'

'Well,' said Whitaker, 'she would have known the contents of this. They had the key.'

'When did they give you the music case?'

'When your father made his will. They asked me to look after it until you were eighteen.'

'And then?'

Whitaker shrugged. 'They didn't say. I suppose they intended to tell you at eighteen that you were adopted—and to give you the case.'

'I can't understand why they didn't tell me years ago and let me grow up with the knowledge,' said Billy, rearranging the collection of mementoes on the bar top, almost as if he felt they might fall into a pattern he would be able to understand. 'It was bound to be a shock, wasn't it?'

'Of course,' said Whitaker. 'But does it really make so much difference.'

'I don't know,' said Billy. 'It's new at the moment—I haven't got used to it yet.'

'What's the piece of glass?'

Billy picked it up and handed it to him. Whitaker held it up to the light, a small owl in transparent glass with a blueish sheen to it. 'Nice little thing,' he said. 'And the locket?'

'Just a silver locket—with some hair in it.'

'The letters?'

'I started to read them...' said Billy. 'I think they're from my father—my real father—to my mother. They're mostly in English, then sometimes they go off into a foreign language. I may—read them properly later.' He passed an envelope to Whitaker. 'They're addressed to Mrs J. Toth.'

Whitaker put on his glasses and peered at the address. 'London NI,' he said. 'That's the City—or Islington.'

'There's another address, too, on the back of one of the envelopes,' said Billy. 'An Elsa Gruber, I think. In Munich.'

Whitaker returned the envelope and Billy put it back in the case. 'I don't want to look any more,' he said. He began to pick up the other things and pack them carefully around the flute. 'It all seems somehow private. Like a time capsule.'

'May I see the photographs?' said Whitaker. Billy handed them to him and tucked the letters and the little owl down the side of the music case.

Whitaker shuffled through the three photographs, looking at the wedding snap, at a shot of the man on his own, and then recoiling with exaggerated horror from the last picture. 'Oh!' he said. 'A revolting baby! Why is it taken for granted that all the world loves a baby? I never did. Thank God, neither did my wife. Noisy... smelly...' He shook his head.

Billy watched him with a slight smile. 'There's writing on the back of that one,' he said.

Whitaker turned the picture over. 'Billy!' he said. 'You see? You were always Billy.'

'Do you think I could find out about them?'

'You have things to go on,' said Whitaker. 'It shouldn't be too difficult. What's that postcard?'

Billy passed it to him.

'Budapest!' said Whitaker. 'I suppose that name is Hungarian—the language in the letters is probably Hungarian, too. They may be dead, of course.'

'But at least I'd know,' said Billy.

'Know what?'

'Who I am.'

'Would you?' said Whitaker. 'Are you so very different from the person you were this morning?' He took a drink of whisky. 'All right,' he said. 'I'll make a few enquiries for you. But I warn you... I'm not cheap.'

Billy nodded. 'Thank you, Mr Whitaker,' he said.

'If you're going to share my house,' said Whitaker, 'You'd better call me Vincent. It's a terrible name... but after seventy years I've grown more or less accustomed to it.' He passed the postcard and snapshots across to Billy, then took the baby picture back for a moment and gazed on it with a kind of fascination. 'Aren't babies hideous!' he said. He reached over and dropped the picture into the flute case with the rest and looked at Billy with an unexpectedly good-humoured smile. 'Thank God you grew up!' he said.

Chapter Three

Back at school, Billy found it easier to cope with his loss in an environment where his parents had never figured anyway, and to get over the horror of sorting through the contents of the family house preparatory to Whitaker selling it for him. 'It was so strange,' he said to Spike. 'I kept coming on mementoes—of me. Things I never knew they kept. Photos, school reports, my old letters home... We threw most of it away. Someone's bought the house already, apparently.'

'How do you feel about that?' said Spike.

Billy shrugged. 'I suppose I'm glad it's not—waiting—anymore,' he said. 'Let's talk about something else.'

But the Christmas holidays approached at a relentless pace. Spike offered an invitation and Billy almost accepted it, but Newcastle, and Whitaker, were his only real links with the life he was used to and it seemed somehow inevitable that that was where he should go.

It wasn't until the school bus dumped him at Carlisle station, early on a Saturday morning at the end of term, that he thought of going to London. It had partly to do with his dread of going home for Christmas for the first time knowing that his mother and father would not be there, partly to do with the Islington address on the letters in the music case, and partly to do with the fact that the London train was announced just before the Newcastle one.

There was no time to think. There was just time to buy a ticket, change platforms and get on the fast train before it pulled out. It was only just after 9.00. Whitaker would not be expecting him until lunchtime. He had a vague idea that he could be down and back before he was missed.

But even the high-speed train took four hours to cover the distance, and it was already lunchtime when it drew into Euston. Billy left his case in a locker and, unsure of direction and feeling short of time, joined the taxi queue.

'You don't want to go there,' said the driver, when Billy told him the address. 'That street's derelict.' Billy got into the cab and slammed the door. 'Don't say I didn't warn you, then,' said the driver. The journey was shorter than Billy had expected. The taxi stopped with a lurch and the driver hung out of his window, reached back and opened the door. 'Told you, didn't I?' he said.

Billy climbed out of the cab. The street was indeed derelict. Every house in the facing terraces had long since been abandoned by its occupants. Some had boarded-up windows, some had their front doors blocked by sheets of corrugated iron, curled and rusting at the edges, most had aggressive graffiti aerosoled onto their brickwork. The street was dead, and waiting for bulldozers to grind up its bones.

Billy handed the driver the sum on the clock plus a couple of extra coins. The driver took the money but didn't immediately pull away. 'Is that enough?' said Billy uncertainly. 'What you want this street for anyway?' said the driver. 'You don't look the squatter type.'

Billy turned away and began to walk down the broken pavement, looking for the number on the letters. 'My mother used to live here,' he said absently. 'I wanted to see...'

The cab kept pace with him. 'Well now you've seen...' said the driver, hoping for the fare back to the station. But Billy ignored him.

'Put up a little blue plate on the wall, will they?' sneered the driver. ' "My Mum lived here." Kids today...oh dear, oh dear!' He put his foot down and the cab droned away, leaving the street empty, but for Billy.

He reached the house, number 29. The downstairs front windows were boarded up but not the door. He put out his hand and pushed it gently. It swung inwards. It had dropped a little on its hinges and it scraped sadly on the hall floor. He walked inside, treading warily on the rotting boards.

The blocked windows made the lower rooms dark, but light filtered down the narrow staircase. Billy climbed it slowly, past faded peeling wallpaper that revealed yet more faded peeling paper behind it. He went into the empty front room at the top, crossing bare dusty boards to look out of the grimy window on to the street.

The room smelt musty and slightly damp. For all he knew, this was the room in which she had read the letters. But it had nothing to tell him now.

Feeling suddenly extremely tired, he sat down in the corner of the room, leaning against the wall and pulling his winter coat around him like a derelict. He took one of the letters out of his pocket and read it, for about the tenth time. 'My dearest Tania,' it said, 'I am very well. Don't worry. I am thinking of you all the time. I write to you in English because that is our language now. We do not belong here any more, I know that. It is cold, and I see no one I know. Kurt is going back into Austria and will post this for me. I have seen Papa. He is not well, as you knew, but he will be all right. We will be with you soon, my dearest love. Soon. I love you so. Jerri.' He folded the letter, returned it to its envelope and then to his pocket, and sat still, staring at nothing.

A siren sounded, suddenly and painfully, making him jump. He stood up and looked out of the window. A police car, blue light flashing, roared through the silence of the street and out of sight, its siren fading into the distance. Billy looked at his watch—two o'clock. He would have been missed by now. He got up and clattered down the stairs. He decided to head straight back the way the taxi had come, find the station and telephone Whitaker before getting on the first train possible.

As he left the house, pulling the door shut behind him, he saw a strange little group turn in at the end of the street and hurry towards him—a West Indian boy of about his own age supported on one side by a white boy and on the other by a slightly older white man with a woolly hat jammed onto his head. Behind them followed a girl, obviously frightened, who kept looking over her shoulder. As they drew nearer Billy saw that the West Indian boy had blood on his head and all over the top of his white rollneck sweater. The police siren sounded in the distance. The man in the woolly hat let go of the boy's arm and went to try the door of one of the abandoned houses. It wouldn't open. 'They've got us!' he said. 'Nowhere to go.'

The girl ran up to Billy. She was almost crying. 'Help us,' she said, 'please. He's hurt.'

Billy hesitated for a moment. Then, 'Come on, back here,' he said. He ran back to number 29, leading them to one door he knew would open. They all piled inside and got the door shut just as the police car turned into the street. They heard it stop and the doors slam, one after the other, as the two policemen got out.

The West Indian boy was leaning slightly forwards in the dim hall, holding his side. His teeth seemed to be clenched and beads of sweat stood out on his forehead. 'He needs a doctor,' said Billy, reaching out automatically to open the door again, to ask the police for help.

In a second the man in the woolly hat was between him and the door. 'Cool it,' he said. 'Give us a few minutes.'

'Please,' said the girl, catching at Billy's arm. 'Please!' Her eyes swam with tears.

'OK,' said Billy doubtfully. 'Come upstairs then. It's—better up there.'

The man in the woolly hat ran up ahead and placed himself at the side of the window, where he could watch the street without being seen. The boy and girl half supported and half carried the West Indian boy up the narrow stairs and into the front room where they lowered him carefully so that he sat on the floor, leaning against the wall. Billy followed uneasily.

'Have they gone?' said the girl fearfully, looking towards the figure at the window.

'Going.'

Outside, one car door slammed, then the next. The engine started, then the siren, and both sounds drew away down the road and into the distance.

'Phew, that was close,' said the man at the window, pulling his woolly hat further down on his head and arching his neck nervously. He turned away from the window, 'I'm Dave, by the way.'

'I'm Sam,' said the white boy, 'and she's Mags.'

They all looked at Billy who automatically introduced himself although the social niceties seemed extraordinarily out of place in the desolate room with its nervous occupants.

Suddenly Mags covered her face with her hands. 'We've got to get away,' she said. Sam crossed to her and put his arm round her. 'It's all right now,' he said. 'It's all over.'

Dave thrust his fists into the pockets of his short combat jacket and moved away from the window in a grotesque little dance, laughing gleefully, 'What a punch up!' he said.

The West Indian boy eyed him from his huddled position on the floor.

'You're trouble,' he said, quite quietly.

'What happened?' said Billy, looking from one to the other.

'This guy just set on him,' said Sam, pointing to the West Indian. 'I don't even know your name...'

'I'm Peter.'

'He just—set on him,' said Sam, almost wonderingly.

'Who did? Where?'

'It was the police. Plain clothes fuzz,' said Dave, bristling with righteous indignation. He was quite different from the others, Billy saw. They were all about his own age, in their Saturday best, frightened and shaken. Dave was several years older, somehow dressed for action in his aggressive little combat jacket and woolly hat, his narrow face bright-eyed and eager as a ferret's. Despite his apparent indignation he, alone, was enjoying himself.

'You don't know it was the police,' said Sam angrily.

'Oh, just stop,' said Mags. She turned to Billy. 'Weren't you on the march?' He shook his head. 'It was a carol festival,' she said. 'We were walking from St Paul's to Parliament Hill. It was anti-apartheid.'

Dave cut in, 'Only not everyone *is* anti-apartheid,' he said.

'We were going to sing carols on Parliament Hill,' said Mags quietly, as if he hadn't interrupted.

'So why did any one attack...'

'They didn't like the colour of my skin, man,' said Peter. 'But honestly, I tried washing...' The blood on his head and sweater had dried but his face was strained and he still held his side.

'But the police would have helped,' said Billy.

Dave snorted contemptuously, walked right up to Billy and peered into his face. 'Where you been hiding, little rich boy?' he said.

Peter looked at Dave. 'I tell you,' he said. 'You're trouble.' He began to cough painfully and Mags went to crouch at his side, wanting to help but not knowing what to do.

'You don't know a friend when you see one,' said Dave.

'All right "Friend",' said Billy, his anger rising. 'Get him a doctor if you're his friend.' He looked down at Peter. 'I'm going for an ambulance,' he said, and started for the door.

Behind him he heard Peter say, on a moan, 'Someone stop him,' and the next second he felt hands on his shoulders and found himself swung round and pinned to the wall by Dave.

'Get your hands off me,' said Billy, hitting Dave's arms away.

'All right,' said Dave in his nasal sneer. 'But before you go breezing off on your white charger, there's something you should know. The bastard who did that to our black friend here is in a pretty bad state himself.'

Billy looked across to Peter. 'I think I killed him, man,' said the West Indian boy, in a whisper.

There was a great stillness in the room. Then, 'I'm going,' said Billy. But Dave nipped round him like a terrier, and blocked the door. 'Not yet,' he said. 'Not till we know what we do next.'

Billy paused. He was bigger than Dave and could probably get past him. On the other hand Dave had proved surprisingly strong and determined, and Sam might join him. 'Why did you come here?' said Sam, as Billy looked across at him.

'I wanted to see it.'

Sam looked round the empty room and spread his hands, half-laughing. 'Why?' he said.

'My mother lived here, before I was born.'

'Isn't that sweet,' said Dave.

Billy gave him a look of such intensity that Sam intervened hurriedly, 'And your Dad?' he said, politely, sociably, cooling things down.

'I don't know,' said Billy grimly. 'I didn't know them.'

'Didn't know your parents,' said Mags, wide-eyed, still on her knees beside Peter.

'I was adopted.'

'My Dad will be so scared,' said Peter. 'Why did I let it happen?'

'Politics,' said Dave, moving over towards him, fixing him with his little bright eyes. 'Our only weapon.'

Peter met his look. 'I don't know who you are,' he said. 'But get off my back, man. Politics! It was people...'

'People *are* politics,' said Dave.

'Yeah, yeah, and all that jazz,' said Peter. 'I lost my temper with him, that's all.'

'You were provoked,' said Dave.

'Just people...' said Peter. 'I lost my temper.' He shifted his position and gave a small involuntary cry of pain.

'Where does it hurt?' said Billy.

'They... he kicked me in the ribs,' said Peter.

'More than one?'

'People like that don't function alone,' said Dave with satisfaction.

Billy rounded on him. 'Will you keep out of it,' he shouted.

'Making you feel good, is it?' said Dave. 'Helping the black man.'

'Go away,' said Mags. 'We don't need you.' She appealed to Sam with a look. 'Yes, go,' said Sam, 'You're not helping.'

Dave gave an exaggerated shrug. 'OK,' he said, 'OK.' He pointed at the slumped figure on the floor. 'But I'm his friend,' he said.

'Thanks a million!' said Peter bitterly.

All Dave's nervous energy seemed to coagulate into a gobbet of rage which he flung at Peter. 'Why were you marching anyway!' he said. 'With your colour! Why? If you weren't provoking?'

Peter spread out his hands in a gesture of mock despair. 'I like singing,' he said mildly.

'And dancing?'

Well—you're on your own, then.' He thrust his fists back into his jacket pockets, looked around the room as if he'd just seen them all for the first time and thoroughly despised them, and hurried out. Mags got up and crossed to the window. She leaned her head wearily on the frame and began to sing in a soft, child's voice 'Oh little town of Bethlehem...' Outside, Dave gave a clenched fist salute to the whole house, then ran off down the road.

His departure lifted a weight off the group. 'Look, we must do something,' said Billy. 'This is ridiculous. He must have medical help.'

'We'll go,' said Sam, reaching out his hand to Mags.'We'll phone an ambulance. You stay with him.' This time Peter made no protest. The fear of what had happened inside his rib cage was overcoming any other fear.

'I'm meant to be in Newcastle,' said Billy, a feeling of

frustration rising in him as he realized this wasn't over yet. 'I should at least make a phone call. Can't you go and she stay?'

'I don't know the area,' said Sam. 'I'm not going alone,' said Mags. They reminded Billy briefly of an illustration he had once seen of the Babes in the Wood, clinging together in an alien world. 'Go on, then,' he said. 'But hurry.'

Mags ran over to Peter, knelt and kissed him on the cheek. 'Be all right, yes?' she said. 'Yeah, yeah,' said Peter.

Mags and Sam scurried out. Early winter dusk was advancing outside. The room was already in deep shadow. For a moment there was silence. Peter broke it. 'Last we'll see of them,' he said.

Billy looked at him, startled. 'They'll get help,' he said.

'You go, man, if you have to,' said Peter.

Billy shook his head. 'I can't,' he said. He went over and sat on the floor beside the other boy.

'Who's waiting for you?' said Peter.

'Mr Whitaker. My guardian.'

Peter half-laughed. 'Not been doing too good a job, today, has he?'

'Is the pain bad?' said Billy.

'It's not good. Talk to me, will you? Take my mind off it?'

'Yes of course,' said Billy, all possible topics of conversation instantly leaving his head. 'What about?'

'Anything. Why you're here. Anything.'

Crouched on the floor in the darkening dusty room Billy told his story; the sailing accident, the music case, the odd little collection of clues to his own past. Peter listened—at first just as a way of passing time until help arrived, then with some interest.

'I must find them,' said Billy at last. 'I want to ask them why they got rid of me.'

'Hey, man!' said Peter. 'Maybe they just had to. Maybe they're dead. Maybe they couldn't keep you. You had nice people to look after you—what more're you asking?'

'I don't know where I belong,' said Billy.

'Join the club,' said the West Indian boy in his East London accent.

Billy looked at him and saw a sympathetic face. 'I don't know who I am, you see,' he said.

'You're you,' said Peter, 'like I'm me.'

'But I don't know who that is.'

'It's just you. Whether you like it or not. I think I killed that man. What's that make me? A murderer? I wasn't a murderer this morning.'

'You were protecting yourself,' said Billy.

Peter lolled his head back against the wall. 'That makes it all right?' he said. 'I'll tell his old woman—I was protecting myself, missus. That's why he's dead.' The tears began to come. 'I hated him,' he said desperately. 'I didn't even know his name and I hated him.' He began to shiver. 'I don't now,' he said. 'I just want to go home.'

'Me too,' said Billy softly.

Peter tried to laugh. 'Oh hell, we *are* a miserable pair,' he said. The sound of a siren grew from the distance and began to echo down the street. 'The boys in blue,' said Peter.

'The ambulance,' said Billy. He jumped up and crossed to the window. The blue light was already flickering across the darkened room. He looked out. 'Police,' he said flatly.

'They shopped me,' said Peter.

Billy turned to him as footsteps sounded on the stairs. 'I can't hide you,' he said.

Peter shook his head. 'Will you telephone my Dad, if I give you the number...?'

'Yes,' said Billy. 'Yes of course.'

By the time he was once more on a train, this time travelling north, Billy felt as though at least a week had passed, rather than only one day. The police had called an ambulance for Peter and then questioned Billy himself for a while before they were sufficiently satisfied to let him go. He had walked back to the station and, since he didn't know the area, not by the quickest route. There he had telephoned Whitaker, who had been curt and unforthcoming, saying only that if Billy arrived home late he should expect to find that he had gone to bed. He had telephoned Peter's father and found himself trying to give just enough detail but not too much to a frightened stranger. Finally he had discovered that he couldn't get a train back to Newcastle from Euston, so he had had to collect his luggage and walk down the road to King's Cross. He slept most of the way to Newcastle Central, and then let himself into the darkened house, where only the hall light burned, as quietly as he could.

Next morning Whitaker listened to his story in a grim silence, staring out of the study window towards the church, hidden behind the gardens, whose bells were ringing out for Sunday service.

'Now I'll tell you what happened here,' he said icily, when Billy had finished. 'When you weren't home by lunchtime I telephoned the school to be told you had left first thing in the morning. Eventually I went to the police station, to report you missing. Miss Price arranged for a neighbour to get tea for her old mother so that she could stay on here, in case of news. The police called in twice to see if we had heard anything. You caused a great deal of trouble to a number of people.'

Billy scowled into the study fire. 'Well, what would you have done?' he said. 'Just left him.'

'It was totally irresponsible to go down to London without letting me know.'

'I've already said I'm sorry. I thought I'd be back in time.'

'I do not like involving the police,' said Whitaker. 'I am Vincent Whitaker, one of the most respected solicitors in the entire north-east. I cannot have a delinquent living here.'

'Is that all you're worried about?' said Billy. 'Your precious reputation!'

Whitaker turned from the window to face him, really angry now. 'How dare you!' he said. 'I was worried about you. Did that occur to you? I was worried about where you were, about what might have happened to you . . .'

'I'm sorry,' said Billy, meaning it for the first time. 'But I couldn't leave him. Honestly I couldn't.'

'Confound those bells!'' said Whitaker.

'Don't take it out on the bells,' said Billy. 'What will happen to him if he did kill that man?'

'Children who play with fire must learn that they can get burned. Was your journey worth it?'

'If you mean did I find out anything about my parents—no.'

'A waste of money, then,' said Whitaker. 'The law will deal with your friend.'

'But the law,' said Billy, 'will never understand Peter's feelings.'

'Feelings are too personal. The law deals with facts.'

'If we were all judged on facts,' said Billy 'there wouldn't be any love.'

Whitaker crossed the room and stood at the other side of the fireplace, following Billy's gaze into the burning coals. 'That's a very long word for a very young man,' he said at last. Then, 'Of course you were right to stay with him. I know a good chap in Gray's Inn who might be able to help.'

Billy looked quickly at him. 'He hasn't got money,' he said.

'No? Well, there are ways round that,' said Whitaker. He sat down in his fireside chair and looked across at Billy. 'I was worried, do you see?' he said, almost apologetically. 'I haven't had anyone to worry about for . . . centuries.'

'I really am sorry,' said Billy. 'It was thoughtless . . . but . . . you see . . .' He sat down on the arm of the chair opposite. 'This is the first time I've been home and they're not here.' He looked down at his hands. 'I hope I'm not going to be a drag about it,' he said.

Whitaker drummed his fingers lightly on the arm of his chair. 'I had planned to greet you with interesting news rather than a wigging,' he said, after a pause. 'I've written to a friend of mine in Munich—Gunter Walser. You'd like him—he used to be what was called a hippy! I asked him about that name, Gruber, in the letters.'

'I wrote to that address twice during the term,' said Billy. 'I never had an answer.'

Whitaker shook his head. 'It appears they've moved,' he said. 'But Gunter seems to think he may be able to trace them. He's a journalist by profession. I've made plans for us to go out there and visit him, see what he's turned up. Just for a weekend—during your spring term.'

'Why must we wait so long?' said Billy, cheering up. 'Why not go now?'

'The Christmas holidays are short,' said Whitaker, 'and a bad time to travel. And if you work as hard for your A levels as you should, a few weeks of next term will pass quickly enough.'

'Do you get over grief?' said Billy suddenly. 'I knew them all my life. I may have been adopted but they were my mother . . . and my father . . .' He stared down at the pattern on the carpet.

'I thought we might spend Christmas at Bamburgh,' said Whitaker evenly, 'if you will invite me to stay in your cottage, Billy?'

Billy smiled across at him. 'I'd like that,' he said shyly.

'Good,' said Whitaker. 'Good. Thank you.' He got up. 'Whisky?'

'I'm under age,' said Billy reprovingly.

'Ah,' sighed Whitaker, pouring one for himself. 'Such delights you have in store.' And still the Sunday bells rang out, peal upon peal.

Chapter Four

On the appointed weekend in early spring, Billy and Whitaker flew Lufthansa to Munich, where a tall good-looking man of about thirty emerged from the anonymous crowd in the reception area of the airport and planted himself in front of them, beaming. 'Vincent!' he said.

'I beg your pardon,' said Whitaker blankly.

The man's smile extended into a laugh. 'Vincent!' he said again. 'It is me—Gunter.'

Whitaker gazed at him wonderingly. 'Good Lord, what happened to you?' he said at last, his eyes travelling from the short haircut to the closely shaven jaw and the smart, though casual, clothes.

'I grew older,' said Gunter apologetically.

'No, much more than that,' said Whitaker. 'You grew respectable. Shame on you!'

Gunter grasped him by the shoulders and attempted to kiss him on the cheek, but Whitaker reared back in alarm and shook himself free. 'For heavens sake, Herr Walser,' he said. 'You're no longer a Flower Child.'

'Well, *you* haven't changed,' said Gunter with delight.

'That's all you know,' said Whitaker. 'I've actually become a good deal older—due mainly to this one. Come along Billy.'

Billy moved forward. 'Gunter Walser, ex crook, meet Billy Stanyon, potential one,' said Whitaker.

Billy and Gunter shook hands and then Gunter shepherded his guests out of the clamour of the airport and into his waiting car. 'Let's go straight to your hotel,' he said, 'and then we can talk properly.'

Whitaker, who detested foreign travel and had been rendered somewhat irritable by the flight, was greatly cheered by the sight of the large airy room Gunter had booked for him. It had a draped four-poster, long windows leading on to a balcony and a spacious sitting area with a bureau and elegant chairs. Billy's more modest, but very comfortable, room adjoined. 'I say,' said Whitaker approvingly, 'we *are* doing things in style.'

'Nothing but the best for my old mentor,' said Gunter. He

turned to Billy. 'He taught me to drink whisky, you know,' he said.

'You're lucky,' Billy grinned. 'He won't let me near the stuff.'

'Our relationships are somewhat different,' said Whitaker. 'You are in my guardianship. That one already had a criminal record.'

'I wasn't *that* black,' said Gunter.

'You were vague about visas,' said Whitaker, turning from his appreciation of the room and choosing a chair. 'There is no greater crime than to ignore red tape.'

'So,' said Gunter. 'Let us all sit down and get to business. How did you first get the name and address of Elsa Gruber, Billy?'

'From a letter my father wrote to my mother,' said Billy. He had taken the stack of letters out of his luggage the moment he had reached his room, and now sat in Whitaker's suite with them in his lap. He shuffled quickly through them, selected the relevant one and slipped it out of its envelope. 'Shall I read it?'

Gunter nodded.

'I may not get back as soon as I'd hoped,' Billy read. 'Phone Mrs Dalgleish in Perthshire. She'll give you the address where letters can be sent. I'm not sure how long I will have to be out here. It depends on when Kurt can do the job. But I will try to be home for the big day...'

'What is the "big day", I wonder,' Gunter interrupted.

'I think,' said Billy, slightly embarrassed, 'it may be my birth. The letter is written about two weeks before. Anyway, I presume my mother contacted Mrs Dalgleish and got the address—see,' he leaned forward and passed the envelope to Gunter. 'It's on the back here, in different handwriting. My mother's, I suppose.'

Gunter looked at the envelope, then handed it back. He had a slightly self-satisfied smile on his face. 'Well,' he said, 'I did as you asked, Vincent. I made enquiries.' He paused for effect.

'And?' said Billy hopefully.

'Nothing spectacular. Or perhaps. Elsa Gruber is—or was, rather—the mother of one Kurt Gruber, presumably the Kurt mentioned in your letter, Billy. Kurt Gruber was killed on the Austro/Hungarian border.'

'Killed?' said Whitaker. 'How killed?'

Gunter shrugged. 'Killed is all I know. It must be on file somewhere—but this is what is interesting. He was killed in December 1963.' He looked across at Billy. 'When were you adopted? Do you know?'

'Alan and Marion Stanyon became his foster parents in March 1964,' said Whitaker. 'He was officially adopted some time later.'

There was a long silence. 'And Elsa Gruber,' said Billy flatly, 'is dead.'

'No,' said Gunter, and his small self-satisfied smile became a positive beam. 'Living with her daughter-in-law near the Chiemsee. I spoke to her daughter-in-law this morning. We are expected tomorrow!'

If he had hoped to give pleasure, he succeeded, but almost too well because Billy had no wish to wait, he wanted to visit Elsa Gruber immediately. But the appointment had been made for the next day and in any case Whitaker was adamant. 'I am a very old man,' he said firmly. 'I have just been hurled—in the most inhuman fashion—from my natural habitat to this far corner of a foreign field. I have no intention of going anywhere until I have had a long, undisturbed nap, followed by several whiskies—Pricey not being here to keep count—an excellent dinner and a good night's sleep. All right?'

Gunter laughed. 'That is what I expected,' he said. 'Come on, Billy, I'll show you the sights of Munich.'

Gunter was a cheerful, informative guide, and it was pleasant to ride in the front of the open Mercedes sports, instead of crouched in the back with the luggage. But Billy was fidgety and inattentive. Gunter tried to awaken some enthusiasm by taking him on a tour of the Olympic Stadium Complex but Billy just stood, woodenly, looking without comment at what he was being shown and then trailed silently behind Gunter to the next point of interest, his mouth sagging in a sulky droop. Eventually even the easy-going Gunter began to lose patience. 'Would you rather go back to the hotel?' he said.

'And sit?' snapped Billy. 'Or maybe you'd like me to lie down and take a nap, like Mr Whitaker.'

'Hey, Billy!' said Gunter.

'I'm sorry,' said Billy. 'I just... I'm sorry.'

Gunter stood still, outside the immense indoor swimming pool, whose crowded interior had aroused no flicker of interest in his guest. 'Come on,' he said. 'We go to the Chiemsee.'

'Now?'

'All part of the conducted tour,' said Gunter, and was rewarded with an instant change of mood and a dazzling smile.

The day was fine and mild and the drive along the motorway, in the fast open car, was exhilarating. It was a beautiful route, through lush wooded countryside, which became even more beautiful when the blueish-white bulk of the Alps themselves rose before them.

'Beyond them is Austria,' said Gunter. 'And then—Hungary!'

'Isn't it weird,' said Billy. 'If things had been different, I might have called there "home".' He turned to look at Gunter. 'Were you really a crook?'

'No,' said Gunter, laughing. 'That was just Vincent. I was —would you believe—a hippy.' He put on an American accent, 'Yeah, man! American words, but we thought England was where it was all happening in the sixties. Make Love Not War. We really meant it, you know. That's what's so sad. It all seemed so hopeful. Or was that just our age? Do you feel hopeful, Billy?' He left no space for an answer. 'Sort of question we can never answer at the time,' he said. 'My visa ran out and I panicked. I had no money, nowhere to live. Eventually I was picked up by the police.'

'What had you done?'

'Pinched some money. Vincent Whitaker defended me for free. He even lent me the money to get home. Said he'd rather have me out of the country.' He shook his head and laughed. 'No—he had a sympathy with our pacifist ideals. As obviously he would, with his background.'

'What do you mean?' said Billy.

Gunter glanced quickly at him, then back at the long, straight road. 'Didn't you know he was a conscientious objector during the war?'

Billy shook his head. Gunter caught the movement out of the corner of his eye. 'You haven't bothered to find out about him, have you?' he said. 'Get to know that man, Billy. It's worth it. Look, here is the Chiemsee.'

They turned off the motorway and Billy leaned slightly forward, looking ahead, barely glancing at the great blue lake, the Chiemsee itself, which gave its name to the surrounding area. Gunter turned down a side road and the lake disappeared, hidden behind trees. He drew into a horseshoe-shaped drive, enclosed by huge banks of glossy-leaved rhododendrons, and pulled up at a pretty white-washed house, hemmed in by trees, with a rather imposing studded wooden front door. They got out of the car and

Gunter rang the bell. Billy stood at his side, watching the door, waiting. Nothing happened. The tree-shaded house, quite silent, seemed to sleep. Gunter shrugged. 'We are not expected today,' he said.

Billy backed away from the door, scanning the impassive house front for some response. A tiny movement at one of the upper windows caught his eye. 'I'm sure I saw a curtain move,' he said to Gunter. 'Try the bell again.'

Gunter pressed the bell. They heard it ring inside the house.

Billy stood where he was, staring at the lace-curtained window where he thought he had seen movement. Dimly, through the broken pattern of the lace, he found he could make out the outline of a head and shoulders, someone at the window, unmoving, looking down. 'Gunter, come here,' he said urgently. Gunter crossed to his side. 'Look,' said Billy. 'I'm sure there's someone watching us from that window.' Gunter looked up briefly and then turned away. 'Perhaps,' he said. 'We must go now. We'll come tomorrow, as arranged.'

'But there's someone in there,' said Billy indignantly.

Gunter strode back to the car. 'And they do not want to answer the door now,' he said. 'They are perfectly at liberty not to, you know. The world does not revolve around your wishes alone.' He climbed into the car and reached across to open the passenger door. 'If you want a lift back, get in. I'm going.'

With the utmost reluctance, Billy joined him in the car. They drove back to the hotel more or less in silence. Gunter left straight away, promising to return next day for a less abortive trip to the Chiemsee. Whitaker was disappointed to find that Gunter was not joining them for dinner in the hotel's exceedingly well-appointed dining-room, though the sight of the extensive menu cheered him. But despite the excellent food, and a wine list which yielded a particularly good claret, Billy's uncompromising frustration and gloom began to dampen his pleasure.

'What *is* the matter?' he said eventually. 'All right, it was a wasted journey, but you saw the country.'

'I didn't come here to sightsee,' said Billy. He ate his perfect steak with a lack of enthusiasm that infuriated Whitaker, who said, 'I'm not surprised Gunter didn't want to spend the evening with us if you were like this all afternoon. No doubt he'd had enough by the time he got you back to the hotel. If you want to take an adult role in an adult world you must behave like an adult. You try my patience.'

Billy set his knife and fork down and shot Whitaker a slightly apologetic look. 'I tried his as well,' he admitted.

Whitaker reached for the bottle and poured himself a little more wine. 'I'm not at all surprised,' he said.

'You must see that it's important to me,' said Billy.

'Yes,' said Whitaker, irritably. 'No one is disputing that.' He drank a little wine and pushed his plate a few inches from him, then sat staring at the wine bottle without seeeing it.

Billy looked at the tense, lined face opposite him and remembered Gunter's words. 'I didn't know you were a conscientious objector,' he said.

Whitaker frowned at the bottle, then poured a few more drops into his glass. 'You did have a heart to heart,' he said.

'You're Gunter's big hero,' said Billy.

'He's far too old to have them any more,' said Whitaker, making a determined effort not to smile.

'You didn't tell me, though.'

'No,' said Whitaker, after a pause. 'It isn't something I usually talk about.' He looked very directly at Billy. 'Besides, I didn't think you'd be interested.' The irony escaped Billy.

'Well—of course I am,' he said.

'Well now you know,' said Whitaker. 'Would you like some cheese, or a pudding?' He leaned back in his chair to catch the waiter's eye.

'Why were you?' said Billy.

'Dear boy!' said Whitaker. 'It was centuries ago.'

The waiter glided to the table and gathered up the plates. 'Just the cheeseboard,' said Whitaker in German. Then, to Billy, 'Something from the trolley?'

'Yes, please.'

But the selecting of cheese and pudding could only go on for just so long and when it was done Billy persisted. 'Was it difficult for you?' he said.

Whitaker seemed to weigh his answer carefully. 'Yes,' he said at last. 'It wouldn't have been if I could have given religious reasons. That was more acceptable. But... I never could see the line between personal conscience and religious belief. I just couldn't hide behind a Christ or a Buddha.' He shrugged. 'It wasn't very nice.'

Billy watched him. 'I shouldn't have asked about it,' he said.

'One never likes to remember the bad times,' said Whitaker. He cut a small piece of cheese, pressed it on to a biscuit and sat looking at it. 'I don't know even now if I was justified,' he said. 'Many people went who felt just as I did.'

'The war had to be fought,' said Billy cautiously.

'There has to be another way,' said Whitaker. He ate his morsel of cheese. 'However,' he said. 'I paid the penalty and nearly finished my career.'

'Why?'

Whitaker leaned back in his chair. 'I was all set for a smart London firm,' he said. 'Chambers in Gray's Inn—wills for the wealthy, divorces for the aristocracy. But the senior partners couldn't see their way to accommodating a conchie. Tyneside was more welcoming—but it took a while to find a firm. I always felt bound to tell them, you see.' He looked at Billy. 'So now you know a little about my past. Does it change who I am?'

'Yes. I know more about you. I have a more rounded picture.'

Whitaker shook his head. 'You don't know more—just a few facts.'

'Do you regret it now?'

'Oh yes. Apart from anything else, it was horrid for my wife.'

'You did what was right for you.'

'If so, only right for me then. Would I have acted differently earlier... or later? Who knows. I didn't and here I am.' He eyed Billy with an unexpected twinkle. 'The picture of respectable old age. Who would think I was a dirty coward at heart?'

'You mustn't joke about it!'

'Yes, I must,' said Whitaker. 'Believe me, I must. And now I suggest we both get some sleep. I should like to be rested for our visit to Frau Gruber.'

This time, the door opened in response to Gunter's ringing and a tall, rather gaunt woman in her forties appeared on the step. *'Guten Morgen,'* said Gunter. *'Ich bin Gunter Walser. Ist dies Frau Gruber?'* But the woman, it turned out, was Elsa Gruber's daughter-in-law — Kurt's widow. She led the visitors inside the house and into the large living-room. The windows were closed and the curtains partially drawn across. In the dim light they saw the figure of an old woman, dressed in black, seated in a wheelchair. She acknowledged their introductions and greetings courteously, but only had eyes for one. 'And you are Billy...' she said, in her soft Austrian accent. Once she had been beautiful, he saw, but her face, although it softened as she looked at him, showed a strength which must have been quite daunting when she was younger.

'Billy Stanyon,' he said, moving over to the wheelchair to hand her the bunch of flowers he had bought for her in the hotel lobby. She accepted them, and thanked him, but still watched his face.

Hilde spoke to her in German and, positioning herself behind the wheelchair, indicated to the others that they should go through the house and out on to the lawn at the back.

'My daughter-in-law has a passion for light and air,' said Elsa Gruber, speaking slowly, rather as though she didn't speak often. 'As you grow older you come to distrust both elements. The air reminds you of life and the light shows up the decay.'

The back of the house looked directly onto the great lake, but although they were shown to garden chairs beneath a delicate willow, on a velvet lawn that sloped gently down to the waterside, with a view across the shining blue to the Alps beyond, it was the regal old figure in the wheelchair which commanded all their attention. The view, beautiful as it was, had no power to distract. Billy sat on a bench opposite her and she talked directly to him. Whitaker and Gunter accepted with grace their role as bystanders.

'Your mother was a pretty woman,' said Elsa. 'Hungarian. She arrived one day carrying a suitcase, and a baby. Not here. I was living in Munich then. She said she was a friend of my son...'

'And my father?' said Billy. 'Jerri? Jerri Toth?'

'I never met. Kurt...my son...he had so many friends, business associates...'

'What was his business?' said Whitaker politely.

Hilde, who was standing like a sentinel at the back of the wheelchair, frowned and leaned forward to rearrange the shawl around Elsa's shoulders. 'Import and export,' said Elsa.

'Of what?' said Whitaker.

Hilde was still busy with the shawl. *'Ach! Hilde!'* said Elsa irritably, shrugging her away. She looked directly at Whitaker. 'Goods,' she said with a note of finality. She returned to Billy. 'She told me that her husband and my son were getting her father out of Hungary. These things do happen. The baby was quite small. She was—highly strung? Is that the right expression? Then Kurt...my son...arrived. He said that the old man, her father, had died before they could move him. Jerri was still in Hungary. There had been trouble.'

Hilde, who had not smiled once since their arrival, seemed to grow more tense as the interview proceeded. *'Ermüde Dich nicht, Schwiegermutter,'* she said.

'I am not tiring myself,' said Elsa impatiently. She sighed. 'But it is all a long time ago now. She left the baby with me. She and Kurt went back to Austria.' She looked across Billy's blond head to the distant mountains. 'That is where I am from.' She paused. 'Later...a long time...they came and told me. A car accident. On the border. They had driven through the barrier at the border post and skidded off the road. The car was burned out and Kurt was dead.'

'I'm sorry,' said Billy.

Elsa smiled sadly at him. 'Hilde came to look after me,' she said. 'A widow and an old woman. I had polio, you know. That is why I am like this. Now, of course, they hardly worry about it.'

'And my mother?' said Billy softly.

'There was a woman's body in the wreckage. The authorities came and took the baby away. Back to England to grow up a little English gentleman.' She stretched out her hand. 'Billy? Is it you?'

Billy gave her his hand. 'Yes,' he said.

She gripped his hand, then released it. 'Dear child,' she said.

'And Jerri?' said Billy. The world seemed to have gone away from him. There was only her face, her answers.

Hilde leaned forward and touched her mother-in-law on the shoulder. *'Wir müssen jetzt gehen. Es wird kalt,'* she said.

'What happened to Jerri?' Billy persisted.

'I don't know,' said Elsa.

'He wasn't in the car?'

'There were two bodies, said Elsa, 'that's all. A woman, and a man they told me was Kurt. Badly burned. So burned I did not know him.'

'But it was Kurt?'

'He had been seen at the barrier, driving the car,' said Elsa. He was recognized. All the evidence points to the body being Kurt's.'

'And Jerri?' said Billy, aware that some kind of invisible wall was rising between them.

'Has not been heard of,' said Elsa firmly. 'I think he must be dead, my dear. Don't search for him.'

'I must,' said Billy simply. 'He's all I've got, you see.'

'Billy.' She stretched out her hand again, but could not quite reach to touch his cheek. 'Don't search for him. I know in my heart he is dead.'

'How?'

'Because... where is he?' She pulled a signet ring from the third finger of her right hand. 'This ring,' she said, 'was given to me by your mother, to cover expenses when I looked after you. Perhaps it was your father's—it is a man's. Now it must come back to you.'

She held it out, but Billy made no move. 'No,' he said, 'she wanted you to have it.'

Hilde grasped the handles of the wheelchair and began to turn it towards the house. The three visitors rose obediently to their feet. 'One day,' said Elsa to Billy, slipping the ring back on her finger, 'it shall be yours. I keep it safe for you.'

The interview was at an end. Hilde wheeled her mother-in-law into the house and then ushered the visitors out of the front door.

In the car, driving once more towards Munich, Billy sat hunched in the back, silent and abstracted. In the front, Gunter and Whitaker talked, and snatches of their conversation came to him through his own thoughts. Gunter began to outline a plan he had just conceived to write an article on Billy's search for his father. He would sell it, he explained, to one of the German glossy magazines, whose readers might find the human-interest aspect appealing. 'If there's anyone around who knows more, it just might arouse a response,' he said. Billy made no comment. Elsa's words were running through his head and an image had come into his mind that he couldn't easily shift; the image of a border post on a misty night—a car racing for the barrier, breaking through it, splinters flying high—Border guards leaping clear, recovering, firing—the car skidding, crashing, exploding into an orange flower of flame, burning vividly against the grey night.

'Are you all right, Billy?' said Whitaker for the second time, twisting in his seat to face him. 'Gunter and I have just been saying—we can pursue all this, if you would like that? Take it a little further, anyway.'

'Yes,' said Billy. 'Thank you.' He seemed to have trouble focusing on Whitaker's face. 'I know,' he said, 'that Frau Gruber wanted to tell me more. I know it.'

Chapter Five

The last few months of school life seemed to Billy to pass with unusual speed; partly because he was unsure of what was going to happen next, but also because the last term was in many ways the busiest, with the extra privileges allowed to seniors, the A level exams, and the preparations for various end of year functions.

Although Hadrian's didn't have a strong reputation for music, there was an enthusiastic school orchestra, and a Saturday afternoon concert was arranged to take place two weeks before the end of term. The last item in a fairly ambitious programme was a Telemann flute concerto, with Billy as soloist. Before the concert started he noticed, among the ranks of well-dressed parents waiting for the entertainment to begin, Vincent Whitaker sitting with a couple he didn't recognize, a rather distinguished-looking man in his fifties and a dark-haired woman. But once he stood at the front of the orchestra, playing the much-rehearsed music, he scarcely noticed anything at all—just a blur of upturned faces enclosed by the massive grey side pillars and long back windows of the assembly hall.

The acoustics were less than perfect, and not a few wrong notes emanated from the earnest-faced orchestra, but for all that the sublime, pure sound of the music filled the room. That is, until the jarring roar of five motorbikes approached up the drive and reverberated around the forecourt. A greater tension showed on the faces of some of the players, but they didn't falter. A few of the more perceptive members of the audience had the impression that the interruption was expected—as in fact it was. The harmonious notes of the music drifted out through the tall windows to the gravel drive below, and the discordant sounds of the bikes, revving and turning, revving and turning, came back in hostile response. The audience, with nothing to do but listen, grew restive.

Suddenly, and wholly unexpectedly, a small rock smashed through one of the great windows, showering the boys at the back of the hall with glittering fragments of glass. One second later, all the motorbikes revved simultaneously, then roared off down the drive and away.

Doggedly, Billy and the orchestra played on, encouraged by those members of the audience, Whitaker and his companions among them, who resisted the urge to look round and instead gave the musicians their full attention. Some of the boys, and even a couple of masters, left the hall at the first impact of stone on glass and vainly gave chase—but they sidled back to their places as the last notes were played, and were in position in time to join in the appreciative applause. As instructed, Billy took a solo bow, and then abandoned his flute and climbed with some relief off the stage to follow the throng into the senior dining-room, where the tables had been moved aside and tea and cakes were available for guests and boys alike. He gathered four cups of tea and a plateful of fancy cakes onto a tray and made his way through the chatting groups of boys and parents to the small oasis of calm by the fireplace that Whitaker and his guests had managed to claim.

'Well done, Billy,' said Whitaker. 'This is my sister-in-law, Mary, and Sir James Little, her husband. He's very "high up" and we lesser mortals must never forget the fact!'

'Don't be naughty, Vincent,' said Mary Little, accepting a cup of tea from the tray. 'You play very well, Billy.'

'Thank you,' said Billy, feeling suddenly shy.

'Yes,' said Sir James. 'Damn shame about the shemozzle outside. You were doing so well.'

They all had their cups and Billy glanced round for somewhere to put the tray, but there was no obvious place near at hand and the plate of cakes still sat invitingly in its centre. So he continued to hold it, quite glad of something to do.

'My sister...' said Mary Little eagerly, 'Vincent's late wife... was very keen on music. She'd have loved this.'

'You make it sound as though you didn't, Mary,' said Whitaker.

'I don't know an awful lot about music,' said Mary Little vaguely.

'I like a good tune,' said Sir James. He was a tall, solid man who looked as though he had decided some years back that he knew what he liked and wasn't going to change any opinions now. Whitaker caught Billy's eye and managed a neat wink which went unnoticed by his two guests. Sir James saw Billy's answering smile, but took it for general good humour. 'What the devil *was* all that rumpus?' he said.

‘It’s been going on for ages,’ said Billy. ‘Group of yobs from the village.’

‘How disgraceful!’ said Mary.

‘Do you know these “yobs” personally,’ said Whitaker, looking at Billy with one eyebrow slightly raised.

‘No,’ said Billy.

‘They might be quite nice,’ said Whitaker.

‘Nice people don’t pitch rocks through other people’s windows,’ said Sir James. ‘We should bring back the birch, I’m convinced of it.’

‘Or hanging, James,’ said Whitaker mildly. ‘We could hang them from the trees... send out a posse...’

‘Still the pacifist, Vincent,’ said Mary. ‘But does it work?’ She cast a quick glance at her husband. ‘They should all get jobs and buckle to,’ she said, and waited for his approval and agreement. But, ‘There aren’t any jobs,’ said Sir James testily, ‘that’s the point.’ ‘Yes, dear,’ said Mary, duly crushed. She turned to Billy, ‘And are you going to take up music professionally?’

‘I don’t know,’ said Billy.

‘He doesn’t know what he’s going to do,’ said Whitaker, frowning, as if he had suddenly remembered something that vexed him. ‘He’s leaving school with no prospects, and at best two A levels.’

‘He’s terrible when he’s roused, isn’t he,’ said Sir James, putting on his jovial manner to lighten the conversation.

‘Perhaps he’d like to join our friends on the motorbikes and fling bricks,’ said Whitaker, not entirely joking.

‘I thought you were all in favour of them,’ said Sir James.

‘Of course not,’ said Whitaker. ‘I just don’t believe punishment is the answer.’

‘Why not take up music?’ said Mary. ‘If you love it?’

Billy glanced doubtfully at Whitaker. ‘I don’t know if I’d be good enough.’

‘Pretty tricky,’ said Sir James, shaking his head sagely, ‘making a living at that sort of game.’

‘That man with the golden flute,’ said Mary brightening, ‘Galway. He’s made a go of it.’

Billy smiled at her. ‘We can’t all be James Galway,’ he said softly.

Whitaker glanced at his watch. ‘We must be on our way,’ he said, ‘if we’re to be in Newcastle in time for that dinner you promised me. Come along, James, tell Billy your news. That's why you're here. You're of no use as a music critic.' He took Mary's arm and began to guide her to the door. Billy followed behind with Sir James, Whitaker's voice drifting back to them as they made for the stairs. 'Did I really hear him say he likes a good tune? He's a total philistine.'

Sir James chuckled to himself, totally unabashed. Billy, walking with him down the stairs, looked at him questioningly. 'Yes,' said Sir James. 'Made a few enquiries about your father. Jerri Toth. Defected to our side in 1955. Just a young chap. Swam ashore off a Russian trawler that had put in to Shetland during a storm. There's not much on him. What there is...' He looked at Billy and seemed to hesistate. They had reached the porch, and begun to cross the forecourt towards the parked cars. Billy kept pace and waited. 'Took British citizenship,' said Sir James. 'Married.'

'Tania,' Billy nodded.

Sir James glanced at him and away again. 'No,' he said. 'No. Charlotte McIntyre, the glass heiress. There was quite a furore over the wedding. Society do. And a bit of a stink, I'm afraid, over the divorce.'

Whitaker and Mary Little had reached the Little's car and were waiting by it. Sir James quickened his step. 'Of course times have changed,' he said lightly. 'We don't make so much of it now. I keep telling Mary if she doesn't behave I'll get rid of her. Fashionable thing to do!'

'He divorced her?' said Billy.

'She divorced him. He admitted adultery.' He was looking more uncomfortable by the minute. 'Sounds worse than it is, really,' he said.

'And then...did he marry Tania?' said Billy.

'Ah, here we are,'' said Sir James with evident relief, joining Whitaker and Mary. He turned back to Billy, 'I'll dig around, see what else I can find out,' he said.

Billy stood still, staring into space, while their goodbyes and renewed congratulations on his performance washed around him. Whitaker was the last to get into the car. 'He's told you?' said Billy.

'On the way up,' said Whitaker. 'Don't forget—facts don't tell you everything.'

Before Billy could answer the air was shaken by the sound of engines as the five bikes roared up the drive once more, taking the groups of shallow steps at speed. They swooped and swerved around the car, with Billy and Whitaker still standing beside it, passing it seemed within a hair's breadth of them, then turned and made for the gate once more, bouncing and lurching down the steps and away.

'Clear off!' yelled Billy, whose patience had been shortened by the general tension of the afternoon.

Whitaker put a hand on his shoulder. 'Steady,' he said as the noise receded into the distance.

'I don't understand them at all,' said Billy angrily.

Whitaker gathered his coat around him and got into the car. 'Envy is a very powerful emotion,' he said.

'Envy?' said Billy. 'Of what?'

'Oh, wake up Billy,' said Whitaker, peering up at him out of the still open door. 'Wake up!'

Billy slammed the door and stood back as Sir James turned the car and drove off, calling out, 'Maybe you could become a pop star flautist. Make a fortune and keep us all.' Left alone, he glared down the drive at the departing car and at the marks left by the motorbike wheels, rattled and angry. But by the time he and Spike were settled in their study for the evening he had largely forgotten the incident. He sat at his desk, writing to Whitaker to ask if he could find out anything about his father's first wife. Spike, who was bored, leaned back in an armchair, his long legs stretched out in front of him, and lobbed darts into the battered dartboard on the wall by the fireplace.

'It's always on Sunday afternoons,' said Spike.

'Shut up, will you,' said Billy, 'I'm trying to write a letter.'

Spike rose languidly, gathered up the darts and sat down again. He began to throw once more, one dart for each word. 'They—always—come—on—Sunday—afternoons.'

'It's the Northern sabbath,' said Billy. 'Bores you to death. Listen—that guy who came with Mr Whitaker said my father was married to an heiress.'

'Your Mum was an heiress?' said Spike, mildly interested.

'No. Before her.'

'Oh, a randy bastard,' said Spike, retrieving the darts again.

'Shut up.'

'Billy—the gang always come here on Sunday afternoons.'

Billy heaved a sigh and pushed his half-written letter aside. 'So?'

he said resignedly.

'Wouldn't you like to get your own back?'

'They come on bloody huge bikes, Spike. What do you suggest we do? Throw ourselves in front of their wheels?'

'What heiress, anyway?' said Spike.

'I don't know.' Billy looked back at his letter. 'All I know is her name. Charlotte McIntyre. Something to do with glass, apparently.'

'McIntyre's glass?' said Spike. 'You must have heard of it. It's collectors' stuff, like Caithness. I think my people know them, actually. I'll ask them if you like.'

'Well, why didn't you say so?' said Billy, crumpling the letter in his hand and dropping it into the wastepaper basket.

'Right,' said Spike. 'That's out of the way. Now, about the motorbike gang. Why don't we get together a party and set up an ambush?'

The basic plan for the ambush was very straightforward. Billy, Spike and four or five others were to lock the main gates and wait in the shrubbery just inside the side gate. They would keep out of sight as the gang rode in, wait until they'd worn themselves out driving around the grounds and shouting obscenities up at the school windows and then, as they drove off out of the side gate, cut off the retreat of at least one by shutting the gate and closing in on the path behind him so he couldn't ride back up towards the school. The plan somehow never evolved beyond that point. In the early stages of its execution it was all light-hearted enough, and most welcome since Sunday boredom was not exclusive to those outside the school boundaries. It worked, too.

The last member of the gang to try to leave by the side gate found it padlocked. As he turned his bike back towards the school grounds, the ambushers leaped out of the rhododendrons at him, to the accompaniment of a theatrical cry of 'HADRIAN'S!' from Spike. He hesitated for half a second, his face under its safety helmet wary and puzzled, then turned the bike towards the gate again. Outside, the other four had stopped and turned back, but there was nothing they could do; the spiked railings were too high to climb. 'Rob!' yelled the leader, then stopped, unable to think of any useful instructions. With the impregnable gate on one side and the advancing line of sixth formers on the other, Rob put the bike into gear and drove straight between two immense rhododendrons and through onto the rough ground, dotted with small trees and large shrubs, on the other side. The boys gave chase. The bike was powerful but it was slowed down by the rough ground and thick vegetation, which were far easier to negotiate on foot. What was more, the ambushers knew the grounds well and there were enough of them to spread out and close in, guided by the sound of the motor. Rob, riding across a small glade away from their shouting advance, had no idea where he was going, and before he had time to think the front wheel hit a rotten branch, half hidden in the long grass. The bike crashed onto its side and the engine cut out. Rob disentangled himself from the machine and limped for the cover of a luxuriant laurel.

By chance, Billy ran in at the other side of the glade just in time to see Rob disappear. Over to the right of the laurel he noticed the bike on its side, partly immersed in nettles. As he opened his mouth to call the others a solid, heavy, gnarled piece of branch hurtled past his head, brushing against the back of his hair, and thudded onto the ground the other side of him. The next second one of his own group of ambushers, Timpson, appeared in the glade. 'Sorry, Stanyon,' he said. 'That was meant for the yob.'

'Are you crazy?' said Billy. 'You could damage someone with that.'

'Where is he, anyway?' said Timpson.

Billy looked at his flushed, excited face. Then, 'he went over there, towards the San. grounds,' he said, pointing away from the bike, which Timpson hadn't noticed.

'Right,' said Timpson, turning and running out of the glade, 'Come on!' He was far too intent on the chase to notice that Billy didn't follow.

Billy watched him duck and dodge out of sight through the entangling vegetation and then turned and walked over to the bike. 'You can come out now,' he said in the general direction of the relevant bush. There was a pause and then Rob appeared, rather cautiously, holding his crash helmet. He didn't attempt to approach Billy and the bike.

'Come on, hurry up,' said Billy irritably.

He lifted the bike upright and stood looking down at it—a 500 cc Triumph in very good condition, gleaming all over apart from a few grass stains where it had fallen. Standing there, actually holding the bike, he began to covet it for the first time. He started to get on it, just to see how it would feel. Instantly Rob was upon him, flinging him to the ground, landing on top and lashing out with his fists. They struggled in total silence in the sunny glade, the bike gleaming beside them. It was a scuffle rather than a fight, and Billy managed without too much difficulty to roll over on top of Rob and pin him down. 'Will you calm down!' he said through clenched teeth into the angry face of his opponent. Rob gave up, not with very good grace, and they got to their feet.

'Go on,' sneered Rob, 'Call the rest. You're nothing without the rest of them.'

'Well neither are you!' said Billy. 'Why do you do it? You're asking for trouble. If not us, then the police.'

'It's a game, isn't it,' said Rob. 'Fills in the time.'

From somewhere behind the wall of rhododendrons Spike's voice called, 'Where are you, Billy?'

'Go on,' said Rob. 'Why don't you tell them?'

'I don't want to,' said Billy. 'Run while you've got the chance.'

'You make me sick,' said Rob, his thin face distorted with contempt. 'Public school! Little gentleman! Pathetic!'

'What would you rather I did,' said Billy, glaring at him with no less hostility. 'Call them—have them set on you?'

'That's what I'd do,' said Rob.

'Billy!' called Spike's voice again, from slightly nearer. There was a crashing in the undergrowth. Billy looked very steadily at Rob. 'Over here, Spike!' he called, without taking his eyes off the other boy.

Rob's sneer faded. 'What'll they do?' he said.

'I don't know,' said Billy. 'We didn't think about that, we just wanted to get our own back.' Rob's expression had changed entirely. He looked quickly round the glade but the unseen attackers seemed to be approaching from all sides at once. 'You're scared,' said Billy.

'Scared?' said Rob. 'Of course I'm scared.'

'Come on,' said Billy. 'You can still make it to the drive.'

'I don't know what you're playing at,' said Rob distrustfully. 'Why're you helping?'

'I don't like what's happening,' said Billy, hauling the bike upright again and shoving it at Rob. 'Come on, hurry!'

Rob got the bike started and Billy pointed out the direction to the main gate. As Spike and the rest eventually met up on one of the paths, lured by the renewed sound of the engine, they were faced with the extraordinary sight of Rob riding for the main gate with

Billy running at full stretch beside him. Billy made it to the gate first, undid the padlock and hauled the gate open just far enough to let the bike pass through. Rob rode clear as the others ran up to Billy, and stopped. They were speechless, and only partly because they were out of breath. Billy shut the gate again, then walked straight past them and up towards the school building. They let him go.

Much later, when he and Spike had finished their regular evening jog around the grounds and were strolling back, Billy said, 'You know Mr Whitaker? He was a conscientious objector during the war. I didn't understand before...'

'Religious reasons?' said Spike.

'No. Conscience. Today I objected to what we were doing. To the "yob", you know?'

'It was just a game,' said Spike.

'Then why do I feel so ashamed?' said Billy. 'You didn't see his face, Spike. He was scared. *I* was frightening him. Why? For a game? Some game!'

'Look, they started it,' said Spike.

'Did they?' said Billy. 'We sit here, behind our big wall, in our big grounds, calling them "yobs". If I was on the other side of that wall, I'd be a "yob" and he'd be my friend. It doesn't make sense.'

Spike gave one of his exaggerated shrugs. 'It's just the way things are,' he said. 'It's not my fault that my father is Lord Melford and that we own half of Dorset. What does it matter?'

'It matters,' said Billy. 'I will never do anything like that again. Never!'

'You just wait,' said Spike. 'It's the survival of the fittest out there.'

They had reached the large gravel forecourt, and suddenly the air was full of the sound of the motorbikes. 'Here they come again!' yelled Spike exultantly. He and Billy sprinted for the main building and reached the safety of the arched doorway just as the bikes slewed to a halt in front of them. The riders raised the visors of their helmets, almost ceremoniously. Their faces were grim. Rob, at the end of the line of riders, pointed to Billy. 'That's him,' he said.

The leader looked straight at Billy. 'You're a marked man!' he said. 'We're going to get you!'

He gave a signal and the riders turned the bikes and roared off down the drive again.

'Eat bloody cake!' Spike yelled after them, laughing. He slapped Billy affectionately on the back. 'That's what comes of helping "yobs",' he said. 'He's marked you now. Just as well you're leaving.' He opened the door and went on inside.

Billy paused in the doorway, looking down the drive at the departing riders, now tiny in the distance. 'It's not a game,' he said quietly.

Chapter Six

At last the school year came to an end. One afternoon the whole school stood in the stained light which filtered through the chapel windows and sang 'Lord dismiss us with Thy blessing,' The sixth formers filed through the chapel door, where the Headmaster waited with a handshake and a special word for each. And then they were outside in the fresh air, officially schoolboys no longer. Billy looked at Spike. 'Now what?' he said.

Spike, as it happened, knew what. He was going to university. The headmaster had wished him luck with his 'further studies'. All he had said to Billy was, 'Keep up the flute. You have a talent.'

At first, Billy didn't feel as much at a loss as he might have because he was so used to long summer holidays. There were times when he could almost persuade himself that this summer was no different from any other, and it was more or less in a holiday frame of mind that he decided on a short expedition. Spike had told him a little more about McIntyre's glass, including the address of the family home of the McIntyres, in the Scottish border country about fifty miles north-west of Newcastle. So early one morning, about a week after the end of term, Billy hitched a couple of lifts and arrived at the southern entrance to the McIntyre property just before lunch time. Apart from a decision to introduce himself as a friend of Lord and Lady Melford who, as Spike had confirmed, were known to the McIntyres, he had no very clear idea of what he was going to say.

His mind was solely concerned with the fact that Charlotte had once been married to his father and so would surely have some information to offer. It didn't really occur to him to wonder how she would feel about being asked for this information.

The gate was unmarked and although the driver of the delivery van which dropped him off assured him that this was the 'McIntyre place', he felt some uncertainty as he walked up the long drive, which curved out of sight behind some ancient oaks. To the right of the drive lay an extensive paddock. It was a hot, sunny day; the gravel of the drive sparkled and hurt the eyes and the cropped grass of the paddock was easier to look at. Not far from the fence, a girl of about twenty in formal riding clothes sat astride a gleaming bay. She had obviously reined him in as Billy appeared and now, when he looked across at her, she walked the horse up to the fence and sat looking down at him.

Yes, she said in answer to his enquiry, this drive did lead to the house and Charlotte McIntyre was at home, though actually her married name was Jameson. She looked puzzled and not altogether friendly, as though strangers were an unwelcome intrusion. As Billy thanked her and walked on she called after him, 'What do you want with her?'

'Just some enquiries,' said Billy.

The house came into view round a corner of the drive, a small elegant mansion set in a beautifully tended garden. A maid opened the door to him and showed him into a well-proportioned living-room with long French windows giving on to a sunny terrace. And only then, waiting alone in the room for Charlotte Jameson, did he begin to feel uneasy. It was almost as if the unease was in the room itself—it was light, airy, even pretty, but there was something oddly oppressive about it. He turned as the door opened.

Charlotte Jameson was an attractive, fair-haired woman in her early forties, wearing the good wool skirt and smart blouse of a country lady. She introduced herself and then said, 'And you're a friend of Lord and Lady Melford?'

'Of their son, actually,' said Billy. 'We were at school together.'

'Ah,' said Charlotte. 'Do sit down.'

Billy sat uncomfortably on the edge of a sofa and Charlotte sat opposite on a delicately carved chair. 'And your name is...?' she said.

She was very gentle, very polite. Billy found himself tongue-tied. 'Billy Stanyon,' he said, and an awkward silence settled on the room.

Charlotte smiled encouragingly. 'I'm afraid, Mr Stanyon, you'll have to give me more of a clue,' she said. 'How can I help you?'

Billy felt himself growing more embarrassed by the second. 'My father was Jerri Toth,' he said.

Charlotte sat quite still. Her face showed no emotion but she no longer smiled. 'Stanyon?' she said.

'I was adopted.'

'Yes. Of course. What do you want?'

'To know about him,' said Billy.

'From me?' said Charlotte. 'From me? I think you've picked the wrong person.'

'But you were married to him.'

Charlotte rose and walked over to the fireplace. She stood with her back to Billy. 'Briefly,' she said, and her voice sounded quite harsh. 'A long time ago. I don't recall any of that time and I don't want to.'

'Is... my father alive?'

'I have no way of knowing,' said Charlotte without turning round. 'We did not part the best of friends. I am not the one to ask about him.' She turned and looked at Billy. She had sounded angry, her words were angry, but her face was full of hurt. 'You have no right to come here,' she said. 'And without even announcing yourself...'

Billy stood up. 'I was afraid if I contacted you first you wouldn't see me,' he said.

'I have no wish to see you,' said Charlotte. 'You are nothing to me. In no way are we connected.'

The door opened and the girl in the riding clothes walked in, saying 'Gramps is arriving, I've just seen his car.' She stopped when she saw Charlotte's expression. 'Are you all right?' she said. When she didn't get an immediate answer she turned sharply to face Billy. 'Who *are* you?'

Charlotte drew a deep breath and smiled across at the girl. 'It's all right, Pamela darling,' she said. 'This is your father's child by... his second wife.'

Billy and Pamela stood staring at each other for a long moment. Then, 'How *could* you come here!' said Pamela. 'How *could* you!'

'I didn't know,' said Billy at a loss, 'that I had a sister.'

'You haven't!' said Pamela.

'It's all right,' said Charlotte again. 'Mr Stanyon, now that you're here you'd better stay to lunch. My father has just arrived. He, no doubt, will have things to say to you.' For the first time there was a note of malice in her voice. For the first time Billy felt more than unease—something like a twinge of fear.

Stanley McIntyre, founder of the McIntyre empire, was a self-made man, a tall robust figure in his sixties whose Scottish accent contrasted oddly with the accents his daughter and grand-daughter had learnt at their expensive private schools. He strode straight up to Billy, holding out his hand and saying, 'And this must be Pamela's new young man.'

Pamela turned and fled, muttering about changing for lunch.

Charlotte said, 'No, Father. This is Jerri's son.'

McIntyre returned his hand abruptly to his side and eyed Billy up and down. 'Is it now?' he said at last. 'Is it now? By which of his fancy women?'

'The Hungarian girl, I suppose,' said Charlotte quietly.

'I'd better go,' said Billy.

'Oh no,' said McIntyre. 'Oh no, my lad. On the contrary, you'd better stay.' He studied Billy's face. 'Yes, you've got the look of him. Pamela was spared that. Now we shall see if you're made of the same stuff.'

'Don't be too hard on him,' said Charlotte quietly. The harshness had gone from her voice. She looked at Billy as though she was beginning to regret having delivered him up to her father.

'I must go,' said Billy, mumbling his words.

'You wouldn't get to the end of the drive,' said McIntyre.

'I don't believe you,' said Billy, trying to laugh.

'Guard dogs,' said McIntyre. He waved an arm to take in the whole of the room. 'Essential. We have some of the most beautiful things money can buy in this house.'

'I didn't see them when I came in.'

'Oh, you can get *in*,' said McIntyre. 'Getting *in* is no problem. What you can't do is get out again.'

'But why do you want me to stay?' said Billy, recovering himself somewhat.

'Why did you come?' countered McIntyre.

'To meet someone who might tell me something about my

father.'

'Exactly. Then "stick around", as they say. You'll hear things about your father that'll curl your little toes. Eh, Charlotte?' He prodded Billy briefly in the chest with a forefinger. 'Never cross a rich man. That's what he didn't learn.'

He was interrupted by the maid who appeared in the doorway and hovered nervously, as if unwilling to come right into the room with McIntyre. 'Lunch is ready, Madam,' she said.

'Splendid!' said McIntyre.

'Thank you, Pat,' said Charlotte. 'Will you lay another place, please.' Pat scurried from the room.

'I shall now go to the lavatory,' said McIntyre to Billy. 'Have you noticed how people avoid speaking of the natural functions? They say "wash my hands" or "powder my nose" when what they mean is "go to the lavatory". Your father was a great one for saying one thing and meaning another.' He pointed at Charlotte, who was now looking as uncomfortable as Billy felt. 'He took that sweet child to have and to hold, in sickness and in health, for richer or poorer... Well, I'm happy to say he didn't get one penny!' He turned and strode out of the room.

When he was out of earshot, Charlotte looked rather sadly at Billy. 'I won't be able to help you,' she said.

Lunch, at the gleaming dining table, formally served by Pat, was a somewhat tense affair, yet not especially because of Billy's presence. Both Charlotte and Pamela were subdued and nervous in McIntyre's presence, and though his attitude towards them exuded pride and affection it was soon apparent that he was the source of the lingering sense of oppression in the house. Throughout the meal he ignored Billy almost entirely and made Pamela the chief focus of his powerful attention.

'How's the jumping going?' he asked her.

'All right,' said Pamela. 'I have trials next week.'

'Good. Where?'

'Surrey.'

McIntyre slapped the table top. 'You show those Sassenachs!' he said. 'And when is the new boyfriend to be revealed?'

Billy, trying to eat and unsure whether he felt hungry or sick, caught the glance that passed between Pamela and Charlotte. 'Miles is arriving tonight, Father,' said Charlotte. 'In time for dinner.'

'Good,' said McIntyre. 'Do I take it you approve?'

'Very much,' said Charlotte. 'A nice boy.'

'Well *that* doesn't necessarily bode well for the future,' said McIntyre. He leaned towards Pamela. 'Your mother isn't known for her good taste in men.' He laughed at his own joke, shovelled in another mouthful of food and said, through it, 'I've been checking on his family.'

'Oh?' said Pamela nervously.

'As far as I can see,' said McIntyre, 'the father bought his knighthood.'

'I'm sure he didn't,' said Pamela, setting down her knife and fork and pushing her plate a little away from her.

'Oh, I approve of that,' said McIntyre. 'Got his priorities right. The boy—Miles—what's he planning on doing for a career?'

'I'm not sure,' said Pamela.

'Not going to follow his father's footsteps into the family firm?' said McIntyre. 'Auctioneers, isn't it?'

'Yes,' said Pamela softly, looking at her plate.

'What's that?'

'Yes,' said Pamela, fractionally louder.

'Doesn't he fancy it?' said McIntyre. He banged on the table, using his pudding spoon as a gavel. 'Going, going, gone?'

'I don't know,' said Pamela.

'Not got his eye on the glass trade, has he?' said McIntyre, leaning forward, peering into her face.

'No!' said Pamela, meeting his eye for the first time since lunch started.

'No?' said McIntyre, flinging himself back in his chair in mock horror. 'Yet one day it will be yours. And he won't help you run it? Tut, tut!'

'I don't know,' said Pamela desperately. 'Yes. I'm not sure. I think he... hopes to.'

McIntyre turned to Billy. 'You'll have heard of our glass?'

'Yes, I have.'

'Ah,' said McIntyre, 'You've been doing your checking as well. Your father thought he'd just... move in. Take over. He was a stable hand, you know. He married her to get the firm. Isn't that so, Charlotte?'

Charlotte didn't answer. She seemed to shrink visibly when the beam of attention was directed on to her, just as Pamela relaxed very slightly now that she was no longer its focus.

'Well it wasn't for love,' said McIntyre, 'for he left you soon enough. Went off...' he rounded unexpectedly on Billy, 'with your mother, I do declare. Though I doubt he ever married her.' He rose abruptly from the table. 'I don't want a pudding,' he said. 'I'll have some coffee in the other room.' He walked out, leaving the door open behind him.

'I'm so sorry,' said Charlotte to Billy, after a pause, trying to achieve a light, social tone. 'Skeletons in cupboards! I'm sure he did marry her. They...loved each other.' She got up and hurried out after her father.

Pamela and Billy were left facing each other across the table. Suddenly they both smiled, for the first time, like two survivors who have weathered the same storm. 'Not what you expected?' said Pamela. 'Coming here?'

'I don't know what I expected,' said Billy. 'I just wanted to hear about...Jerri.'

Pamela made a face.

'Aren't you curious about him?' said Billy. 'He's your father as well.'

Pamela shook her head. 'He never was,' she said. 'He was leaving her even as I was being born. I was only three when Mother married again. I call him "Daddy"—I think of him as my father.'

'Who?'

'David Jameson. He works at the shop.' She shrugged. 'We always call the factory the shop. I don't know why.'

Through the open door behind Pamela, Billy saw McIntyre approaching across the hall having, presumably, decided to forego coffee. He stopped short of the doorway when he caught Billy's eye and gestured with his arm. 'Come along,' he said.

Pamela jumped slightly when she heard his voice, but she didn't look round. 'You'd better go with him,' she said quietly to Billy. And then, 'Don't come back.'

'What?' said Billy, surprised since he had felt she was growing slightly friendlier.

'Don't come back,' said Pamela. She got up, walked over to the window and stood looking out of it with her back resolutely turned. Billy got up and went into the hall. As he approached, McIntyre turned and led the way out of the front door. He crossed the drive and got into his car, leaning across to open the passenger door. 'Hop in,' he said.

Billy obeyed. The force of McIntyre's personality was such that obedience was virtually automatic. 'Where are we going?' said Billy.

'To see the family firm,' said McIntyre.

The glassworks was on the far side of the huge paddock, still within the mansion grounds. After the strange peacefulness of the house and grounds, it came as a shock to Billy to find himself in an extremely busy factory which was, in effect, just down the drive. McIntyre gave him the standard visitor's tour around the furnaces and workshops, explaining how the molten glass was blown and shaped and cooled and the results stored, never once touching on personal matters. Interested despite himself, Billy began to relax. From the factory, McIntyre shepherded him into his large office, with its views across the paddock and the surrounding countryside. A great mahogany desk dominated the room and the walls were lined with showcases in which stood shelf upon shelf of perfect glass objects, the light from the window playing and reflecting and dancing across their surfaces. Billy began to understand why both the house and the office had such large windows—light was an integral part of the design of the delicate bowls and goblets he was looking at. Though he knew nothing about glass he found, as he worked his way slowly along the showcases, that its beauty was catching his imagination. McIntyre's voice continued from behind him:

'That piece of glass is said to have been used by James VI. Early seventeenth century...or even late sixteenth. I tremble when I think of it... that it's lasted so long. And over there, in the cabinet behind you...our most recent designs. I don't allow garish colours, you'll notice. Glass is a receptacle of light which should not be obscured by the whim of a craftsman. You have the look of your father.' The sudden change in subject took Billy by surprise and he turned to look at McIntyre, who went on, 'He walked round these cases just as you are doing. Is it money you want?'

'No!' said Billy, surprised.

'You don't need to look so shocked,' said McIntyre. 'It usually is. What is it then?'

'I want to know about him,' said Billy. 'If he's still alive. Where he is.'

'Has it occurred to you,' said McIntyre, moving round his desk to sit in the large leather chair behind it, 'that if he's still alive he doesn't seem to be caring about your welfare? Which wouldn't surprise me at all. He always showed little regard for the feelings of others. Charlotte was nearly destroyed when he left.'

'Why did he go?'

'He took up with your mother. You're the product of a deal of lust! Oh, don't look so old-fashioned. Am I embarrassing you? And now... suddenly... you turn up. Billy Toth. And what am I to make of that? I wasn't born yesterday.' Before Billy could think of an answer, McIntyre had already lost interest in that line of conversation. He gazed round at his showcases with sudden immense pride. 'You know,' he said, 'in all the years I've worked with glass, I have never broken a single piece. That's a record. And another record is that I started as a factory hand, cleaning the floors, and now I own all this. It bears my name. Some of the most delicate artefacts made by men... and dealers throughout the world will say "Oh, that's a piece of McIntyre glass..." ' A knock on the door interrupted his flow and a middle-aged man with a handsome but rather weak face came in. 'Sorry to disturb you,' he said. 'The Grant consignment is ready for you to check.'

'Good,' said McIntyre. 'David, this is Toth's son. Keep him company, will you.' He went out of the room, closing the door behind him.

'My wife telephoned to say you were here,' said Jameson, after a pause.

'I'm just going,' said Billy.

'Got what you camc for?' said Jamcson.

'I don't think I've ever been anywhere so... unhappy,' said Billy. 'I don't know why anybody stays here, with him.'

Jameson laughed, quite pleasantly. 'Don't you?' he said. 'It's quite simple. It's because we've all got what we want.' He walked over to the door of the drinks cabinet and tried it. It was locked. He seemed unsurprised. 'Me, for instance,' he said. 'Life with the woman I love, a nice job at the end of the drive, plenty of money. If anyone ever flies through your window and offers to grant your dearest wish... run! Your father was right to get out, but it's hard. She'll never leave, you see. Charlotte.' He wandered over to the window and looked out. 'He had a son who left once—but he came back. The old man took him back into the fold.'

'What happened to him?'

'Shot himself. Not much of a life here, you know. "Daddy" does it all.'

'Why did he come back?'

'Same reason Charlotte will never leave. Greed. One day it will all be hers. And meanwhile, it's not so bad, not for her. It is, after all, what she's always known. But your father couldn't take the dogsbody life...'

'And Pamela...?' said Billy.

'Loves her horses. Can't have a horse in a bed-sit in Edinburgh, living off a gas ring with the man you love.'

'Then you do without,' said Billy.

'Easy to say. But the alternative is more attractive. Invite the man you love to join you. That way, you have "everything you want". Only snag—"Daddy" is the head of the family.'

'But I'm sure Pamela is unhappy here,' said Billy.

'Come over here,' said Jameson. Billy joined him at the window and found he could see across the paddock where Pamela and Charlotte were taking the bay and a beautiful roan over a series of jumps in the tranquil afternoon sunlight. 'They're both unhappy,' said Jameson. 'But they put all their hope in their men—and what can any man offer more than they have already got?'

The door opened again and McIntyre came back into the room. 'I've passed it,' he said. 'I take it you two have been having a good chinwag. David's a great talker.'

'I'm going now,' said Billy firmly. The tour round the factory had distracted him—now he remembered that he had been wanting to get away since a few moments after his arrival.

'Wait,' said McIntyre. He went over to one of the cabinets and took out a small glass owl. He held it out to Billy. 'Our visitors are all given one,' he said, with a slightly quizzical smile on his face. 'We make them out of scraps. Nothing is wasted.'

Billy looked at the owl, but didn't put out his hand for it.'I already have one, thank you,' he said. 'There was one among my mother's possessions.'

The smile disappeared. 'I can see you wouldn't want two,' said McIntyre, returning it to the case. 'How droll that the only thing he took with him was our giveaway gift.' He brightened, thrust a hand into his pocket, 'Now! I must give you the money for your fare.'

'No thank you,' said Billy.

'You're sure?' said McIntyre, visibly taken aback.

'Quite sure,' said Billy. 'Goodbye, Mr Jameson.' He turned and walked out of the room, and the factory.

Behind him McIntyre was saying, 'I'd like the design of the giveaway gift changed. This little owl has lost its fascination for me.' He picked it up once more, looked at it rather sadly, then quite deliberately dropped it on the floor where it broke into three pieces. He set his heel on the pieces and ground them down to a fine powder. 'Pity,' he said quietly.

More at ease now he was out of the old man's immediate jurisdiction, Billy stopped at the paddock fence, on his way down the long drive, and called across to Pamela, 'If I find out anything about Jerri . . . shall I let you know?'

Pamela rode over to the fence. 'No,' she said. 'Go away.'

'All you have to do is leave,' said Billy. 'You don't need all this.'

Pamela looked down from the bay with an odd little smile on her face. 'Isn't it funny,' she said, 'how the "have-nots" always want to persuade the "haves" to give up what they've got. I told you, don't come back.'

Billy turned from her and walked on down the drive. Pamela's new boyfriend Miles, arriving in his smart red Morgan, passed him travelling the other way, up the drive, bright and hopeful, cheerfully unaware that rejection or suffocation were the only possible ends to his journey.

Outside the gates of the McIntyre property Billy thumbed a lift. As he got into the car that stopped for him, which was hot and stuffy and smelt strongly of dog from the border collie that panted on the back seat, he felt that this was the first fresh air he'd breathed since walking in at the gates that morning.

Chapter Seven

But in fact this summer was not like any other, and Billy couldn't go on pretending that it was. Nor could he endure hanging about uselessly in Whitaker's house all day, especially as he knew there was a busy office functioning just the other side of the wall. Whitaker offered no criticism but Billy sensed that some kind of action was, not unreasonably, expected of him. He had passed his A levels, just, but they didn't seem to point him in any particular direction—until he saw an extremely neat and discreet notice posted in the window of a bookshop about twenty minutes walk from Whitaker's house: Assistant Required. Apply Within.

The manageress, Miss Moreton, an austere dragon-lady in her fifties, took him on promptly. She loathed being short-staffed and in any case Billy appealed to her. She liked his public school accent and manners. Also, although she didn't admit this to herself, she was not unaware that his particular brand of blond, blue-eyed good looks would go down very well with her female customers, who were in the majority.

Whitaker was pleased about the job. And one evening, perhaps as a way of expressing his approval, he announced that he had arranged to introduce Billy to Dr Jolland, a retired flautist who might be able to offer advice about Billy's chances of taking up the flute professionally.

Whitaker collected Dr Jolland in the Rover late one Friday evening while Billy set up his music stand and tried to decide what to play for him, settling in the end on a Bach sonata.

When he arrived, Dr Jolland turned out to have something of the archetypal music teacher about him. He was a man in his early seventies whose bald head was fringed with white hair which hung just over his collar, and whose white moustache and goatee beard gave a solemnity to his face that, in the circumstances, Billy found quite alarming. He had no interest in polite preliminaries. He put his coat and scarf over a chair by the sitting-room door before Whitaker could offer to take them from him, nodded at Billy, then went to stand by the fire, lit to take the chill off the late summer evening, plainly waiting for what he was required to hear.

Whitaker sat down in his usual chair, which meant that his back was to Billy and the music stand, and watched Dr Jolland for his reaction. He was every bit as nervous as his ward and, in a sense, in a worse situation because there was nothing he could do but wait. While Billy played, Dr Jolland stood with his hands on the mantlepiece and stared into the flames. Nothing about him gave any indication of his feelings. Billy finished the first movement of the sonata and lowered the flute, looking across at the two elderly men by the hearth, unsure whether to continue or wait.

Whitaker looked up at Jolland. 'He was nervous tonight,' he

said.

Dr Jolland glared at him over his half-spectacles. 'Let me be the judge,' he said severely, 'You're an expert on the flute?'

'No,' said Whitaker, crushed.

Dr Jolland clasped his hands behind his back and walked across to Billy. 'You were nervous?' he said.

'A bit. Yes.'

'Hm,' said Jolland. 'Play me some more, then.' He paced back towards the fire as Billy turned the page and started on the second movement, then raised his hand abruptly saying, 'Stop, stop, stop.'

Billy lowered the flute once more.

'Let the music speak, ' said Jolland. 'The flute is your voice. You are speaking the music. It doesn't need your additions.'

'No, Sir,' said Billy quietly. The room was silent apart from the sounds of the flames busy among the coals.

At last Whitaker said, with the utmost caution, 'Well?'

'He's good,' said Jolland grudgingly.

Whitaker's face broke into a smile of pure delight and he smacked the arm of his chair and craned round to beam at Billy, still at the stand behind him.

'But,' said Jolland, obviously disapproving of such excess, 'he'll have to be much better if he's going to make a living out of it.'

'I would like to go somewhere like the Royal College...' said Billy.

'Yes,' said Dr Jolland, 'I daresay you would. Well you must *earn* your place at such an establishment. Do you practice every day?'

'No,' said Billy uncomfortably.

'Then don't waste my time. I'm an old man. I have no wish to entertain a dilettante.'

'Oh, I must protest,' said Whitaker, defending.

Jolland rounded on him. 'You want a virtuoso?' he said. 'Then be prepared to suffer.'

'You'll take him on?' said Whitaker, hopefully.

'I can't teach him,' said Jolland. 'But I can prepare him to be taught.'

'And his talent is worth that?'

Dr Jolland crossed over to the chair by the door and began to tug his scarf out from where it lay, under his coat. 'Talent?' he said, winding the scarf round his neck, 'he has no talent. A skill for blowing, that's all. His talent has yet to emerge.' He shrugged on his great coat and peered across the room at Billy. 'What are you doing this weekend?'

Billy hesitated. 'Going up to the cottage at Bamburgh,' he said.

'A rich dilettante,' said Jolland. 'Worse and worse. You have a job?'

'I work in a bookshop.'

'Good. Be at my house at seven o'clock on Monday. Spend the weekend on the Bach you played me. If I don't see an improvement, I'm not interested.' He looked at Whitaker. 'I must go. Are you taking me?'

Whitaker, who had fallen into a pleased sort of trance in his chair, leaped to his feet. 'Of course,' he said.

'Well come along then,' said Jolland. 'I'm a very old man and at this rate I may die before you get me home.'

Whitaker followed him out of the room, then stuck his head back round the door for just long enough to give Billy a large wink.

By the time Whitaker got back, Billy was sitting in front of the fire drinking cocoa and reading, the picture of relaxation. 'Do you want a cocoa?' he said, as Whitaker irrupted into the room and made straight for the drinks cabinet. 'After that evening?' said Whitaker. 'I do not. I want an extremely liberal Scottish. Wasn't he *awful!'*

'But he's going to take me on,' said Billy smugly, watching as Whitaker poured himself something more than a double and added an extremely modest quantity of Malvern water.

'You must be a masochist.'

'He is good, isn't he?'

'He used to be a good player,' said Whitaker, taking himself and his whisky to his fireside chair. 'How much he knows about the flute now, I couldn't say. Still, I expect it's a little like riding a bike. You never entirely forget.'

'I've never heard of him,' said Billy.

'Before your time, dear child,' said Whitaker. He took a drink of whisky and stretched out his legs comfortably. 'God,' he said, 'you must be getting heartily sick of geriatric old men. My fault. All my contemporaries grew old along with me.' He drank again and raised his eyebrows at Billy. 'More's the pity,' he said. 'The very old are almost as revolting as the very young. Well, are you satisfied?'

Billy grinned at him. 'I'm amazed! How many more people do you know?'

Whitaker smiled to himself. 'A few,' he said. 'But this is just a stop-gap. He was saying in the car – he has a contact at an Academy in Salzburg. Says he might put your name forward...'

'Salzburg!' said Billy.

'Yes. I thought that might make you perk up.'

'But if I was in Salzburg I'd be quite near Hungary.'

'Oh, just nip in, I suppose,' said Whitaker.

'Why not? My father did.'

'And hasn't been heard of since.'

'No,' said Billy deflated. He got up and went to kick one of the coals from the edge of the fire into its glowing heart. The glow became flames. 'We don't get any further forward, do we? Perhaps we never will.'

Whitaker stood, too, and put his almost empty glass on the edge of the mantlepiece. He hadn't intended to be dampening. 'Then you'll just have to content yourself with being a brilliantly famous fluter,' he said.

'Flautist!'

'Fluter!' said Whitaker. The rapidly downed whisky had made him very slightly pixilated. He chanted in a rhythmic monotone:

A fluter who tutored the flute
Tried to tutor two tooters to toot...

'I'm going to bed,' said Billy laughing.

Whitaker continued unabashed, beating time with one hand:

Said the two to the tutor
Is it harder to toot
Or to tutor two tooters to toot?

'It *must* be second childhood,' said Billy, still laughing, making for the door.

Whitaker made a dismissing gesture with his time-beating hand. 'Early start in the morning,' he said. 'I want to be in Bamburgh in time for my morning constitutional.'

Billy went out of the door and then stuck his head back into the room, in imitation of Whitaker's earlier exit in the wake of Dr Jolland. 'All the way to the pub,' he said, and vanished.

'Be gone!' Whitaker shouted after him: then turned towards

the drinks cabinet. 'I'll just have one more little one...' he said contentedly.

Bamburgh was lying low under a heavy sea mist that seemed to press down the contours of the already fairly flat landscape. The sea itself was invisible and the sand and even the usually vivid dune grass looked grey and drear. It was not the day for a constitutional, even to the pub. Whitaker parked the Rover outside the cottage and paused to reach for his briefcase from the back seat. Billy got straight out and went to the door, his key ready, wanting to get in and light a fire as soon as possible. But something about the door struck him as odd. He stretched out his hand and pushed it. It swung open.

'Hey!' he said in surprise.

Whitaker shut the car door and followed him. 'What?'

He joined Billy in the doorway and the two of them stood side by side looking around the living-room. There were dirty plates and cushions around the hearth, as though people had eaten a meal in front of the fire, which was grey and dead but had not been raked out. A used mug stood on the low mantlepiece, a doll lay in the corner of the sofa looking up at them with wide tragic eyes, the chairs were somehow not quite in their usual places.

'Visitors,' said Whitaker. 'What a mess!'

Billy ran upstairs to check. The twin beds in the front room and the single in the back room had all been slept in and left unmade. 'More than one!' he called down the stairs.

From the sitting-room below came Whitaker's voice, unmistakably rattled, 'Hell and damnation!'

Billy leaped down the stairs and swung round the banister post into the room. 'What is it?' he said anxiously.

Whitaker, still in his hat and coat, was at the drinks cupboard, holding a bottle which was about two thirds full. 'They've opened my malt,' he said. 'I was saving that for Christmas. Oh—fiends!'

'What do we do?' said Billy.

'Ask to use someone's telephone and contact the police,' said Whitaker. 'Or stroll along to the station ourselves.'

'I'll go,' said Billy.

'We'll both go,' said Whitaker firmly. 'They may come back. And what is more, they may be large and not very friendly.'

At that moment the front door swung open and crashed back against the wall, making them both jump. A fair-haired boy of about five ran in from outside.

Billy began to laugh. He squatted down to be on a level with the startled, snubby-nosed face. 'What are you doing here?' he said.

'I live here,' said the boy gravely. 'Are you burglars?' Abruptly he turned and started to yell, 'Mam! Mam! There's men here.' He made a dash for the door but Billy grabbed him and half carried him outside, Whitaker following.

A woman in her twenties and a small girl of about seven were toiling across the dunes towards the cottage, emerging damply from the mist like two lost souls. The woman stopped in her tracks, seeing Billy with the child, and screamed out: 'Jason!'

The boy wriggled round in Billy's grasp and delivered him a hefty kick on the shin. Billy grunted and let go in surprise, and the child ran. At the same moment the woman began to run towards him, caught him by the arm and began hitting out, wildly, hysterically, screaming, 'I told you, Jason, didn't I? didn't I? I told you not to run on.' The girl was making hopeless efforts to pull Jason clear of the flailing hands and both children were sobbing. Billy ran to the woman and caught her from behind, pinning her arms to her sides. 'Stop it,' he said. 'Please stop it. Don't hurt them.'

All the anger drained out of her and she sagged against him, beginning to cry. Whitaker signalled to the two terrified children to come into the cottage. 'Come along,' he said. 'Noise like that'll frighten the seagulls.' The girl led the whimpering Jason nervously towards Whitaker, and Billy followed, supporting the woman, who was sobbing over and over again, 'What am I going to do? What am I going to do?'

Once the damp, bedraggled little family was inside the cottage, the woman seemed calmer. She sat in Whitaker's chair in her cheap, fake leopardskin jacket and worn denims, her long frizzy hair dry and dead yet sparkling with droplets of mist, and watched as Billy cleared the fire and lit a new one. The children sat on the sofa, close together, and Whitaker collected up the dirty crockery, asking one or two careful questions as he did so. She was May Tanner, she told them. The children were Lucy who was seven and Jason who was five. They were hers. They had been put into a home because she had been ill, had been in hospital, but now she was well again and she'd taken them out. She didn't look well. Her face was pale and there were violet smudges under her eyes.

Billy went out to the kitchen to heat up some soup. Whitaker followed him, leaving the adjoining door open. Behind them they heard Lucy say, in her serious voice, 'You promised you wouldn't hit us.'

'I won't hit you,' said May, and her voice was gentle and very sad. 'I never meant to. You're my babies.'

Lucy got up and went over to her, touched her face, then climbed onto her knee. May put her arms round her and held her close, rocking her slightly. 'Big baby,' she said softly.

Billy carried two mugs of soup into the room. He gave one to Jason and one to Lucy. May pushed gently at her, 'Get off while you drink your soup,' she said. She looked up at Billy. 'Jason likes it here,' she said. 'Don't you, Jason?'

'It's by the seaside,' said Jason.

Billy went back for the third mug, brought it in and gave it to May. Whitaker let himself, quite quietly, out of the front door. 'I took them to the beach this morning,' said May helplessly, accepting the mug. 'But they were cold. Kept on about being cold.' She shivered.

Billy sat on the end of the sofa, next to the chidren. May turned her large sad eyes on him. 'Where's the old chap gone?' she said.

'Out,' said Billy.

'For the police?'

'You can't keep running,' said Billy gently. 'You are running, aren't you?'

May turned and gazed into the fire. 'They say I'm not suitable,' she said. 'To look after the kiddies.' She looked back at him. 'You live here?'

'Sometimes.'

May smiled wistfully at him. 'It must be nice to have a house for sometimes.'

'I mean,' said Billy embarrassed, 'when I'm not working.'

'Is he your Daddy?' said Jason suddenly. 'That old man?'

'No,' said Billy.

'Who's your Daddy?'

Billy smiled at him and got up. 'This is...' he said, crossing to the small bureau where he kept the photograph of Jerri and Tania, newly framed. But it wasn't there.

'That's funny,' said Billy. 'There was a photograph.'

'I don't know nothing about it,' said May, too quickly.

Billy turned to look at her, puzzled and uneasy. 'Where is it?' he said. 'It's all I had of them. I never knew them.'

'They don't know their Daddies either,' said May. 'Better off that way.'

'Where is it?' said Billy, growing more impatient. 'You don't want it. Where is it?'

May had turned right away from him. 'Awful old photograph,' she said into the fire.

Lucy got up and crossed over to the bureau. She picked up the wastepaper basket from beside it, brought it over to Billy, and shyly handed it to him. He took it and looked down into it. At the bottom lay the buckled picture frame and the photograph itself, torn into little pieces and all mixed up with slivers of broken glass. 'No!' he said. 'No!'

'Old picture,' said May into the fire. 'Don't want that.'

Billy stared down at its shattered remains and the image Elsa Gruber had planted in his mind came back – a border post on a misty night – a car racing for the barrier, breaking through it, splinters flying high – Border guards leaping clear, recovering, firing - the car skidding, crashing – exploding into an orange flower of flame. He flung the waste paper basket down and advanced on May. 'It was *mine*!' he said. 'All I had of them. How *could* you . . .'

May rounded on him, lips drawn back over her teeth, spitting with anger like a cat, 'Go on, then, hit me,' she said. 'See how easy it is. They don't understand that. They say you're not fit to look after your kids. But look at you . . . you're itching to take a swipe, aren't you!'

Jason began to scream which made Billy aware that Lucy, too, was shrinking back on the sofa, crying. 'I'm sorry,' he said to them gently. 'It's all right. I'm sorry.'

May got up and walked over to look out of the misty window. 'Pictures of couples,' she said bitterly. 'All lovey-dovey. God what a load of . . . her Dad went off one day – never came back. I don't know where he is. I don't care. Good riddance!' She pushed her hair back. Her nails were bitten down to the quick. Some still had smears of red varnish on them. 'I'm not bothered, don't you worry,' she said. 'Love? Flowers in your button-hole? Don't make me laugh. His Dad – I don't even know his name. He was just comfort.' She began to cry. 'God what a mess we make.' She turned round. 'And now they're in a home.'

'I liked it there,' said Jason solemnly. 'I had a friend with funny eyes.'

'He was Chinese,' said Lucy. 'I'm going to marry him.'

'No, I am,' said Jason.

'Men can't marry men, silly,' said Lucy, giggling.

'He's my friend,' said Jason stubbornly. 'He makes me laugh.'

'They're all right, you see,' said May. 'But what about me?'

Jason's eye was caught by the flute case, which Billy had dumped on the small sideboard when he first arrived. 'What's that?' he said. 'Is it a gun?'

'It's a flute,' said Billy. He went over to get the case and brought it back to the sofa.

'It's a gun,' said Jason firmly, climbing from the seat of the sofa onto its back to look over Billy's shoulder.

'No,' said Billy. 'Look,' and he opened the case, took out the flute and played a rippling scale on it.

Jason gave a peal of delighted laughter and Lucy leaned forward and began to smile, too. 'Do it again,' said Jason. Billy played the scale in reverse.

Lucy held out her hands. 'I want to do it,' she said.

Billy wiped the flute and passed it to her. She held it to her lips and blew but could only produce a faint, hoarse, rushing sound. Billy looked at May, hunched by the fire. 'I'm sorry,' he said.

'You're too soft, that's your trouble,' said May.

Lucy handed the flute back to Billy. 'You do it,' she said.

Sitting on the arm of the sofa Billy thought for a moment, then began to play Debussy's 'Syrinx', very softly. The children sat quite silently, their eyes round, listening. May Tanner still sat gazing into the fire, her eyes glittering with tears. 'That's . . . lovely,' she said.

Billy heard the police car draw up outside, but he didn't stop playing until Whitaker, who had returned with them, came into the cottage. 'They're waiting outside,' said Whitaker. 'I didn't want to frighten the children.'

May went without protest, leading the two children one by each hand. Lucy carried her doll. Billy and Whitaker followed them out of the cottage. One policeman stood by the car, the other came forward, 'You are May Tanner?' he said.

'Yes,' said May wearily. 'I'm May Tanner. Come on kids.' The policeman opened the back door of the car and the two children, subdued and silent, climbed in.

May stopped at the car door, then looked back at Billy. 'You satisfied?' she said.

'For the children's sake,' said Billy. 'They'll be all right...'

'Oh, they'll be all right,' said May. 'But what about me? How'll they deal with me? A few more drugs and sweep me under the carpet? Eh?'

'Come along, Mrs Tanner,' said the policeman.

'Miss,' said May viciously, getting into the car. 'I didn't have that pleasure.'

As the car drove off, Jason and Lucy knelt on the back seat, staring back out of the rear window to where Billy and Whitaker stood at the cottage door. Billy swallowed hard.

'She walked out of a home for the mentally disturbed, yesterday,' said Whitaker, quietly. 'Took the children from a care centre in Gateshead.' Billy stared after the fast disappearing car, the two small faces in the back window now just pale blobs in the distance. 'Apparently she nearly killed the little lad...'

'Yes, yes. All right,' said Billy. He walked a few paces down the lane, the way the car had travelled. 'Poor May,' he said. 'She's so right. We'd rather not know...'

The next time he played the Debussy was in Dr Jolland's study on the following Monday evening. When he had finished, Jolland said, 'Not bad. Not good, but not bad.'

'I don't see that it matters,' said Billy, staring down at the flute in his hands.

'Mr Stanyon,' said Dr Jolland, 'you must not waste my time — at my age it is a most valuable commodity. You have regaled me with your touching story about the weekend but you should not expect that to be an excuse for not having practised.'

Billy opened his mouth to protest, but Jolland waved an impatient hand at him. 'Hear me out. You will not be a performer unless you want that above all else.'

'But, when you're faced...' Billy began.

'With such misery? Such heartbreak?' said Jolland. 'Do you help by moaning about it to me?' He softened, 'Those little children,' he said, 'will remember a funny man who tootled tunes long after all the rest is a vague nightmare. And the woman... she sat by the fire and listened to music. It's not about pretty tunes, Billy. Through music you touch the spirit. It is both a gift and a responsibility. Now! Play again from the beginning. I shall work you till you drop.'

Billy looked at him thoughtfully for a moment or two. Then he raised the flute and began to play.

Chapter Eight

The letter from France was totally unexpected. The writer, Giselle de Beauvoir, explained that her husband Henri had chanced to pick up a German magazine while on business in Frankfurt. In it he had found the article Gunter Walser had written about Billy and his search for his parents. They had both, she went on, known Billy's parents many years ago, before he was born. If he would care to visit them at their chateau they would be happy to tell him what little they could about Tania and Jerri.

Billy passed the letter to Whitaker across the breakfast table. 'I'd like to go at once,' he said, 'but I'm not due for any holiday from the shop yet. I could only go for a weekend.'

'That's no bad thing,' said Whitaker. 'Staying with strangers can be most pleasant or quite hideous, so the shorter the better. You can always go again.'

'Will you come?' said Billy.

'No,' said Whitaker. 'In my experience, staying with strangers is *always* hideous.'

Billy arrived at the Chateau Beauvoir in the midst of such a strange occasion that for a moment he thought he must be jet-lagged and imagining what he saw. He had taken a night flight, then a train, then had been driven by one of the estate workers through lush summer countryside, past the carefully-tended vineyards of the Beauvoir Estate, and into the grounds of the Chateau. Now he stood on the large, immaculate lawn and gazed at a dream-like scene.

Right in the middle of the grass, and quite by itself, was a table spread with a white cloth. It bore several gleaming tulip-shaped glasses at one end and a dozen bottles of champagne at the other. Scattered about the lawn in groups of five or six, quite still and silent, stood the estate workers, gardeners and indoor staff. Right in the centre of the lawn stood Henri de Beauvoir, a tall good-looking man in his forties. A little to one side, away from the workers and from her husband, stood Giselle. Everyone, apart only from Giselle, was staring up at the roof of the Chateau. It was small as chateaux go, but pretty and ornate, with a complex of sloping roofs and a single pointed tower on the top of which a weather-vane glinted in the sun. And creeping slowly along the ridge of one of the roofs, the focus of all attention, was the small slim figure of a boy, a child of about eleven or twelve. Billy put his bag on the grass and watched too, allowing himself to be frozen into the tableau with the rest.

Giselle, because she was deliberately looking away from the roof, noticed Billy quite quickly and moved over to greet him. 'That is René, my son, up there,' she said. 'I can't look. Tell me, is he all right?'

'He's all right,' said Billy, but at that moment René slipped. The gasp from the assembly on the lawn made Giselle turn. She put her hands to her face but still did not look up. René slithered three or four feet and then stopped, caught in an angle of the roof. 'Mama!' he called. 'Mama! Mama!' Giselle began to run towards the Chateau but Henri caught her as she passed him and restrained her. The child seemed to calm down, but did not continue the way he had been going. He crawled back towards an open window that Billy had not noticed before, and climbed inside. There was a sense of anticlimax on the lawn. The people began to disperse quietly and the young butler started to clear the solitary table.

Giselle recovered herself and turned to call Billy towards her. She introduced him to Henri who shook his hand and then said, with a smile so forced as to be almost unpleasant, 'So sorry. I thought you were about to witness an historic moment in the Beauvoir family. The champagne must wait for another day. I will see you at luncheon. Excuse me, please.' He strode away across the grass towards the Chateau, looking neither to right nor left.

'Please, come with me. I will show you your room,' said Giselle. 'I am so sorry that we did not welcome you immediately.'

Billy looked across at the table. 'Champagne?' he said.

'Everyone who works on the estate drinks a toast in champagne after the climb,' said Giselle. 'It's all part of the tradition.'

'How often does this happen?' said Billy, as they walked towards the open front door.

'Only once!' said Giselle. 'I couldn't stand the strain otherwise. Before the son and heir of the Beauvoir estate reaches his thirteenth birthday he has to climb to the top of the tower in full view of the assembled workers—and for all I know in the sight of God.'

Billy looked up at the tower as he walked. It was a tall, narrow cone-shape, with hang-tiling which afforded no footholds whatsoever. 'But that's stupid, it's not possible,' he said. 'What if he can't do it?'

'Oh, he will.'

'How do you know?'

'They always do,' said Giselle simply.

When she had shown him around, and he had left his bag in his room, Giselle asked Billy to go and fetch René for lunch. 'We lead quite a solitary life here,' she said. 'He has been so looking forward to our visitor. You may take his mind off—just now.' She directed Billy to a room at the very top, the room of the window from which René had made his attempt on the tower. It was a kind of attic, full of dust and sunbeams. René half-lay astride an aged rocking horse, his arms around its neck, his cheek pressed to its cheek. He had been crying but now he was silent.

'Your mother sent me to find you,' said Billy. 'It's time for lunch.'

René made no response.

Billy crossed to the small window and squinted out at the tower which rose before him, three sloping roofs away. 'Perhaps there's another way up,' he said doubtfully.

'Is Papa angry?' said René softly, into the horse's amiable wooden face.

'I'm sure not,' said Billy. 'Why should he be?'

'Because I was afraid.'

'I expect he was, when he climbed the tower,' said Billy.

'But...I showed it.' He sat up a little. 'How long will you stay?'

'I must go tomorrow. I only came for the weekend.'

'What is a *courtisane?'* said René unexpectedly.

"Sorry?" said Billy, taken aback.

'Papa told Mama that your mother was *une courtisane,'* said René. 'I did not know what it meant.'

Billy turned and made for the stairs. 'Come on,' he said curtly, and hurried down.

By the time he took his place at the head of the lunch table, Henri had come to terms with his disappointment. He spoke encouragingly to René, using English as a courtesy to Billy. 'You don't just dash in without thinking it out, René,' he said. 'Would Everest have been conquered if they had not first known the route they were going to take?'

'No, Papa,' said René, still subdued.

'Of course not. Believe me, there is only one way to get to the top of that tower. I know, I have done it. I went the way my father went, as he went the way of his father—right back to Giles de Beauvoir, who made the mark.'

'Yes, Papa.'

Henri turned to Billy. 'You see, not only does René have to climb the tower, he must see the mark at the top. Only I know what that mark is—and when he knows it he will never tell it to anyone. He will wait for the day when his son will whisper it in his ear, as I now wait for René.' He smiled. 'It is foolish, I am sure,' he said, lightly and entirely unconvincingly, 'but it is a tradition as old as the Chateau. You are enjoying your visit?'

'Yes. Thank you.'

'When I read that article, I contacted the journalist—Gunter Walser. He once wrote an article on the Chateau which was quite good. He gave us your address. The son of Tania Szabo!' He smiled across the table at Giselle.

'Your mother and I were very close friends,' said Giselle. 'We shared a flat just off the Gloucester Road. In Rosary Gardens, do you know it?'

'No, I don't know London very well,' said Billy.

'Tania and I were in the orchestra at the Opera House,' said Giselle dreamily.

'My wife plays the violin most beautifully.'

'You exaggerate, Henri.'

He spread his hands in mock capitulation. 'Only my opinion, of course.'

'And you knew my father?' said Billy.

'Not so well.' Giselle rang a small handbell and a maid appeared and began to clear the lunch dishes. Henri gave René permission to leave the table, but he had begun to gaze at Billy with undisguised admiration and seemed reluctant to go. Giselle shooed him gently away, promising that, after his rest, she would help him to give Billy a conducted tour of the grounds. 'René is not very strong,' she said half-apologetically to Billy, when the child had left the room and the maid had placed the coffee things in front of her. 'He is asthmatic.'

'Psychological,' said Henri complacently. 'He'll grow out of it.'

Giselle began to pour coffee. 'Were they married?' said Billy, prompting.

'Your parents?' said Giselle. 'Not when I knew them.'

'Ever?'

'Oh, I expect so. Cream and sugar?'

'No sugar, thank you.' He accepted his cup and then said, very directly, 'Why don't people like to talk about them?'

'It was all so long ago,' said Giselle.

'Ah, Giselle,' said Henri, 'We have brought him here, we must tell him what he wants to know.' He turned to Billy. 'There was quite a scandal. The papers made much of it. Your mother defected from Hungary in pursuit of her childhood sweetheart. When she got to England she found he had married.'

'Charlotte McIntyre?'

'You know her?'

Billy paused. 'I've met her,' he said.

Giselle leaned forward. 'Tania had been a solo instrumentalist in her own country. Her reputation followed her. She took work at the Opera, as a temporary measure—but the scandal put an end to it.'

Henri chuckled to himself. 'Tania more or less marched up to the McIntyre family seat and demanded her sweetheart back,' he said.

'Oh, it wasn't quite like that,' said Giselle reprovingly, but smiling too.

'Near enough,' said Henri.

Billy watched them as they wrangled affectionately over their memories, then said, 'Did she love him?'

'Very much,' said Giselle, without hesitation, turning her smile on Billy.

Billy found her far more approachable than Henri whose manner was slightly sardonic and who also had a way of studying him intently which Billy found faintly unnerving. Giselle seemed more aware of the importance to him of anything that was said about his parents, and when she strolled around the grounds with him that afternoon—René darting from them and back again, sometimes examining the tower from however great a distance, sometimes playing hide and seek—she said, 'I am sorry if we seemed hard about Tania and Jerri Toth. I remember your mother as a good friend of the days when I was young and Henri was wooing me, with roses.' She laughed. 'Always roses, even in winter. I was very impressed.'

René bobbed out at them from behind a large shrub. Billy grinned at him and he grinned back and ran off again. 'Does he seem very young for his years?' said Giselle. 'We have kept him too much here, I think. It was a difficult birth...and he was so asthmatic when he was little. He has a tutor but we think he will go to school soon.' She smiled almost guiltily at Billy. 'I even dread that! Is it such a terrible crime to be a doting parent? You see, I couldn't conceive again, after René. He is our only one.'

'How fortunate,' said Billy, with an edge to his voice, 'that he was a boy. Or there would have been no Beauvoir to climb the tower.'

'You think it is all a nonsense?' said Giselle.

Billy paused, not wanting to be rude but unable to find a polite way of saying what he thought. 'Yes,' he said at last. 'I don't think it's being fair to René.'

Giselle stopped walking, looking across at a side view of the Chateau. 'Look,' she said. 'That is a part of René. It is what family is—future and past. He will do the climb and he will run the vineyard and he will marry and have a son...it is part of him, like the shape of his nose or the colour of his hair.'

'But what if he wants something different?'

'We don't just take or do what we want,' said Giselle. 'We take what is ours and do what is expected of us.'

'But he was scared,' said Billy. 'Why must he do something so unnecessary if he's scared. I wouldn't.'

'No?' said Giselle. She began to walk on again, slowly. 'René does it for his father, and for his family honour.'

There was a silence between them. 'And I have no family?' said Billy.

Partly to break the awkward moment, Giselle called, 'René!' He came running back to her and put his arm round her waist. 'Monsieur Billy says you shouldn't climb the tower if you don't want to,' said Giselle, stroking his hair.

'Not want to?' said René, pulling away from his mother. 'I am René de Beauvoir.' Giselle glanced at Billy with a small smile. 'When I have climbed to the top,' said René, 'Everyone will cheer. And I will come down and whisper to Papa what I have seen. And he will say,' he planted himself in front of them and spread out his arms, '*"Un Beauvoir a vu!"* ' He smiled almost condescendingly up at Billy. 'That means "A Beauvoir has seen",' he explained, and instantly ran ahead again, running his hand down the line of a hedge.

René and Giselle entertained him for the rest of the day and Billy was unable to speak alone with Henri until after dinner. It was Henri's custom to smoke a last cigar out of doors on warm evenings, and to listen to the familiar night sounds. Billy followed him out, tense with something he wanted to say. Unaware and relaxed, Henri sniffed appreciatively at the balmy air. 'I love this place, he said. 'When I am away from it I feel only half alive. You understand?'

'Yes,' said Billy, partly out of politeness but partly because Henri de Beauvoir's sense of place was so apparent. But, 'Do you?' said Henri, doubting. 'An estate like this takes every ounce of a person. Like a demanding mistress.' He smiled a private smile. 'No, I have always found them less insistent.' A dog barked in the distance. 'That dog,' said Henri, 'I could tell you exactly where on the estate he is... somewhere near the third year vines, coursing a hare...'

'Why did you tell René that my mother was *une courtisane,'* said Billy.

'Did I? Surely not.'

'He heard you say it to Madame de Beauvoir,' said Billy steadily.

'Oh well, perhaps. She was a pretty little thing, but intense. Not unlike you in that department.'

'Did she turn you down, Monsieur?' said Billy.

Henri glanced at him with an amused smile. 'On the contrary,' he said.

'I bet she told you to stuff your Chateau in France,' said Billy, his eyes glinting in the light which flowed out from the hall behind, 'and your champagne, and your roses in winter.'

'No, she didn't, Billy,' said Henri, his voice quite serious. 'Not at all. But Giselle came from a good family, and that is what matters when you are taking a wife.'

'Why did you invite me here?'

Henri turned to face him, gave him his full attention. 'Giselle did it for an old friend,' he said. 'I did it for an old mistress.'

'I don't believe you,' said Billy.

'Oh, yes, Billy,' said Henri. 'Yes indeed. And so naturally I was intrigued. I wanted to see you.'

Billy stared at him. There was an empty echoing silence

between them which he felt he might fall into. Frogs croaked in the distance. The dog barked once more. Henri held the moment cruelly, then broke it with a smile. 'You could only be Jerri Toth's son, Billy,' he said. Billy drew in a long breath. 'You have his look,' said Henri. 'He was a merchant seaman, you know. A peasant.'

'So,' said Billy. 'You've seen.'

Henri laughed. *'Un Beavoir a vu!'* he said and turned away to gaze across the dark estates.

Billy turned on his heel and went indoors.

He was up and dressed soon after dawn and making his way to the attic room where the rocking horse gazed uncritically at him. He opened the window, climbed out onto the first of the sloping roofs and began his assault on the tower. The day before, had he even considered doing such a thing, it would have been in an attempt to find a safe route for René, to save him from needless fear and danger. Today he wanted nothing more than to vandalize the traditions of the *famille de Beauvoir.* He was afraid of heights, but the rage he felt towards Henri, and towards the miniature Henri they called René, kept his feet and hands steady. Sharp, indignant cries from below told him that he had been noticed. He glanced down briefly to see Henri and his son approaching the Chateau, a dog at their heels, guns over their arms. He could not make out any words but it was obvious that René was enraged, Henri calming him.

At the base of the tower he stood carefully upright on the roof ridge, his hands pressed against the smooth tiled slope, and looked up at the seemingly hopeless ascent. Then something caught his eye, something half hidden by an angle of roof, and quite invisible from below. He reached out and drew it towards him — a rope ladder which hung down from the very top of the tower.

Carefully and steadily he climbed it, to the top—and there examined the weather-vane, the tiles, everything. But, 'There is no mark,' he said to himself in quiet fury. 'How stupid!' He climbed down again, and when he jumped in through the window he found René waiting for him, feet apart, hands on hips, shaking with rage.

'There is no mark,' said Billy fiercely.

'How dare you climb my tower?' cried René.

'It's easy,' said Billy. 'There's a ladder. And there is no mark at the top. It's just a stupid game.'

René clapped his hands over his ears. 'You're taking away my birthright,' he screamed. 'Papa, come quickly!'

Henri, already near the top of the stairs, strode into the room. 'He has told me!' said René, beginning to sob.

Henri shook him. 'You forget yourself,' he said. Then, more coldly, 'Told you what?'

'That there's a ladder to climb.'

Henri seemed to relax. 'It's all right,' he said. 'You would have found it.'

'There is no mark at the top,' said Billy.

'No?' said Henri. 'How would you know? You are not a Beavoir. Come René, I think today there will be champagne.' He led René out of the room and down the stairs.

Billy was left alone in the room, with the dust and sunbeams. For a moment he put his hands over his face, then he aimed a vicious kick at the rocking horse but regretted it at once and reached out to stroke the worn head.

As he prepared to leave the Chateau, he saw that the tableau that had greeted his arrival had reformed itself. The table stood beneath its champagne, the estate workers stood in their silent groups, Henri stood proud and upright in the centre; Giselle, as before, stood apart, not watching. But this time René had left the sloping roofs behind him, was already working his way up the tower itself by the ancient rope ladder. Billy crossed to Giselle. 'I came to say goodbye,' he said.

'You will not stay for the climb?'

He shook his head. 'I lost my temper. I'm...I'm very sorry.'

He looked up at the tower. René was already half-way up it when one of the struts of the ladder, weakened by Billy's weight, gave way. He almost fell, clung on with his hands, legs kicking for a foothold. Giselle, looking up at the Chateau roof for the first time, reached out and gripped Billy's arm, her fingers almost clawing at him. Then René found the next rung with his feet—and edged on upwards. The assembly, which had drawn in its breath in horror, let it out again in a sigh of admiration.

Then René was at the top, methodically examining the weather-vane, on all sides. Suddenly he raised one arm and his voice carried down to them. *'Un Beauvoir a vu.'* Applause began on the lawn.

Giselle watched René's descent, and waited until her son was led across the lawn by his father. She began to move towards them, then checked herself.

Father and son stood alone before all. Henri stooped and René whispered in his ear. Henri stood upright. *'Un Beauvoir a vu!'* he cried. Amid the sound of cheering and champagne corks, René stared straight across at Billy, eyes blazing.

Billy walked up to him and extended a hand. 'Congratulations,' he said.

'Thank you,' said René, taking his hand, suddenly very adult.

'You saw a mark?'

'Of course. You didn't?'

Billy shook his head.

'You are not a Beauvoir,' said René.

Henri approached with champagne for his son. For a moment his eyes met Billy's, then he turned René so that they both faced the assembly. Giselle smiled at Billy briefly, then she, too, joined the group. Henri was raising his glass, toasting his son; the estate workers, smiling and laughing, were echoing the toast.

Billy picked up his pack and walked away, across the lawns. No one looked after him and he did not look back.

Chapter Nine

It was Friday afternoon and Billy was at work in the bookshop. As he was half-way up a ladder, propped against Religion and Philosophy, he did not see the apparition that swept in through the double glass doors and up to the counter where Miss Moreton stood. Miss Moreton, however, looked up to see an extremely tall and slim young man, in heavy make-up, wearing a loose purple shirt and shocking-pink harem pants, bearing down upon her. He rested his shiny purple shoulder bag on the counter and said, most politely and in extremely cultured tones, 'Do you sell pornography?'

'Certainly not,' said Miss Moreton, looking at him ominously through her spectacles.

'Pity,' he said. 'What can you suggest?'

'We have nothing of that nature.'

He sighed. 'May I look round?' he said. 'I might find a copy of Chaucer.'

'The Classical Section,' said Miss Moreton, surprised, 'is over there.'

'So you do have Chaucer?'

'Of course!'

'Aha,' said the glamorous young man, 'What did I tell you? Can be rude, you know.' He swept off in the direction of the Classics. As he went he cast a quick glance at Billy, now descending the ladder with a paperback, watched admiringly by a rather dowdy middle-aged customer.

Billy carried the book to the counter, wrapped it, took the money and handed over the parcel. 'Thank you so much,' said the customer, as she accepted it and slipped it into her bag. 'I'm sorry to have been a trouble.'

'Not at all,' said Billy. 'The shelves are very high.'

The customer smiled at Miss Moreton. 'Such a charming young man,' she said as she went.

'Thank you, Madam,' said Miss Moreton, gratified.

Billy watched the woman with an amused smile as she made her way out of the shop. 'What *does* a woman like that want with the Tibetan Book Of The Dead?' he said.

Humour had never played any part in Miss Moreton's life. 'She is no doubt doing an Open University course,' she said.

'On Tibetan Buddhism?'

Miss Moreton looked at him severely. 'The paperback shelves are in fearful disarray,' she said, by way of command.

'Yes, Miss Moreton,' said Billy. He went to the nearest of the high, free-standing bookcases that held the paperbacks and had just begun to re-arrange them when a movement caught his eye. A book from the Science Fiction section, open and with its spine towards him, was moving slowly round the bookcase at eye level, apparently of its own volition. Billy stared in fascination at the horned creature on the lurid cover. As it came further round the bookcase he could see it was actually held by human hand, whose owner must be standing just behind the shelves. Then a head came round the case, the face hidden by the open paperback, and a muffled voice said, 'Ve vill ex-ter-min-ate her for you.'

'I beg your pardon?' said Billy.

'Se sour-faced prune at ze seat of custom,' said the book. 'Ve vill...aaargh!' To the accompaniment of a fearful throttling sound the book was lowered and Billy found himself gazing at the heavily made-up face of the young man in shocking pink. He stared blankly for half a second, then his face lit up with pleasure. 'Spike!' he cried. Spike slipped the book back onto its shelf and they hugged each other, laughing.

Miss Moreton leaned across her counter. 'What do you think you're doing, Mr Stanyon?' she said.

'Sorry, Miss Moreton,' said Billy, 'He's a friend of mine.'

'Is he indeed,' said Miss Moreton witheringly.

'His father's a lord,' said Billy.

'Oh, Stanyon!' said Spike. 'You always were such a snob!'

'No, honestly, Miss Moreton,' said Billy, still laughing. 'He's Lord Melford's son. They own half of Dorset!'

'Well he's not in Dorset now,' said Miss Moreton. 'You were going to do the shelves, Mr Stanyon.' She turned away to serve a customer.

'I don't think she likes me,' said Spike.

'What are you doing here?' said Billy.

'Looking up an old friend,' said Spike. He bent down and peered up the front of Billy's sweater. 'Very interestink!'

'You'll get me sacked!' said Billy, pushing him away.

Spike spread his arms to indicate the entire shop. 'You actually work here?'

'Oh no,' said Billy. 'I'm having an illicit relationship with Miss Moreton and this is the only way we manage to meet! Yes, I work here. But why are you here? I thought you were the leading light of a red-brick university.' He stepped back and looked at Spike more carefully. 'One thing's certain,' he said, 'you don't manage the family estate. You'd frighten the sheep.'

'Cattle, please!' said Spike.

'You *are* going to a fancy dress party?' said Billy, knowing the answer.

'No, ducky,' said Spike. 'This is street drag. Can I stay the night?'

'Where?'

'What do you mean "where"? In your cave, your pad, your shack... what do you do? Swing from a tree?'

Miss Moreton's voice cut through the air. 'Mr Stanyon. Would you serve, please?' She indicated a rather lost-looking woman who was pawing helplessly at the fiction shelves. Billy went over to her, Spike following. 'Forget it if it's too much trouble,' said Spike.

'Course it isn't,' said Billy. 'Look Spike, I'm busy now. Come back at 5.30, OK?' He reached the customer. 'Can I help you?' he said.

'Oh I do hope so,' she said rather desperately. 'I'm looking for something for a very poorly lady in hospital. Something amusing and, well, cheerful.'

Spike leaned towards her over Billy's shoulder. 'Try the Karma Sutra,' he said. 'My mother loved it.'

'Oh, thank you,' said the customer.

'5.30, Spike,' said Billy, threateningly.

'And I can stay?'

'Yes. *Goodbye.*'

'I'll go and collect the cabin trunks, then,' said Spike. He strode out of the shop, treating Miss Moreton to a sweeping bow in passing.

'What a charming speaking voice,' said the customer, looking after the silky pink and mauve apparition as it shimmered out of the door. 'Surprising, really. Do you sell this... Carmen Soutrer?'

Billy only managed to keep his face straight with the greatest difficulty. 'The Karma Sutra,' he said, 'is a collection of erotic writings from the early Vedic tradition of Hinduism. I don't think it's quite what you're looking for... unless, of course, your friend is with the Open University?'

'Good gracious, no,' said the customer. 'She's had an appendectomy!'

'Then perhaps something a little lighter...' said Billy, turning to the shelves.

The shop was busy for the rest of the day, and in any case Billy was well aware of Miss Moreton's attitude towards private telephone calls, so the first Whitaker knew about an overnight guest was when Billy and Spike arrived back at the house. He lived an ordered life by choice and was never at his best when taken by surprise. When the two boys flopped into chairs in the living-room and began to talk, clearly expecting dinner to materialize without any effort on their part, his patience was stretched to its limit. And when, alone in the kitchen in a fluster, he managed to burn two pieces of toast and let the soup boil all over the top of the stove simultaneously, his patience snapped. 'Billy!' he shouted. 'Billy!'

After a pause, Billy wandered into the kitchen and, leaning against the draining board, watched Whitaker frantically mop at the mess. 'What?' he said.

'This is too much,' said Whitaker. 'You stand there and say "what?" This is not an hotel.'

'You said I should entertain him,' said Billy.

'I didn't know I was expected to produce a three-course meal.'

'No one asked you to,' said Billy, infuriatingly reasonable.

Whitaker flung the wet cloth he had been using into the sink and turned to glare at him. 'What is the alternative?' he said. 'Sling a sliced loaf on the table and tell him to get on with it? Have you put sheets on his bed? Have you laid the table in the dining-room? Did it even occur to you to pop in here and see if everything was all right?' Whitaker had removed his jacket and tied a flowery apron over his dark waistcoat and trousers, but neither he nor Billy was in the mood to see the funny side of it. Billy, already somewhat unsettled by the casual way in which Spike had diminished his job in the bookshop, had caught Whitaker's anger, and they were both shouting now. 'He's the first friend I've had to stay here,' he said.

'Nice friends!' said Whitaker.

'How dare you judge him when you don't know him. You of all people.'

'And what does that mean?'

'Well, you weren't exactly regular yourself, were you?' said Billy. Then, suddenly afraid he had gone too far, 'Sorry. I shouldn't have said that.'

'I just think it's a downright imposition,' said Whitaker, 'to turn up with a guest with no warning whatever. You could have telephoned.'

'Miss Moreton doesn't like me using the phone.'

'I'm not surprised,' said Whitaker. 'You don't have to pay the bills.'

'Oh,' said Billy, exploding again, 'stuff the bills! You make it all so *dreary.*'

'Oh really? I personally?'

'No. All of you. You, Miss Moreton, the lot. I'm fed up with the shop and living here and everything...' He turned round and slammed out of the kitchen, dragged his jacket off its hook in the hall and called, 'Spike! Come on!'

Spike appeared in the sitting-room doorway, looking surprised. 'Where?'

'Out!' said Billy, hauling the front door open. 'Out to eat. You coming or not?'

'All right, all right,' said Spike, following him. 'I'm coming.'

The front door slammed behind them. Whitaker stood alone in the middle of the untidy kitchen. He untied his flowery pinny, set it neatly over the back of a chair and looked down at it, his face sad and tired. 'Damn,' he said to himself, very softly.

They ate in a hamburger parlour, Billy very aware of the mixture of amused and horrified glances that Spike's appearance attracted. Later they went to a disco and there it was Billy who looked odd and out of place in his grey slacks and plain pullover. Spike danced with extrovert enthusiasm, snaking his long limbs to the beat, eyeing up the talent. Billy sat alone at a table, watching, out of it, hating it. The flashing lights, the frenzied movements of the dancers, the relentless throb of the music seemed to him the very personification of a headache. The lights and beat grated their way into his skull and created a separate and personal headache inside. He endured as long as he could, then suddenly got up and pushed his way through the nightmare of dancers, their faces grotesque in the flashing strobe lights, and out into the street; cool air—silence—

Spike caught him up. 'What is it?' he said.

'I didn't like it in there,' said Billy, walking on down the road.

Spike kept pace. 'No,' he agreed. 'It was rather a grotty one.'

'Was it?' said Billy. 'It's the first time I've been anywhere like that.'

'You're joking!'

'I am not!'

They walked on in silence. 'So?' said Spike. 'What does it matter?'

'You make me feel it matters.'

'Why?'

Billy stopped abruptly. 'Oh, Spike,' he said. 'I'm making such a mess of it all. Working in that stupid bookshop...'

'It's only temporary,' said Spike reassuringly.

'Temporary till when?'

Spike grinned at him, then gave him an affectionate thump on the shoulder. 'Come on,' he said. 'We can't stand around here—we'll be had up for loitering.'

It was after midnight when they got back. Whitaker was in the sitting-room with the door to the hall wide open. An empty glass was at his side and so was the whisky bottle. The level in the bottle was quite low. He appeared to be reading *The Times,* which he did not lower as they came into the room. 'Good morning,' he said from behind it.

'It's not all that late,' said Billy, brightly.

'Not at all,' said Whitaker. 'If anything I'd have said it was early. The next day.'

'My fault, I'm afraid,' said Spike. 'I wanted to see the scene.'

'You go up, Spike,' said Billy. 'You know where your room is.'

'Sure,' said Spike. 'Goodnight, Mr Whitaker.'

'Goodnight,' said Whitaker.

Billy closed the door behind Spike. Whitaker continued to stare at the paper, holding it high so that he was quite obscured by it.

'Surely you've finished reading that by now?' said Billy.

'Almost.'

'You're usually in bed by eleven.'

'And so are you.'

'Precisely!' said Billy angrily.

Whitaker lowered the paper and looked at him. 'Have you had a good time?' he said mildly. Billy didn't answer. 'Where did you go?'

'Out.'

'How surprising!' said Whitaker.

Billy punched the back of the sofa. 'Why are you so angry?' he said. 'Because I'm not tucked up in my cot? Bed by eleven, up by seven. Work in a bookshop, practice the flute, weekends at Bamburgh. I haven't got a single friend. You realize that? Not one!'

'And you blame me for that?' said Whitaker.

'Of course I don't.'

'William!' said Whitaker, quite gently. 'You left in anger, you're very late – naturally I was worried. And you're behaving like an idiot now.'

'Am I?'

'I shall lose my patience.'

'So?' said Billy, pacing about behind the sofa, too restless to sit down. 'Then we can have another row.'

'No harm in a row once in a while,' said Whitaker, 'so long as you make up afterwards. What's the matter? Is it that you wish you were like Spike? Free? Or is it aimless?'

'I used to be like him,' said Billy. 'At school.'

'And now?'

'We went to a disco. At first I pretended I went often.'

'Why?' said Whitaker, genuinely surprised.

'Because I didn't want to admit...oh, I don't know why. He makes me feel so boring.'

Whitaker looked into the fire for a moment, then nodded thoughtfully.

'Thanks!' said Billy, with a glimmer of humour.

'What?'

'You could have said "no, no, you're not".'

'Doesn't need saying,' said Whitaker. 'Did you enjoy the disco?'

Billy shook his head.

'Dr Jolland telephoned,' said Whitaker. 'You missed your lesson tonight.'

'Oh my God! I forgot. Was he angry?'

'Terrifying! I couldn't last two minutes with that man. He scares me to death!'

'What *am* I doing?' said Billy, 'working as a shop assistant and practising the flute. What's it all for?'

'Well,' said Whitaker, 'working in the shop pays for the lessons.'

'But why have the lessons?'

'I thought you enjoyed the flute. There's certainly no point if you don't.'

'It seems so stupid working for a future. I mean, what about now?' He came round the sofa and slumped down onto it.

Whitaker looked at him carefully. 'You haven't talked about your search for your parents since you came back from France,' he said. 'Why?'

'Because I'm not getting anywhere,' said Billy. 'My mother slept around...and my father ran off with her and left his wife and baby daughter. Fantastic!'

'Is that what people say?' said Whitaker. 'Do they say if he loved her? If it was easy to leave his wife and daughter? If he was happy?'

'I don't know,' said Billy. 'I'm bored with it all. I'm bored with being conscientious and *dull.'* He picked at bits of fluff on the sofa arm. 'All right,' he said, 'I don't know *what* I want. Is that so surprising?'

'Of course it isn't,' said Whitaker. 'I still don't. Go to bed, Billy. Things always look better in daylight.'

'Yes,' said Billy. He got up, went to the door, then paused. 'Have you ever been lonely, Mr Whitaker?'

'Yes,' said Whitaker, after a moment.

'Tonight, in the disco... I think I was lonely.'

'Good night, Billy,' said Whitaker firmly. Billy went out of the room. Whitaker rose rather stiffly from his chair, picked up the whisky bottle to put it away, then set it down again and stared at it. 'Had enough,' he muttered to himself. He pomm'd a little tune. Then, 'Oh, hell and damnation,' he said. 'If I want another I shall have another.' He poured it, neat. Took a small sip, still standing there, by the fire. 'Oh, Billy,' he said, softly. 'All your emotional energy's been going into your search for your real parents. That's what's kept your mind off Alan and Marion... If you stop the search, what will sustain you then?' He downed the whisky at a swallow, swung the guard in front of the fire, and took himself off to bed.

Spike emerged next morning some time after Billy had left for work, still in his amazing outfit but with his face washed clean of make-up. Whitaker, regretting his anger of the evening before, provided breakfast without complaint.

'I'm sorry about last night,' said Spike.

'I think we all are,' said Whitaker. 'I certainly lost my temper. Billy said he'd see you at lunchtime.'

Spike shook his head. 'I must go and see the old man.'

'And tell him you've walked out of university?' said Whitaker.

'Wouldn't be so bad if that was the truth,' said Spike. 'Actually, I've been sent down.'

'In the middle of term?'

'Incessant offensive behaviour.'

'My dear child!' said Whitaker.

'Don't "dear child" me,' snapped Spike.

'Forgive me,' said Whitaker. 'I forgot the young never like to be called young.'

'Do the old like to be called old?'

Whitaker considered the proposition. 'Within moderation I quite enjoy it,' he said. '"Old" I dont mind one little bit. "Decrepit" irritates. "Senior citizen" sends me into a rage.'

'Why?' said Spike, amused.

'It's hypocritical and evasive. Also it sounds like a brand of cigarettes or a two-ring gas stove. "The Senior Citizen Saves on Fuel".'

Spike laughed outright. 'I like you.'

'Thanks,' said Whitaker. 'I don't believe a word about the "offensive behaviour".'

'No,' said Spike. 'It's much more pathetic that that. I just haven't done any work.'

'But to be sent down in the middle of term...'

'Last term. I needed time to break the tidings.'

'What have you been doing?'

'Waiting in a restaurant.'

'How splendid!' said Whitaker. 'Why didn't you tell Billy?'

Spike shrugged. 'I didn't want to be the failure.'

'Dear chap, failure is only in the mind. And now?'

'Plead with pater not to cut me off—what else is there? I'm not like Billy. I don't have anything I'm good at.' He picked at his shiny purple lapel, 'Except looking crazy. And that's getting harder.'

'Do say goodbye to Billy before you go,' said Whitaker. 'He's fond of you. He thinks you're a success, how he would like to be. Your visit has disturbed him.'

'Maybe that's why I came,' said Spike, 'to build up my morale...'

'By making him feel inferior?'

Spike rose from the table. 'Surely his inferiority is only in the mind,' he said.

'Touché,' said Whitaker but he wasn't smiling.

In the bookshop, Miss Moreton called Billy from the stockroom where he was unpacking a new consignment of paperbacks. 'Mr Stanyon,' she said, 'Your "friend" is outside. Kindly get rid of him. I realize you have every right to whatever type of friend you care to make... but off these premises. Is that clear?'

'Thank you very much,' said Billy, extricating himself from a tangle of corrugated paper, 'but I can't actually see what's wrong with him, apart from a fairly freaky exterior.'

'People like that are no respecters of order,' said Miss Moreton, narrowing her eyes. 'When order goes, the state declines. He came in here and asked for pornography. In *this* shop. With a special display of the works of James Herriot in the window.'

'I think he meant it as a joke,' said Billy.

'Oh hootingly funny,' said Miss Moreton. 'He must make a small fortune as a wit.'

Billy went out of the shop, to where Spike waited on the pavement. Neither of them quite knew how to say goodbye, both were aware of Miss Moreton watching them frostily through the glass. They agreed to stay in touch and Billy walked slowly back into the shop.

'Is he really a Duke's son?' said Miss Moreton, as she and Billy stood side by side watching Spike's retreat.

'A lord,' said Billy. 'They own half Dorset.'

'Oh, only a lord,' said Miss Moreton, with some relief.

'And only half Dorset,' said Billy.

'Well I thought he was a thoroughly objectionable young man,' said Miss Moreton, taking her place behind the counter.

'He was my best friend, once,' said Billy, quietly, to himself.

Chapter Ten

Billy sat at the dining table watching as Whitaker, standing, sank a serving spoon into a cottage pie. He leaned forward, sniffing at the steam, 'Mmm, that smells good.'

'The proof is in the eating,' said Whitaker, serving a generous portion and passing it to him. 'Have a good day?'

'All right. The shop was busy. And...' He watched as Whitaker served himself and sat down.

'And?' said Whitaker, encouragingly.

'You're not going to like it.'

'Try me.'

Billy took a mouthful of food. 'Mm!' he said. 'It *is* good.'

'Billy!' said Whitaker, 'Don't be infuriating.'

Billy swallowed the food and then said, very fast, 'I've put a down-payment on a motorbike.'

'Surprise, surprise,' said Whitaker, pouring himself a modest glass of wine.

'Well—aren't you?' said Billy.

'Dear boy!' said Whitaker. 'Why would I be? The study is knee-deep in *Motorbike Weekly* and *Exchange and Mart.'*

'And you don't mind?'

'Would it make any difference if I did?'

'Not a lot.'

'Quite,' said Whitaker peaceably. 'You go and smash yourself up, if that's what you want.'

'It's potentially more hazardous crossing the street to post a letter . . . ' Billy began, slightly pompously.

'Ah,' said Whitaker, pointing at him with a forkful of food, 'Thank you.'

'For what?'

'You've reminded me. You've got one. A letter. On top of my desk.'

Billy got up and went through to the study. He came back with a square brown envelope with something slightly bulky inside. He sat down at the table again and looked at it dubiously. 'It's from Germany,' he said, 'but it's not Gunter's writing. What on earth can it be? Do you suppose it's a letter bomb . . .?'

'Oh, open the confounded thing,' said Whitaker. 'You're so like your father.'

'How do you know?' said Billy.

'All right, your adopted father, then. He used to dither and speculate about letters.'

Billy opened the envelope and took out a small parcel of tissue paper. He put it beside his plate and peered down into the envelope. 'No letter,' he said. He began to unwrap the tissue, 'Just this . . . ' Carefully he folded back the tissue till it lay flat, and revealed the signet ring that Elsa Gruber had tried to give him. He set it on the palm of his hand and held it out towards Whitaker. They both stared at it.

'Now why has she sent you that,' said Whitaker.

'And with no letter,' said Billy. 'I've written to her three times, and this is the first time I've had anything back. What shall I do?'

Whitaker continued to gaze at the ring. 'Whistle and I'll come to you, my lad,' he said thoughtfully.

There was something so dramatic about the unexpected and unexplained arrival of the ring that all Billy's enthusiasm for the hunt was rekindled. He still had not worked at the shop for long enough to be entitled to any leave, but Miss Moreton, rather grudgingly, allowed him a single day, on the strict understanding that his weekly pay packet would reflect his absence. He managed to book himself two consecutive night flights to Munich, and Whitaker contacted Gunter. Gunter arrived, smiling, to meet his plane, which landed just before first light, and drove him home for breakfast.

'I'm sorry it's such short notice,' said Billy.

Gunter grinned at him. 'One of the depressing things about being a free-lance journalist,' he said, 'is that you are so often free. What's the plan?'

'You're sure you can spare the time?'

'I told you—I don't think this is the day to start my epic novel. I'll start that tomorrow!'

'Can we go to the Chiemsee, then?'

'Ought we to telephone first?'

'I don't think so.'

'Right,' said Gunter, getting up from the table. 'Let us go. By the way—did some people called Beauvoir contact you?'

'Yes!'

'Oh! So you also suffered at their hands. I did an interview with them for the magazine. Were they helpful?'

'Not really.'

'So you're no further forward in finding your father?'

'Not at all.'

'It's all down to Elsa Gruber, then,' said Gunter. But Elsa Gruber, it turned out when they reached her house, was not so readily accessible. Gunter rang the bell at the side of the wooden front door and, after something of a pause, Hilde opened it.

'Guten Morgen, Frau Gruber,' said Gunter. *'Ist Ihre Schwiegermutter daheim?'*

'Sie ist nicht zu Hause,' said Hilde.

'Kommt sie bald wieder?'

'Nein. Sie ist fort. Es tut mir Leid.'

'What's she saying?' Billy asked impatiently.

'She says that her mother-in-law is away,' Gunter translated. He turned back and continued to speak to Hilde in German. Billy backed away from them and looked up at the impassive house front, as he had before. Although he half-hoped to see something he was nevertheless quite surprised when the net curtain of the upper room was twitched aside and he found himself looking straight up into Elsa Gruber's face. He was about to call out to Gunter when she raised a finger to her lips in an unmistakable gesture of warning, then let the curtain drop again. Billy looked quickly across at Hilde, but she was too busy talking to Gunter to notice anything else. Then Gunter turned away from her and called down the path to Billy, 'Now what do we do? Frau Gruber says that her mother-in-law is visiting relatives in Austria and will be away for some considerable time.'

'Too bad, then,' said Billy casually, wandering up to join Gunter. He smiled at Hilde. 'Perhaps you could tell her that we just called on the off-chance... and ask her to give our best wishes to Frau Gruber?'

Gunter looked at him for a moment, then nodded. 'All right, then.' He turned back to Hilde. *'Wir waren in der Nähe, und wollten Frau Gruber besuchen,'* he said, as Billy sauntered back to the car. *'Bitte geben Sie ihr unsere besten Wünsce wenn sie zurück kommt.'*

Billy climbed into the car and then, as Hilde shut the door, raised his arm and waved briefly, directly at the upper window. Gunter loped down the path and got into the driving seat. 'That was fairly useless,' he said. 'Now what?'

'Can you drive off just far enough to make it look as though we've gone?' said Billy.

'Yes, sir,' said Gunter amused.

'I saw Elsa,' said Billy, as Gunter turned the car out of the drive. 'She was looking out of her window again. She signalled to me.'

'I see,' said Gunter. 'So Hilde was deliberately lying. How interesting!' He pulled the car into the side of the road and parked on the grass verge. 'Far enough, I think,' he said. 'Let's go back on foot and see if we can figure something out.'

It was not hard to get quite close to the house without being seen because the half-wild shrubbery at the side of the drive gave very good cover. Billy and Gunter arranged themselves comfortably among the leaves with a good view of the front door, and were both wondering what on earth they thought they were going to do next, when the door opened and Hilde came out. It was a warm day and she wore no coat over her slacks and sweater, nor did she carry a shopping basket. But she did have her shoulder bag with her and she did lock the door, hurry down the drive to the road, and disappear in the direction of the village.

'Thank you, Hilde,' whispered Billy. 'Gunter—you follow her.'

'In broad daylight?' said Gunter, aghast. 'I'm a journalist, not a reporter. I'm no good at cloak and dagger stuff . . . '

'Hurry, please, said Billy. 'I want to get in and see Elsa on her own. I need you to warn me if Hilde is coming back.'

'Can't I just "keep watch" here?'

'She might come back the other way, by the lake entrance.'

'All right,' said Gunter, 'If she comes, I will whistle.' He pushed through the foliage onto the drive, and set off at a steady jog in Hilde's wake.

Billy ran up to the front door and rang the bell, rang it again, and then banged impatiently on the door with the flat of his hand. He stepped back and looked up. 'Frau Gruber,' he called. 'It's me. Billy. Billy Toth.' Behind the lace curtain he could see movement—Elsa was struggling to open the casement window. At last she managed it and, her head framed in the opening, shushed him anxiously. 'I will not be alone very long,' she said. 'It is not safe.'

'Frau Gruber, you sent me the ring,' said Billy. 'Please let me in. I must speak to you.'

She looked thoughtfully down at him for a moment. 'And I to you,' she said. 'There is a door round the back. Wait for me there.'

Billy ran round to the glass garden door at the back of the house. He tried it, but it too was locked. He waited restlessly by it, half-listening for Gunter's signal, looking through the glass at a small scullery and beyond it to part of the tiled hall and the foot of the stairs. And as he looked something very strange came into his line of vision, something he could not immediately make sense of. It looked for a moment as though a black coat had been hung over the banisters at the top of the stairs and was now sliding very slowly down them, catching on each stair as it came. But as it neared the foot of the stairs he saw that it was Elsa Gruber, in her long black dress, using her arms and chest to work herself down the rail, her legs dragging helplessly from step to step. At the bottom she allowed herself to sink gently into a heap on the floor and then began to crawl across the tiles towards him, using only her arms, looking rather like a slim black seal. He watched in horrified fascination. At the door she raised and supported herself on one hand, reached up with the other to turn the key, and then let herself fall back again. Billy opened the door a few careful inches and sidled in. 'Frau Gruber!' he said, concerned. But she was chuckling to herself with huge satisfaction. As he knelt at her side she grinned up at him. 'They have no idea what I get up to,' she said. 'They think I am secure upstairs! But I have much more difficulty getting back. So! You will carry me?'

'Of course,' said Billy, half-laughing with relief. He lifted her easily and took her back up to her room.

'Is this how you posted me the ring?' he said.

'Oh yes. I knew Hilde would be out for some time that day, and there is my downstairs wheelchair in the hall, you see.'

Billy sat her carefully in her upstairs wheelchair, by the window. 'Why did Hilde tell us you were away?' he said.

Her face clouded over. 'Hilde is a fool!' she said, more to herself than to him. 'She is being destroyed, and she is letting it happen.'

He opened his mouth to speak, but she cut in. 'Listen to me, Billy. Listen. It is not safe for you to keep looking for your father, you understand me? That is what I wanted to say to you. And I wanted you to know that I am thinking of you, Billy. For a little while you were like my baby.' She looked up at him, almost as if she might cry. 'I didn't want to let you go.'

Billy crouched down in front of her chair. 'And you sent me the ring to bring me here?'

'No,' she said, softly. 'No. I thought you should have it...it should be yours.'

'I know there are things you could tell me,' said Billy, almost pleadingly. 'Why won't you?'

Elsa looked down at her hands in her lap. 'I am a very old lady,' she said. 'The things I know cannot distress me any more. But you will only find unhappiness if you go on searching—and I don't want that for you.'

'Jerri is alive, isn't he?' said Billy. 'Is he in trouble?'

'He was in trouble from the day he met my son,' said Elsa. 'It is not nice for a mother to have to admit it, but Kurt is a wicked...' She stopped herself. 'It is not good to think ill of the dead. But...he made money out of other people's suffering. Much money. And he made suffering, too. His wife...his mother...much suffering. Do not inherit that, Billy. I will tell you nothing.' She reached for his hand and held it between both of hers. 'Go home to England and forget about us. Wear that ring to the memory of your mother and father who loved each other and who . . . got trapped . . . like flies in a web.'

'There is so much you could tell me,' said Billy wistfully.

'And never will!' said Elsa, pushing his hand away. 'You don't listen to me. Your father is dead. Your mother is dead. You cannot bring them back to life. I will not see you again. I will not answer your letters. I have returned the ring . . . and I am free of you. Now go, Billy, please.'

A soft long-drawn-out whistle sounded in the garden below, like a drowsy mid-day bird. 'That's Gunter,' said Billy. 'Hilde's coming back.'

Elsa spun the wheels of her chair with her hands, retreating from him and in the same movement turning to face the window, her vantage point. 'Quickly, down the stairs and out through the back door,' she said.

'Frau Gruber . . . ' said Billy.

'Goodbye, Billy Toth,' said Elsa firmly. 'She is coming. Don't give me away. Go . . . please.'

Hilde's key clicked into the lock. Billy flung himself down the stairs, across the hall and had just reached the little scullery when the front door opened. From upstairs Elsa called, *'Hilde! Hilde! Komm Schnell!'* Hilde ran to the stairs and up them, in response to the urgent summons, and Billy was able to slip unnoticed out of the back door. Once out he didn't stop running until he bumped into Gunter, in the shrubbery near the road, driven by exhilaration rather than fear. He grabbed Gunter by the arms and swung him round. 'That was the craziest thing I've *ever* done,' he said, laughing. 'Hey! Shh!' said Gunter, laughing too, then, when they'd both calmed down, 'Was it worth it?'

'No!' said Billy. He put on a stage German accent. 'It vould be better if I stopped searchink!'

'Oh reahlly!' said Gunter, in a stage upper-class English accent. 'How *fascinating!'*

They began to walk back to the car. 'Is that really what she said?' Gunter asked.

'Yes. "It is dangerous to try to trace your father". Which of course makes me more anxious than ever to do just that.'

'Of course,' said Gunter more seriously. He waited until they were sitting in the car then produced a slip of paper. 'Look what I got!' he said with glee.

'What is it?' said Billy, taking it from him.

'I turned out to be a better spy than I thought. Hilde had gone to send a telegram. This is the sheet of paper that was immediately beneath the telegraph form she filled in. I pencilled over the marks that her writing made. We spies know all the tricks!'

Billy stared at it. 'My name,' he said. 'I can't read the rest, but there's my name.'

Gunter took it back from him. ' "Toth," ' he read, ' "Toth something—I—can't—read it here." '

'The address?' said Billy.

Gunter shook his head. 'Can't read it at all—except—I think—*Osterreich.*'

Billy looked at him questioningly.

'Austria,' said Gunter.

'Austria,' said Billy. 'There is someone over there who had to be told I was here.' He looked at Gunter. 'My father?'

'We don't know.'

'She said he was dead, but I don't believe it. How can we find out? It's all tied up with Kurt Gruber—Elsa's son—the man who was killed in the crash with my mother. Elsa said that my father was in trouble from the day he met Kurt.' He paused. 'Maybe he's in trouble still,' he said more quietly.

'Maybe,' said Gunter gently. He turned the key in the ignition and began to drive in the direction of Munich.

Back in Newcastle after his second night flight Billy breakfasted with Whitaker and tried, without much success, to get himself into the mood for work. Whitaker listened gravely to his story of his visit to Elsa. At its end he said, 'I would like to know more about Kurt.'

'So would I,' said Billy. 'But how?'

'How did Jerri first get in touch with him?' said Whitaker. 'It's mentioned in one of the letters, isn't it?'

Billy nodded. 'Through a Mrs Dalgleish in Perthshire,' he said. 'He tells Tania to phone her for Elsa Gruber's address. Tania wrote the address on the side of the same letter—that's how we first heard of Elsa's name...'

'Hm,' said Whitaker, looking at Billy with a glint in his eye.

'Oh no,' said Billy, half-laughing. 'There must be thousands of Dalgleishes in Perthshire. Besides...what if Elsa is right and it really is dangerous for me to continue the search?'

'There are two things you can do with danger,' said Whitaker.

'Avoid it or face it.'

'And that's your idea of being my guardian?'

'I can only offer you the options,' said Whitaker. 'And by the way, talking of danger, you were expected at Dr Jolland's last night.'

Billy looked at him in blank horror. 'He changed the day...' he said.

'He says you will never make a professional flautist,' said Whitaker. 'Your attitude is that of the dilettante...or worse... the amateur!'

'Was he furious?'

'He was not pleased.'

Billy buried his head in his hands. 'Oh what should I do?' he said. 'Oh I do dread him when he's furious.'

Whitaker began to laugh, not unkindly. 'Well, I think this is one danger you'd better face,' he said. And then, as Billy caught his laughter, 'But...oh, I *am* glad I'm not you!'

Chapter Eleven

By the early autumn Billy had paid for the bike and passed his test. The peace of the cul-de-sac was shattered regularly, as he drove off and returned. The noise made Whitaker flinch but he managed to refrain from comment. On the first Saturday in October Billy set off on the bike to spend a weekend at Bamburgh on his own. With jeans pushed into boots, leather jacket and gloves, crash helmet and goggles, he was even better kitted out than Rob had been and his bike, though the same make as Rob's, was slightly more powerful. Whitaker stood in the doorway and solemnly waved goodbye, then turned and went inside, trying not to think about road accident statistics.

The day was crisp and bright but with the memory of mist wafting across the low ground and hanging among trees in hollows. Billy drove fast, enjoying the noise, the speed, the rush of air, the sensation that it was possible to go on forever. But he slowed down before he reached Bamburgh, at a tiny roadside copse, and nosed the bike slowly amongst the trees, stopping in the shaded interior. He got off the bike, set it on its mount and was just pulling off his gloves when he noticed a figure standing beside a silver birch: a girl, tall and pale and very young, with long straight blonde hair. For a moment, standing there so still in the dappled light, she looked more like a dream or a ghost than a person. 'Hallo,' said Billy uncertainly.

'Help me,' said the girl in a small voice.

Billy went over to her. 'What's the matter?' he said. 'Are you lost?'

She shook her head. From close to she looked less ethereal, in her pale blue jeans and anorak, but she was very pretty.

'It's all right,' said Billy, trying to sound reassuring.

'Why did you stop?'

He smiled. 'I'll show you,' he said. He walked through the tiny copse to a gate with a field beyond. 'Come and look.' She came, very cautiously. Billy pointed over the gate and across the field to a glimmering line in the distance. 'I always stop here,' he said. 'It's my first sight of the sea.' She looked at the sea, then at him. 'Where are you going?'

'To Bamburgh.'

'What's there?'

'Oh... a castle.... and the sands...'

'No, I mean why are you going there?'

'Oh, I see. I have a cottage there. Well, it was my parents'...'

'Are they there?'

'They're both dead.'

She reached out her hand and touched his arm very lightly. 'I'm sorry,' she said. Then, 'Will you take me there?'

He looked at her thoughtfully. 'I don't know. How did you get here?'

She walked a little way away, between two trees. 'It's so complicated.'

'It can't be all that hard explaining why you're standing in a lay-by on the A1!' said Billy lightly.

'I hitched a lift.'

'To here?'

'No. I got scared. I asked to be put down... we happened to be passing here.'

'No luggage?'

'Back there in the trees. It's only a small pack. Please take me. I won't be any trouble.'

'I still don't know what you're doing here,' said Billy, 'or why you asked me for help.'

'Do you own this lay-by?' said the girl unexpectedly. She turned her back on him. 'People are always asking questions.'

'Not me,' said Billy, losing patience, going back to the bike.

'You were!'

He climbed on to the bike and started to put on his helmet. The girl followed him. 'You did ask,' she persisted. 'You wanted to know what I was doing here.'

Billy pulled the helmet on to his head and buckled it into place, the visor still open. 'OK! OK!' he said. 'I'm going.'

But she caught at his arm. He could see that she was near to tears. 'I'm sorry,' she said. 'I will tell you. But not here... don't leave me here, please.'

'Have you run away?' said Billy.

She nodded almost imperceptibly. 'If you must know,' she said, subdued, 'my father is a policeman and I am sixteen and I live in Durham. I suppose now you think you know me.'

He looked at her for a moment. 'Well,' he said, 'I can't leave you here on the side of the road. I just hope your father doesn't catch up with us.'

'What?'

'It's illegal to ride without a crash helmet. Come on, we'll risk it.'

She smiled at him for the first time, a lovely open smile, and ran back into the trees to collect her pack. 'You didn't tell me your name,' he called after her.

'Sarah,' she said as she came back and got on to the bike behind him. She put her arms round his waist and Billy kicked the engine into life and rejoined the road to Bamburgh.

At Bamburgh, they walked on the beach; then at dusk, lit a fire in the cottage and cooked a meal. Billy found himself telling Sarah all about himself, his life with Whitaker, his search for his parents. She turned out to be a very good listener and by the time they'd had supper he had told her more than he had told any other person.

They sat side by side on the floor in front of the fire, leaning back against the sofa, the music case and its contents spread on the floor between them, and listened to the sound of the sea.

'Can we go to the castle in the morning?' said Sarah.

'Well . . . ,' said Billy. 'I did intend to go to Scotland. Just for the day.'

'Why?'

'There's a woman up there I want to see, a Mrs Dalgleish. She was connected in some way with my parents. You know the people in France I told you about? I got her address from them.'

'Is she expecting you?'

'No.'

She gave him a mischievous smile. 'I think you should write first. Then we can go to the castle tomorrow.'

Billy looked at her and smiled back.

'I hope you do find your father,' she said. Her eyes were very soft and brown.

'Oh . . . I don't know . . .' said Billy, suddenly dejected. 'He's not exactly looking for me, is he? That's if he's alive. And if he isn't there's not much point.'

'It's not just finding him, though, is it?' said Sarah. 'It's knowing who you are. In a way, it's you you're looking for, isn't it?'

Billy looked at her very steadily in the firelight until she looked away, embarrassed, and picked up the little glass owl. 'Isn't it sweet,' she said. She held it up, watching the firelight through it.

'Won't the entire police force of Newcastle and Durham be looking for you?' said Billy.

'Well, they won't find me here,' said Sarah. 'And you've got plenty of food in the freezer.' She put the little owl gently down on the carpet. 'I know,' she said. 'I know I can't stay. But let me pretend for a bit . . .' She began to cry, quite quietly. Not knowing what to do, Billy stared into the fire. 'I don't know where to go,' said Sarah. 'I'm frightened . . .'

'Don't cry,' said Billy. He didn't look at her, but he knew she hadn't stopped. Abruptly he turned and put his arm round her. She put her head against his shoulder and sniffed. 'I'm sorry,' she said, her voice muffled by his jersey.

'It's all right,' said Billy. 'Wouldn't it help to tell me . . . ?'

She pulled away from him and rubbed her eyes with the back of her hand. Then drew up her knees and sat with her chin on them, staring into the fire. 'I have a friend called Marianne Farmer,' she said. 'She's two years older than me, but we've always been friends, for as long as I can remember. Anyway, she's got a boyfriend called Alec. Marianne went to visit her sister in Lytham

St Anne's and . . . Alec came round and asked me out.'

She paused. 'So?' said Billy.

'I went out with him. He's really nice . . . you know? I knew about him and Marianne . . . but he seemed to want to see me. For a bit we didn't tell her . . . but she found out, of course.'

She stopped again. Then, 'She was my best friend,' she said quietly.

'Not any more?'

'She really liked him, you see.'

'Do you still see him?' said Billy.

She shook her head.

'Why not?'

'He wanted . . . you know . . .'

'And you didn't?'

She shook her head. 'I don't know.'

'Is that why you ran away?'

'I had no one to talk to.'

'Your mother and father?'

'Oh, Billy! Talk to them about that? I couldn't. You don't know them!'

'They'll be worried sick,' said Billy.

Still looking into the fire Sarah said, in a very quiet voice, 'I wanted to—with Alec. Is that awful?' she glanced quickly at Billy's profile, outlined by the glow from the fire, but the reassurance she wanted didn't come. 'I don't know,' said Billy eventually.

She got up quickly and went to her pack which she had left in a corner of the room. 'There's no need for you to make up a bed for me,' she said brightly. 'I've got my sleeping bag. I can sleep on this sofa.'

'Sarah, what about your parents?' said Billy urgently.

'If I telephone them tomorrow they'll come and collect me. How long will it take?'

'From Durham? About three hours.'

'Good, we can go the castle first, then. Does your Mr Whitaker worry about you?'

Billy smiled. 'Yes. He says I'm the only person he's had to worry about for centuries. I think he finds it a bit of a strain, actually.'

'Do you worry about him?'

Billy looked surprised. 'No,' he said. 'No one worries about him, he's all right.' He had a sudden comforting mental picture of Whitaker sitting in his chair, reading, a whisky at his elbow, the clock ticking peacefully on the mantlepiece.

In fact, Whitaker was sitting at the desk in his study, some documents open in front of him and a used plate and wineglass on the corner of the desk. His head had dropped forward onto his chest and he was dozing. The front door opened and closed again, very quietly. A moment later, Miss Price appeared in the study, still in her coat. She looked at the scene for a moment and then went over to the desk and collected up the plate, the glass and a half empty wine bottle. As she tiptoed towards the door with them, Whitaker woke with a jump.

'What?' he said.

'It's all right,' said Miss Price soothingly. 'Go back to sleep.'

'I was not asleep.'

'Of course not,' said Miss Price, 'just thinking with your eyes closed.' She went out of the room and closed the door behind her.

Whitaker glared at the closed door, then got up and followed her out of it. He found her in the kitchen. Her coat was hanging behind the door, she was wearing his flowery pinny and red rubber gloves, and she was washing up.

'What in the name of thunder are you doing in my house?' said Whitaker, still half asleep.

'Washing up,' said Miss Price mildly. 'Though whether it is in the name of thunder, I couldn't honestly say. I shouldn't think you've washed up for a month.'

'I have a lot of dinner services.'

'Why you can't let Billy do some of it, I don't know,' said Miss Price, running a greasy plate under the tap.

'Let him?' said Whitaker. 'You make it sound as if I stop him!'

'You're too soft with him,' said Miss Price. 'If you're going to stand there you could do some of the drying up.'

'They dry on their own. Miss Price, you belong next door in the office, not here, and certainly not on a Saturday evening!'

'Mother has had her supper,' said Miss Price, washing and rinsing imperturbably. 'She eats earlier and earlier. She's almost ready for breakfast before she goes to sleep.'

'Shouldn't you be with her? For company?'

'She has the television,' said Miss Price, with an edge to her voice. 'They make a perfect couple.'

'So you thought you'd come round here and... *what?*'

'I needed the notes you took at the meeting with Mr Armstrong.'

'I haven't finished with them,' said Whitaker, 'and on a Saturday, Pricey?'

Miss Price continued to wash up in silence. She was most methodical and the stack of clean and rinsed dishes was already far larger than the pile of dirty ones on the other side of her. 'I can't sit all evening watching television,' she said briskly.

'Oh, Pricey,' said Whitaker, softening. 'Look... leave all that and come by the fire.' He went out of the room and back to the study, where the fire had burned quite low. He stooped and added some coal, rearranging the older glowing coals with the end of the shovel. Miss Price didn't follow him. He clunked the shovel back into the coal bin and went back to the kitchen. Miss Price had finished the washing up and was drying the plates and stacking them on the table. 'I said to leave that,' said Whitaker.

'Yes, Mr Whitaker,' said Miss Price, wiping and stacking, wiping and stacking. 'You should have gone to Bamburgh with Billy.'

'He's driving to Scotland in the morning and I have no intention of riding pillion. Besides, it does him good to get away on his own.'

'He's only a child,' said Miss Price. 'I swear he'll have an accident on that machine.'

'I wouldn't be at all surprised,' said Whitaker irritably. 'Oh, stop faffing, woman.'

'There,' said Miss Price, looking with some satisfaction at the pile of clean dishes. 'I'll leave you to put them away.' She removed the pinny and gloves and took her coat down from the back of the door. 'Now,' she said, putting it on, 'if you'll just let me have those papers...' She walked through into the study, Whitaker following helplessly in her wake.

'Confound it, woman,' he said. 'You can't go into the office now. It's past your bed-time.'

'I have my portable at home,' said Miss Price. She crossed to his desk and extricated the papers she wanted in a matter of seconds, without disturbing anything else.

'Stay and have a sherry,' said Whitaker, going to the cabinet.

'I don't like leaving mother for too long.'

'Your mother!' He poured a small sherry and carried it carefully across to the middle of the room where Miss Price stood.

'You should have gone with Billy to Bamburgh,' she said, 'if you're lonely.' She made no attempt to take the proffered glass.

'I'm not lonely,' said Whitaker, a little too vehemently. He took her hand, pushed the sherry glass into it and forcibly closed her fingers around the stem. 'It's wonderful having the place to myself.'

'Then why do you need my company?'

'I don't! I simply thought a small medium sherry...' He turned away exasperated. 'Oh... it doesn't matter.'

'What is it?' said Miss Price, more gently.

'I'm worried about Billy.'

'Oh, Billy.' she sounded disappointed.

'I don't like him riding about on that bike,' said Whitaker, walking over to look into the fire and then walking back again. 'Oh listen to me, Pricey, clucking away like an old hen. But it's a responsibility. I mean... should he be... I don't know... doing more with his life...'

Miss Price stood quite still, holding the papers in one hand and the sherry in the other, somehow isolated in the middle of the room. 'The young need guidance,' she said cautiously.

'I wouldn't dare.'

'But you do, by example.'

'I hope I don't,' said Whitaker. He went back to the cabinet and began to pour a whisky, without much enthusiasm. 'I don't want him like me.'

'What do you want?'

'Really it's too much,' said Whitaker, crossing to the desk to put the glass of whisky down on it, then pacing back to the fire again. 'I'm far too old and far too self-centred to have to worry about him. He must work things out for himself.'

'Yes, Mr Whitaker,' said Miss Price, watching him with a kind of amiable amusement.

'I want him to be happy, Pricey,' said Whitaker. 'No... I want him to be himself.'

'But he *is* being,' said Miss Price. 'Don't you remember being that age?'

'Of course I don't. It was centuries ago.'

'Any minute now,' said Miss Price, 'he'll be bringing his first girl home. I trust you'll be able to cope with that!'

'He makes me feel so old,' Whitaker wailed.

'You are old,' said Miss Price unsympathetically.

Whitaker glared at her. 'I don't know why you stay with me if you find me so tiresome,' he said.

An odd expression passed across Miss Price's face. She placed her sherry glass, untouched, on the table by the door. 'Habit,' she said. 'I don't like change. Goodnight, Mr Whitaker.'

'Goodnight, Pricey,' said Whitaker, at a loss, addressing her retreating back.

In the cottage Sarah sat by the fire, her sleeping bag ready on the sofa. Upstairs in his room Billy stood at his music stand, playing the flute, intensely aware of Sarah listening below.

The next morning they walked together to the nearest call box and Sarah telephoned her parents while Billy waited outside. When she had finished, he put his arm round her and they walked down to the beach. 'All right?' he said.

'I spoke to Dad. They're driving down. He said he loved me...'

They walked over the dunes to the hard wet sand left by the retreating tide. 'Do you suppose we'll meet again,' said Billy. He tried to look into her face, but she was watching the waves.

'I think I've had enough adventures for a bit,' she said. She suddenly pulled free of him. 'Let's race to the castle,' she said, and was off, a small, light figure, yellow hair against yellow sand.

Billy stood where he was. 'I want to see you again,' he called across the distance.

'Why?' came back her voice, faint against the sea. 'Come on.'

'I don't know why,' said Billy to himself. He began to run after her.

Sarah explored the castle with delight, walking along the battlements, touching the great stones of the walls, looking out at the views from the different sides. Billy followed, looking at her more than he looked at anything else.

'This Alec,' he said. 'Did you... love him?'

'I thought I did.'

'Not now?'

'I don't know. It's all a muddle.'

They stopped to rest high on the ramparts, overlooking the sea. 'If we were to meet again...' said Billy.

'I'm scared.'

'There's nothing to be scared about. We could meet just to talk. We can talk, you and I. Last night you understood so much.'

'Did I?'

'When I was talking about tracing my father. You said I was looking for me. That's what I believed. You understood. I think my mother and father must have been just like us. You know? Feeling...like this.' The wind was blowing her hair across her face. He reached out and pushed it back. But she didn't smile. She turned away and examined the texture of the stone wall. 'I thought about it all last night,' she said. 'I don't want to see you again.'

'Why, Sarah?'

'Because that's what happened with Alec.' She faced him again. The wind was making her eyes water. 'I don't want to get serious,' she said.

'I'm only suggesting we get to know each other,' said Billy gently.

She shook her head. 'I can't explain. With you it's all too... It would get serious too quickly. I know. I just want it ordinary, Billy. I just want to go home.'

Billy looked at her steadily, with no expression on his face. Then he glanced at his watch. 'You'd better go down to the road,' he said. 'He'll be here, I think.'

'I'm very sorry,' said Sarah.

'I wanted to give you a present,' said Billy.

'No.'

He reached into the pocket of his anorak and took out the little glass owl. He held it out to her. 'Please,' he said. 'I want you to have it.'

'I can't. It was your mother's.'

'Please.' He put it into her hand. She stood looking down at it. 'You've made me understand so much. People say terrible things about my parents, but they loved each other, Sarah. Please take it. It'll help you remember me. The one who gave you the little glass owl...' He smiled. 'Maybe that's what he said to her.'

'I don't understand, Billy.'

He took her face in his hands and kissed her, very briefly. 'Just...' he said, 'just...that no one is to blame. You can't help your feelings. You're right about us. We couldn't just be friends. I couldn't. Goodbye, Sarah.'

She stood and looked at him for a moment. Then put the owl into her pocket, turned and ran.

From high up on the ramparts Billy looked down at the castle gates. He saw Sarah come out of the castle and hurry towards a waiting car. A man and a woman, who had been standing by it, ran to meet her. Even from so far away, their relief and affection were quite apparent. They led her to the car, and all three got in. Billy stood, the wind stinging his face, and watched as they drove away.

Sarah did not know he was watching. So it did not occur to her to look back.

Chapter Twelve

The following Saturday morning, at quarter past eleven, a car turned slowly into the street where Whitaker's house and office stood side by side; an ancient, gleaming, yellow and black Rolls, which made stately progress down the terrace and came to a smooth stop, the passenger door precisely aligned with the brass plate of *Whitaker, Belton and Stanyon.* A chauffeur stepped out. He was in his twenties, tall and good-looking, wearing an immaculate grey uniform which was, perhaps, a shade too tight, and glossy black boots. He strode in at the main door and up the stairs, following the sign that directed visitors to Whitaker's office. Without preamble he walked straight into Miss Price's office and up to her desk. 'Mrs Dalgleish to see Mr Vincent Whitaker,' he said, most formally, in his soft Scottish accent. He leaned forward from the waist and set a visiting card before Miss Price's surprised gaze.

'Is she expected?' said Miss Price.

The chauffeur seemed nonplussed. 'Well, she's here, isn't she?' he said. 'She's out in the limousine.'

Miss Price rose from her desk and ushered him subtly but firmly back down the stairs again. 'What is it about?' she said. 'We don't usually see people on Saturdays. The office isn't officially open.'

By now they were standing in the doorway together and Miss Price found herself gazing on the full glory of the 1928

Rolls-Royce, which looked as though it had been driven straight out of a particularly well-stocked motor museum. As she looked, the back window of the car was lowered and the face of the occupant became visible.

She was an extremely beautiful woman, her hair drawn back from her forehead beneath a black silk turban, her eyes heavily shadowed and mascara'd, her mouth gleaming with lip gloss. 'What seems to be the trouble, Jonathan?' she called. Her voice was the voice of a girl and she spoke with a uniquely blended accent, created when she, Hungarian-born as she was, had learned her English from a lowland Scot.

'You should have an appointment,' said Jonathan, crossing the pavement to open the car door for her.

Mrs Dalgleish emerged from the yellow Rolls-Royce, her black mink flowing open to reveal a silk dress, strikingly stripped in black and white. She approached Miss Price with a dazzling smile. 'An appointment?' she said. 'I'm sure he'll see me.'

'He is very busy,' said Miss Price, in her neat blouse and skirt, her sensible shoes.

'Yes, of course,' said Mrs Dalgleish soothingly, sweeping past Miss Price into the hall. 'But not for me.' She stood back, her stance plainly indicating that she expected Miss Price to lead the way to the relevant office. 'Tell him I want to talk to him about Jerri Toth.'

Bowing to the inevitable, Miss Price reluctantly gave way, delivered the splendid stranger to a surprised Whitaker, and withdrew.

Mrs Dalgleish settled herself upon the sofa in Whitaker's office, allowed her mink to slide gently off her shoulders and crossed her long and beautiful legs. The air around her shimmered with expensive perfume.

'May I... offer you something?' said Whitaker, quite dazzled by the spectacle.

'Most kind,' said Mrs Dalgleish, her eye lighting upon the bottle which stood on its tray on a side table. 'Mr Dalgleish was a whisky baron.'

'Really?' said Whitaker, bemused. He dispensed whisky. Mrs Dalgleish received her glass in an elegantly gloved hand. *'Egészégére!'* she said in Hungarian. She tossed the whisky back in one, and seemed for a moment to be about to throw the glass over her shoulder—but instead she laughed and set it down.

'That's a drop of the good stuff.'

'Another?' said Whitaker, amazed.

'Naughty!' said Mrs Dalgleish. 'You want me tiddly.'

At that moment the door opened and Miss Price walked in, carrying a tray with a coffee pot and cups. 'I've made you some coffee,' she said, unnecessarily.

'Oh...' Whitaker began guiltily, but Mrs Dalgleish cut in. 'Coffee would be very pleasant. Black. No sugar. Thank you.' She accepted the cup and then leaned forward to gaze intently at Whitaker. 'I expected someone older,' she said.

Miss Price's eyebrows shot up her forehead, but she passed Whitaker his coffee without comment. 'I couldn't be much older,' he said, becoming rather pink.

Miss Price thrust a plate under his nose. 'Biscuit?' she said.

'No, thank you,' said Whitaker, recovering himself. 'That will be all, Miss Price. We can manage.'

'I'm sure you can,' said Miss Price acidly.

Mrs Dalgleish treated her to a small conspiratorial giggle. 'Men!' she said.

Miss Price responded with a basilisk stare. 'I'll go, then,' she said.

'Go?' said Whitaker, suddenly alarmed. 'Not completely?'

'I will be next door,' said Miss Price, closing the door behind her with a firm little click.

Whitaker cleared his throat. 'Jerri Toth..?' he said.

Mrs Dalgleish glanced around the room as if she expected to see someone hiding in a corner. 'Where is the boy?' she said. 'Jerri's son?'

'Oh...he's up at Bamburgh. He has a cottage there.'

'On his own?'

'Well—I'm going up this afternoon.'

'But it is not safe for him,' said Mrs Dalgleish.

'He is an adult,' said Whitaker.

'Ach, pooh—adult!' She made a dismissive gesture with one hand. 'For some people it is not safe to be alone. Jerri Toth's son is one...You will take me to him now.' She rose to her feet and set down her coffee cup. 'We will go in the auto.'

'But...' began Whitaker, getting up hastily.

'Don't concern yourself. We will have refreshments as we go. How far is...Bumbrow?'

'Fifty miles.'

'Nae more than a stroll by the bonnie banks of Doon,' said Mrs Dalgleish. She giggled. 'Mr Dalgleish knew Henry Lauder!'

'Harry,' said Whitaker.

'No rush,' said Mrs Dalgleish airily. She swept out of the office and paused by Miss Price's desk. 'Thank you for the coffee,' she said. 'Next time it should be stronger. My coat is on the chair.'

Miss Price rose slowly to her feet, but before she had time to speak Whitaker appeared behind Mrs Dalgleish, holding the coat. 'Ah, so kind,' she said; then instantly sank to the brink of tears. 'Poor mink!' She stroked the fur. 'Perhaps they were already dead, you think? Natural old age?' She slipped into the coat. 'I will wait for you in my limousine.' And she was gone, down the stairs, leaving a drift of perfume hanging on the air behind her.

'Where are you going?' said Miss Price.

Whitaker was already on his way downstairs in her wake. 'Bumbrow,' he said firmly.

'Now? With her?'

'Apparently. I'd better collect my things from the house. Miss Price, can you lock up here?'

'I thought we were going to "get a lot done" today!'

'We were. But that was before the arrival of Mrs Dalgleish. Sorry. Another time.'

Miss Price stood on the landing and watched him disappear out of the front door. 'Men!' she said witheringly.

In the car en route for Bamburgh Mrs Dalgleish cast back the lid of a hamper with a graceful movement and proceeded to press delicacies upon her willing guest. Whitaker sat at her side, a chicken leg in one hand, a glass of excellent champagne in the other and a beatific smile on his face. Mrs Dalgleish did not eat, but she matched him glass for glass with the champagne.

'So you were originally from Hungary, Mrs Dalgleish?' said Whitaker, forcing himself to recall the point of the exercise.

'Yes,' she said, looking ahead past Jonathan's shoulder. 'I was a singer. Opera.'

'And you left...'

'A long time ago. I marry Mr Dalgleish. He like my singing.'

'Have you ever been back?'

'To Hungary? How could I? I am an exile. Have some salmon.' Whitaker, his mouth full, shook his head and waved the chicken leg discreetly by way of explanation. 'No, I have never gone back,' said Mrs Dalgleish sadly. 'I am Mrs Dalgleish. I live in a castle. It is very draughty. My husband, Mr Dalgleish, was a property baron. We were going to put in central heating, but he died. People say I betrayed my country. I should have...spoken out.' She shrugged helplessly. 'I did not know what to say.'

'Did you leave before the revolution?'

'There have been so many revolutions. Poor bleeding country. Like an old lady who has been to the operating table too many times.' She shuddered. 'I do not like this talk.' She leaned forward and rapped on the glass behind the chauffeur. 'Jonathan, drive slower. We have plenty of time.' She turned her smile upon Whitaker. 'I don't like rush,' she said. 'Why rush? We are all going to end up in the same place one day.'

'How did you hear about..?'

She interrupted, 'About Billy Toth? And you? There is very little I do not hear about in time.' She refilled his champagne glass. 'From Giselle. You know, Giselle de Beauvoir? I believe Billy visited them in France. Giselle still writes to me. I have money — that makes me socially acceptable. The French have their priorities.' Chancing to look out of the window she caught sight of something that made her cry out with pleasure. 'The sea!' She clasped her hands like a child. 'Look! Look! The sea! Are we here?'

'Not far now,' said Whitaker, beaming at her indulgently.

'Oh, I should have brought a costume,' said Mrs Dalgleish, sitting on the edge of her seat as if that would bring her nearer to the ocean. 'Mr Dalgleish used to like the watch me swimming. He was a very *visual* man.'

Whitaker spotted Billy before the car reached the cottage, a lonely figure walking by the edge of the sea. Billy didn't see him until he was at the foot of the dunes and approaching across the sand: when he saw he waved, and broke into a run. 'You're early,' he called as he came within earshot.

'Checking up on you,' said Whitaker. 'I thought you were going to spend the day practising.'

'I have been. I needed some air.'

'We are not alone,' said Whitaker very softly, mouthing the words. He inclined his head slightly.

Billy followed the direction of the gesture and saw the distant figure of Mrs Dalgleish, straight and dark in her mink, standing on the sands, gazing out to sea and holding a parasol over her head, the fringe moving in the chill autumn wind. As he watched, she gestured with the parasol and the immaculate figure of Jonathan stepped forward from the dunes and took it and held it over her, although the warmth from the sun was minimal.

'Who is she?' said Billy, amazed.

'Mrs Dalgleish,' said Whitaker. He put on a mid-European accent. 'She is so anxious to meet with you.'

'I don't understand,' said Billy, as they began to walk towards her. 'I never wrote to her.'

'Never underestimate the French connection,' said Whitaker cryptically.

With the practised ease of someone used to giving orders, Mrs Dalgleish caused Jonathan to set the scene. Within minutes she and Whitaker were seated on chairs produced from the boot of the car, plaid rugs over their knees, and another wondrously stocked hamper open on the sands between them. Billy sat on a third rug, at Mrs Dalgleish's feet. Jonathan opened more champagne and poured three glasses, then disappeared in the direction of the yellow Rolls, out of sight on the road at the back of the dunes. Mrs Dalgleish turned her attention to Billy and launched into her story, while Whitaker beamed upon them both and worked his way rapturously through the champagne.

'Your mother's name was Szabo,' she said. 'It is an usual name...but hers was an unusual family. Her father was a conductor. Is that what you say? A *chef d'orchestre.* He was the *maestro.* Szabo.' She shook her head. 'I don't like memories.' She smiled down at Billy. 'But for you...' She held out her empty glass. Billy refilled it for her. 'You are very handsome,' she said. 'Do you drive a car?'

'Not yet.'

'You're so young. When you are old enough to drive a car, perhaps you would like to be my chauffeur? I pay well.' Billy caught Whitaker's quizzical expression and had to suppress a laugh. Mrs Dalgleish swept on without waiting for a response. 'Eat. Eat. There is another hamper in the limousine. Jerri Toth was not musical. Perhaps he didn't need to be. They were... sweethearts. When he came to this country he came to see me. Tania was left behind, you see. I couldn't help him. Mr Dalgleish didn't like me to become involved. Secretly I think he was afraid that Jerri Toth might charm me too much.' She sighed. 'Silly man!' She leaned towards Billy. 'Mr Dalgleish could never believe that I was entirely his,' she said in conspiratorial tones. She shrugged. 'So. Much later, your mother is writing to me from London . . . and the rest you know. Jerri was married . . . there was a scandal . . . and here you are.'

'Yes, I've pieced together that much,' said Billy.

Mrs Dalgleish shivered suddenly. 'It is cold.'

'There's a fire in the cottage,' said Billy.

She shook her head, turning up the luxurious collar of her coat. 'I do not like to be inside. At home I am always inside. Home!' She gave a bitter little laugh. 'I call a small castle in Scotland home. Mr Dalgleish bought it for me. It isn't very old, but it is very draughty. Mr Dalgleish died there and left me everything. He was a money baron. But it isn't home.'

'Where is home?' said Billy.

Mrs Dalgleish leaned towards him again, her fine-boned face pinched in the autumn air. 'I don't have one,' she whispered. She sank back in her chair. 'I am not welcome in Hungary because I ran away. The communists do like me because I would not acknowledge them. The dissidents do not like me because I deserted them. I live in a small draughty castle in Scotland and Mr Dalgleish is dead. I have no home.' From near tears she suddenly beamed. 'But I have a lot of money,' she said with satisfaction. 'Tania Szabo came to me. Mr Dalgleish was not long dead. I wore black.' She shrugged. 'It suited me. Tania was there'—she flung her arms dramatically wide—'we cried and cried! I had not seen her since she was a little girl and I was a *Prima Donna Assoluta.* Once I took twenty-four curtain calls after the third act of *Bohème* . . . and that isn't even the end of the opera!' Her face became serious. 'Does it seem ridiculous to you? Old people's memories?'

'No,' said Billy gently, just as entranced as Whitaker.

She smiled at him. 'And you are a virtuoso flautist. So was your mother, at home in Hungary. Here . . . she scratched a living. Who is your teacher?'

'Ernest Jolland.'

'I never heard of him.'

'But I'm hoping to go to Karl Zuckmayer in Salzburg, if I can get a scholarship.'

'I will write to him,' said Mrs Dalgleish. 'I don't know him, but perhaps my name . . . She told me that her father, the great Szabo, was dying in Hungary. She wanted to get him to the West, but how?' Abruptly she rose to her feet. 'Too much air,' she said. 'I must go back to the limousine. Leave everything. Jonathan will clear.' Abandoning her rug she marched off across the sands, towards the dunes and the road. Billy and Whitaker struggled hastily to their feet, Whitaker still holding a half-full glass of champagne. 'Met your match?' he said softly.

Billy looked after her retreating figure. 'You have to work so hard to keep up with her,' he said.

Whitaker drained his glass. 'She has a superb cellar!' he said contentedly as they followed her tracks back to the car.

Whitaker climbed straight into the Rolls, glad to be out of the wind, but Billy paused to say to Jonathan, 'I'll help you with the picnic things.'

'No, you won't.' said Jonathan. 'That's my job. And by the by...if she goes offering you employment, just you remember—there isn't a vacancy.' He gave Billy a dark look and then turned and walked down the beach.

As Billy got into the car and sat on the bucket seat, facing the other two, Mrs Dalgleish said, 'Dear Jonathan. So loyal...so insanely jealous. We have a perfect contract. I pay him well and he gets a little bonus at the end of the year...if I'm satisfied.' From a small hamper at Whitaker's feet she selected a bottle of whisky and a glass. 'Isn't this cosy?' she said, pouring. 'I once said to Mr Dalgleish, let's sell the castle and live in the car. He was quite a small man, it could have worked. Whisky?'

'No, thank you,' said Billy.

'I've had enough,' said Whitaker.

'Good heavens!' said Billy, with exaggerated amazement. Whitaker gave him a quelling look.

'Ah well,' said Mrs Dalgleish. She tossed back a double in one swallow and handed the glass and bottle to Whitaker who put them away for her. 'I said to her,' she went on, 'yes, I want to help you. The *Maestro* ill in that cold country! But my contact—his price was dear.' She turned to look out of the window, her gloved hand over her mouth. 'I cannot speak for a moment,' she said, her voice muffled. Her eyes glittered. She turned back. 'He got me out of the country, took all my money...and went away. I thought he was my lover, you see...but it was only the money. Later—when I marry Mr Dalgleish—he became a great nuisance.'

'Who was he?' said Billy.

'Kurt Gruber.'

'You introduced my parents to Kurt Gruber?'

'Oh yes,' said Mrs Dalgleish. 'You know him?'

'He's dead.'

'No!'

'Along with my mother, seventeen years ago...'

Mrs Dalgleish's hands flew up to her face. 'Tania is dead...' she whispered.

'They were escaping over the border out of Hungary into Austria,' said Billy. 'Their car crashed.'

'And *he's* dead,' cried Mrs Dalgleish, clasping her hands with glee, 'Oh, I breathe again.' She narrowed her eyes. 'And yet I would like to see the body.'

'It was burned in the car explosion.'

'Kurt Gruber would not be easy to kill,' said Mrs Dalgleish in a sombre voice. 'Like a snake he slips through the fingers...'

'But he *is* dead.'

She shook her head, subdued. 'Take no person's word for it,' she said. 'So. Kurt agreed to help Jerri Toth. But why, I asked Jerri, why? You have no money—why is he helping you? Believe me, he is getting something out of it.' She gazed mistily at Billy. 'Jerri, who was so gentle,' she said. 'Where is he now?'

'I don't know. Since my mother's death he hasn't been heard of.'

'And where was he then?'

'Somewhere in Hungary. My mother went there with Kurt Gruber to meet him.'

'I thought I was his girl—his *Prima Donna Assoluta*... I came to the West, but I did not work so much. Then Mr Dalgleish found me. Mr Dalgleish like my singing.' She closed her eyes, her mouth in a smile at the memory. There was a silence. Billy and Whitaker both watched her, fascinated. Slowly, slowly her head drooped to one side and came to rest on Whitaker's shoulder. He sat very still. Billy touched her arm gently. She woke with a start. 'Now—I must go back to my castle,' she said. 'When you are in Scotland, you will visit me? Goodbye, Mr Whitaker.' She held out her hand and, rather to his own surprise, Whitaker kissed it. 'And Billy,' said Mrs Dalgleish. She put her arms around his neck, and kissed him on the cheek. 'I hope you find what you are looking for. Though I don't know why you try. You have friends—you have a bonny life. I only knew Mr Dalgleish... and now...'

They climbed out of the car and closed the door. Jonathan, who had been leaning against the rear bumper, got into the driving seat. Mrs Dalgleish rolled down her window and handed Billy her card. 'If you need anything,' she said, 'you are to ask me.'

'Mrs Dalgleish,' said Billy, 'my mother...was she...' He shook his head. 'It doesn't matter.'

Mrs Dalgleish gave him a long serious look. 'How would you describe anyone?' she said. 'Me? What would you say about me? There are as many pictures as there are people describing. You will never know her, Billy Toth. She is dead. Let her rest in peace.' She rapped on the glass behind Jonathan. 'Drive on!' she called. The yellow Rolls moved slowly off, leaving Billy and Whitaker standing in the cool wind, staring after it. After a moment they looked at each other and began to laugh. Then a thought struck Billy. 'How did you come?'

Whitaker waved his stick in the air. 'In the auto,' he said, in an approximation of a mid-European accent.

Billy nodded at him, smiling. 'And how will you get back?'

Whitaker's levity faded. 'Oh my God!'

'Oh Mr Whitaker,' said Billy, 'at long last your chance to ride pillion on my motorbike!'

'No, no, I positively refuse,' said Whitaker, stumping off in the direction of the cottage, Billy at his heels. Then the situation and the champagne overcame him again, and by the time they reached the cottage door they were leaning on each other, both laughing weakly.

Chapter Thirteen

It was late on a December evening and Whitaker and Billy were in the study, playing chess in an atmosphere of silence and intense concentration. The game, in fact, was nearly over, with Whitaker moving in for the kill. Hand poised, he looked at Billy, a demonic smile on his face. 'I don't believe it,' said Billy, seeing what was about to happen. Whitaker began to chuckle as he made his final move. 'Checkmate!' he cried in triumph. 'You *always* win,' said Billy. Whitaker rose from the table. 'This old dog knows a few tricks,' he said gleefully. Then, his smile faded and he stared at Billy with a look of disbelief that began to turn into fear. 'Mr Whitaker?' said Billy, starting to get up. Whitaker opened his mouth as if to speak, leaned forward to support himself on the table with both hands, made a small choking sound in his throat and slumped across the table. Chessmen scattered in all directions. *'Mr Whitaker!'* said Billy, but before he could reach him Whitaker had fallen to the floor. There he lay, quite still and white, his eyes closed.

Billy came out of a confused nightmare made up of a telephone call, a fast drive in an ambulance with lights flashing, and a variety of doctors and nurses. He was sitting on a long bench in an otherwise deserted waiting area on the second floor of the hospital. A ward sister sat at his side holding a clipboard with a form attached to it. 'Next of kin?' she was saying.

Billy looked at her blankly.

'His family?' she said.

Billy shook his head. 'He hasn't any.'

'And you are..?'

'Stanyon. Billy Stanyon.'

'Are you related, Mr Stanyon?'

'No,' said Billy. The area they were in was so large and empty it seemed that echoes were waiting to come out of its walls. 'Well...not exactly,' he muttered. He was unsure how loudly he should speak.

The sister put her hand on his arm. 'It's all right,' she said. 'We're doing all we can.'

'It was just an ordinary evening,' said Billy. 'We were playing chess. He'd just beaten me.'

'Help me get the details,' said the sister gently.

'He's my guardian. I'm his...ward, I suppose.'

'And he has no family?'

'I'm his family,' Billy snapped, fear making him irritable. 'Is all this necessary?'

'I'm afraid it is. Hospitals are run on forms.'

'But how is he?' said Billy. 'That's all that matters.'

'Alive,' said the sister calmly, 'which is always a good sign.' She was quite young and she had a reassuringly round and sensible face. 'I should go home and get some rest,' she said.

'Rest!'

'It *is* the middle of the night. Far better if you get some rest and come back in the morning. We'll telephone you if there's any change.'

Billy shook his head. 'I'd rather stay.'

'I promise you there's nothing you can do...'

'I want to stay,' said Billy. 'He's not just...he's all the family I've got.'

The sister looked at him for a moment, then nodded. 'I'll see if I can rustle you up a cup of coffee,' she said. Her footsteps clicked away, across the waiting area and down a corridor. There was silence. Billy closed his eyes for a moment, in an effort to ward off the headache that was beginning to form behind them. When he opened them again he found that his head had lolled to one side, he was stiff all over, and a plastic cup of coffee stood at his feet, cold and greyish. The curtains that had covered the huge windows had been drawn back and cold daylight was washing in. He realized what had woken him—someone had come to sit on the bench beside him and had said his name. He straightened up and looked round.

'It's only me,' said Miss Price, sitting neatly upright, her outdoor coat buttoned to the neck.

Billy rubbed his eyes with the palms of his hands. 'How is he?' he said. His voice sounded hoarse.

'They say "comfortable". Have you been here all night?'

'Yes.' He yawned. 'Oh, I feel *awful.*'

'I should think you do,' said Miss Price. 'Sleeping sitting up!'

'Can we see him?'

'*I* don't know,' said Miss Price. 'Perhaps you should ask.'

'He is all right?' said Billy, something about her tone making him uncertain.

'Yes,' said Miss Price.

'You wouldn't lie to me?'

She looked him straight in the eye. 'Of course I wouldn't.'

'But...there's something.'

Miss Price looked away again. 'He's had a stroke,' she said, in clipped tones. 'He has not yet regained consciousness.'

'What does that mean?' said Billy desperately. 'I don't know what any of it means. I don't even know what a stroke *is.*'

'A stroke is...' said Miss Price. She paused. 'A blood vessel ruptures...in the brain, and...' She stopped, looking straight ahead, without expression.

'And?' said Billy.

She shook her head.

'You seem to know all about "strokes",' said Billy angrily. 'I'm sorry. I don't. I'm not that clever.'

'Oh yes,' said Miss Price, 'I know about them. I've lived with one. We should go now.'

'I want to see him.'

'Why?' said Miss Price. 'What good will seeing him do?' She looked down at the handbag on her lap. 'Mother had a stroke,' she said. 'Oh, a long time ago now. She talks with a funny slur... which gets on my nerves. She guzzles her food and gawps at the television. I try...' her voice sounded odd. 'What good will seeing him do? He's...' she shook her head crossly. 'You only see the outside. That isn't him.' Her hands, on the bag, were tightly clenched. She noticed this and consciously relaxed them. 'You should have telephoned me, Billy.'

'I didn't want to disturb you,' said Billy.

She looked at him for a moment. 'How thoughtful,' she said curtly.

A nurse clacked importantly down the corridor towards them. 'He's conscious,' she said. 'You can go in for a moment.'

They both got to their feet, but Miss Price said, 'You go. I really must get back to the office.'

Billy stared at her. 'I don't understand you,' he said.

'No?' said Miss Price. 'I have work to do. Mr Whitaker had an interview booked for 11.30.'

'What does it matter about the office?' said Billy.

'Excuse me,' said Miss Price. She walked away, towards the swing doors and the outside world. Billy stood looking after her. The nurse touched his arm. 'I'll show you the way,' she said. 'But it's only a look, mind.'

Billy turned and followed her. So he didn't see Miss Price falter just before she reached the swing doors. She stood for a moment with her head down, one hand pressed over her mouth, steadying herself with the other hand against the wall. A girl coming through the swing doors with a vase of flowers paused, concerned. 'Are you all right?' she said. 'Yes, thank you,' said Miss Price. She adjusted the collar of her coat and gave the girl a brief, forced smile. 'I just need some air.' She went through the swing doors and made her way to the lift, upright, brisk and efficient once more.

Billy got back to the house at about lunchtime. Another empty house. Whitaker had been conscious, but asleep. The distinction had been too subtle for Billy. He left the hospital but didn't feel much better when he got home. Eventually he went next door to the office. The sound of typing came from Miss Price's room. He knocked on the door and went in. She stopped typing to look up at him, but her hands were still poised over the keyboard.

'Am I disturbing you?' said Billy. 'I just wanted company.'

'I thought perhaps you'd sleep,' said Miss Price, putting her hands in her lap with an air of resignation.

He shook his head. 'Will you come back with me this afternoon?'

'No,' said Miss Price. 'I really must catch up on work. Besides, Rita is away at the moment and there's a temporary on the switchboard. Mr Belton will be going this evening. Perhaps you could go with him..?'

'Don't you care?' said Billy, suddenly angry.

'Care?'

'The work can't be that important.'

'I'd only be in the way,' said Miss Price firmly. 'I am Mr Whitaker's secretary. I belong here. Oh, by the way,' she reached across her desk to an envelope which rested on the corner, 'I brought the mail in from the house and there was a letter for you.' She handed it to him. 'From Germany. If you don't want the stamp, could I have it? My neighbour's daughter collects them.'

Billy took the letter. 'I don't understand you,' he said.

'Why should you expect to,' said Miss Price. 'I'm getting on with my job, Billy.'

'I thought Mr Whitaker was more than just an employer to you.'

She looked at him for a moment, then started typing again. Billy gave up. He slit open his letter and carried it over to the window to read it. 'Oh no,' he said, quite quietly.

The typewriter stopped. 'What is it?' said Miss Price.

'Someone I knew in Germany,' said Billy, still staring at the letter. 'Frau Gruber. Gunter says she was found drowned.'

'Oh dear,' said Miss Price. 'An accident?'

'Suicide, they think.'

'Did you know her well?'

'No—but I felt I did. She looked after me for a while, soon after I was born . . .' Suddenly he started to shake.

'Billy?' said Miss Price.

He stood there, staring out of the window, visibly trembling. Miss Price pushed back her chair and got up. 'Billy?' she said, alarmed, going over to him.

'I don't want to lose him,' said Billy, clenching his teeth to try to stop their chattering.

'No,' said Miss Price, standing beside him but not touching him. 'Well you haven't. He's . . .''

Billy interrupted. 'What is he? Will he be like your mother? Paralysed and unable to speak . . .'

'We don't know yet. They'll be doing tests.'

'But what if he is!'

'We must wait until we hear,' said Miss Price.

Billy looked at her. His eyes were very large and bright. 'I lose everyone, you see,' he said simply. 'I don't want to lose him.'

'I do understand,' said Miss Price, more gently.

'Do you?' said Billy. 'You don't act as though you do. You keep so calm.'

Miss Price returned to her desk and sat at it. 'I'll come and see to your tea before I go home at six,' she said, staring at the sheet of paper in her typewriter.

Billy folded the letter and stuffed it into his pocket. 'I'm really quite capable of getting my own tea, thank you, Miss Price,' he said. He walked out of the office and closed the door loudly behind him. As he went down the stairs he heard the keys of the machine begin to clatter once more.

At a loss, he returned to his vigil on the long bench in the hospital. Waiting was such an uneasy pastime anyway that it seemed more bearable to pursue it in an area designed for it than to try to endure it at home. It was mid-afternoon and the hospital was crowded in contrast to the night before, not only with staff and walking-wounded but with visitors as well. However, Whitaker was not in a ward, to be visited, but tucked away in Intensive Care, with a saline drip running into his arm and his heartbeat monitored on a small screen at the head of the bed. So while other visitors waited a while and were then admitted, Billy just waited.

After some time he saw the young sister of the night before hurrying past him. He jumped to his feet and called out to her.

'You here again?' she said, coming over to him. 'You know we'll telephone you.'

'Is there any more news?'

'There are a lot more tests we have to do,' she said. 'But be thankful he's conscious. Concussion, you see. He bashed his head when he fell... and of course he's an old man.'

'Not so very old,' said Billy defensively. 'Can I go and see him? Then I'll go home, really.'

'Well...' she looked doubtful. Then she smiled. 'Come on, then. But just a quick look and don't you dare wake him.'

She led the way into Whitaker's room and stood beside Billy at the bedside.

Billy looked at the impassive face on the pillow. 'You bloody well get better, Vincent Whitaker,' he said, very quietly. 'You hear me? Bloody well.'

'The language of the child!' said the sister, in mock horror. 'Come on... out.' She went out of the room and Billy, with one last look at the still figure, followed her. But just as he reached the doorway he heard a whisper from the bed behind him. It sounded like his name. He turned round. Whitaker's eyes were still closed but his mouth moved very slightly. 'Billy?' he said. 'Is that you?'

'Yes,' said Billy, holding on to the door, staring.

And without opening his eyes Whitaker said, in an extremely soft but absolutely clear voice, 'Where's my whisky? A large one.'

Billy stood where he was for a moment longer, then turned and ran out of the room calling, 'Sister! Sister!' She hurried back towards him, looking concerned. Billy began to laugh, 'It's Mr Whitaker,' he said. 'He wants a large whisky...' He followed her back into the room, laughing as though he would cry any second.

They wouldn't let him stay on, but he didn't really need to any more. He ran the entire way home, through the early winter dusk, and burst in at the front door, pink in the face and out of breath. To have found an empty house would have been an anti-climax, but there was a light in the hall and the chinking of china came from the sink in the kitchen.

'Pricey!' he shouted. 'Pricey!'

She came, drying her hands on a tea towel, surprised to hear herself called by that name. Billy grabbed her by the waist and spun her in a half circle. 'Billy!' she said, with steely calm, 'let go of me!'

'I won't ever,' said Billy, spinning her the other way and then giving her a great hug. 'He's all right, Pricey! He asked me for a whisky!'

'He can talk?' said Miss Price, managing to disentangle herself from his embrace. 'Properly? Talk properly?'

'I think so,' said Billy, 'I don't care. He's talking!'

'*You* heard him?' said Miss Price, examining his face intently.

'*Yes!* He said my name and everything.' Miss Price hurried across the hall and began to struggle into her coat. Billy burbled on, 'This sister, she said I could go in, but just for a minute, she's really nice, anyway, I went in and he talked. That's good isn't it? I mean... isn't it?'

Her coat was on, her bag was over her arm, she was already dragging at the front door. 'I'm going back to the office, now,' she said. 'There's a casserole in the oven. It should be ready at 7.30.'

'Oh *God*!' said Billy, excitement turning to frustration. 'Can't you be glad?'

'I'm very glad,' said Miss Price evenly. 'Now, if you'll excuse me...'

As she hurried out of the front door Billy yelled after her, 'Do you *have* to be the perfect secretary *all* the time? Can't you show *any* emotion?'

He stood in the hall for a few moments, glaring at the front door. Then he stopped glaring and just looked at it. Then he shrugged to himself and followed Miss Price through it.

He found her in Whitaker's office. Still in her coat, she was sitting bolt upright in the chair which faced the large desk, looking across at the empty swivel chair behind it. Her back was to the door. Billy crossed the room until he stood beside her, but not close to her. She didn't look round. Her face was expressionless. 'I'm sorry,' he said. 'I shouldn't have spoken to you like that. You were the only person I could tell, you see.'

'Show emotion?' said Miss Price, as though she hadn't heard him. 'After thirty years I've schooled myself never to show emotion.'

'I'm... sorry,' said Billy.

'He'll have to retire,' said Miss Price, to the empty chair. 'He won't like that. He won't be good in retirement. And I... I will have to find another job. I couldn't work for Mr Belton, and anyway, without Mr Whitaker here, the firm is bound to change.'

'Can't we just be happy that he's all right?' said Billy, almost pleadingly. 'He talked to me, Pricey. I thought he was dead, when it happened.'

She turned to look at him for the first time. 'You didn't think to telephone me, though, did you?' she said. 'Because I'm just Miss Price... who is awfully good in the office.'

'I didn't want to disturb you.'

'Didn't you? But you let me go into the house this morning, looking for him. You let me find the lights on... chess pieces everywhere... the telephone off the hook...' She turned away. Tears were very near. 'I thought I'd just work on here for a little while,' she said.

'Shouldn't you go home?' said Billy gently. 'Your mother..?'

She smiled. 'You sound just like him! Vincent blamed mother for everything.'

'You called him Vincent,' said Billy.

'I think of him as Vincent. I speak of him as Mr Whitaker.'

'So do I,' said Billy quietly.

There was a brief silence in the office. Then, 'I telephoned my neighbour,' said Miss Price, becoming more matter-of-fact. 'The one with the child who collects stamps... remember? She's been a good friend. She's quite used to mother-sitting.'

'Have supper with me,' said Billy on an impulse.

The matter-of-fact approach left her. She looked sad and tired. 'I really need to be alone, Billy,' she said. 'I so rarely am, you see, with mother...'

Billy nodded. 'I'll go, then,' he said.

But she stopped him as he got to the door, twisting round in her chair. 'Wait,' she said. 'I would like to have supper with you. Thank you. But... let me just stay here a little longer?'

'You come in when you're ready,' said Billy, opening the door. But she stopped him again. 'I'm sorry about the woman in Germany,' she said. 'Such a shock for you.'

'Well... I didn't really know her,' said Billy, still holding the door. 'But I liked her. And I always hoped she'd tell me about my father and mother...'

Miss Price sank back a little in her chair. 'I could tell you about your adopted parents,' she said, gazing across the room with a dreamy expression on her face. 'they had such a good marriage. I used to envy married people. It's a terrible waste, envy. So exhausting.'

'Did you know Mr Whitaker's wife?' said Billy, coming further into the room.

'Yes. She and I were great friends,' said Miss Price, rather too brightly.

'I can't imagine him with a wife.'

'That's because you're used to him without one. Surely you remember her?'

He shook his head. 'Not really.'

'Of course you were only a child when she died. She was... a very nice woman. That's what made it so difficult.'

Billy wandered back to the side of Whitaker's desk and stood looking at her. Eventually she returned his look and gave him a brief smile. 'This is where I belong, Billy,' she said. 'Here in his office, where there's a job to do. He needs me here. I am... expected here.' But she was not doing a job. She was sitting, isolated, in her coat, facing a desk which had an empty chair on the other side of it. 'When Mrs Whitaker died,' she said, 'he was so distraught that I thought he might...' She shook her head. 'Poor woman. Your German woman. Suicide must be such a lonely moment.' She looked down at the tidy desk top. 'We used to work late into the night, after her death. Of course he was very busy in those days. I used to think he was fighting everyone's battles for them—the young, the underdog, people like Gunter Walser—and how they all adored him. They all pulled him through... and I suppose I helped.' Unexpectedly, her voice hardened. 'And then mother had her stroke! The irony that he should have one...'

'But only a little one,' said Billy. He squatted down by her chair and put his arms round her. 'He *is* going to be all right.' She tried to pull away from him, but he wouldn't let her. 'I love him too,' he said. She relaxed slightly. 'You'll have us both crying,' she said.

'You should have married him,' said Billy. He stood up again.

'He's such a stubborn man!' said Miss Price. 'And I suppose neither of us wanted to risk it. We already have something that is so good, you see. Monday to Friday, nine to six, and a half day on Saturday.' She looked up at him with a watery smile. 'How many married couples can boast as much?'

Billy touched her shoulder. 'Come and have supper.'

'You go in. I'll join you. I just have some clearing up to do.'

He hesitated for a moment, then nodded and left her. Miss Price sat on in her upright chair and let the tears roll down her face until they were finished. 'Now look what you've done, Vincent,' she said, to the empty chair. 'I'm crying...'

Whitaker's progress was steady. By the following day he was sitting up in bed, waiting to be visited. The lines at each side of his mouth seemed to have deepened, and he spoke slowly as if he was tired, but there was no slurring.

'How did a woman in a wheelchair drown herself in a lake?' he said, when Billy told him Gunter's news.

'What are you suggesting?' said Billy.

'I'm not suggesting anything,' said Whitaker, crustily. 'Just asking questions. Tell Pricey, when she comes, to bring my diary. And you might point out that it's about time she put in an appearance. What are you grinning at?'

'You,' said Billy, cheerfully. 'You're getting better. Or worse. We'll all be dreading you again quite soon. She's outside, shall I fetch her?'

Whitaker passed his hand across his chin. 'I haven't had a shave,' he said doubtfully. Billy ignored him and went to the door. Miss Price came in, carrying her briefcase. 'I haven't had a shave,' said Whitaker again.

'I can see that,' said Miss Price.

'I've been lucky,' said Whitaker, suddenly subdued. 'Just a little warning. Can't move my left arm much, but they think that'll come back.' He brightened. 'And I use my right for lifting the glass.'

'Perhaps,' said Miss Price crisply, 'if you were to stop lifting the glass...'

'...pigs might fly,' said Whitaker. He beamed at them both. 'Dear children! I've been a nuisance, I can tell. How long have I got till we go to Salzburg, Billy?'

'About five weeks.'

Miss Price plonked the briefcase down on the bedside table. 'Don't you think that considering flying to Austria,' she said, 'is a bit like considering walking before you can crawl?'

'Probably,' said Whitaker. 'But when he gets that scholarship, I want to be the first to know.'

'*If...*' said Billy.

'*When...*' said Whitaker.

'Then I agree with you,' said Billy. 'You'd better be there. I'm off, now. I should put in an appearance at the shop. Miss Moreton doesn't really allow compassionate leave.'

'It's half-day closing...' began Miss Price, then stopped and smiled briefly at Billy, who pointed a severe finger at her and said, 'Did you bring his diary?'

'Yes?'

He flopped against the door in exaggerated relief. 'I thought you were in for a wigging!' He looked across at Whitaker. 'I'll see you tomorrow,' he said. 'And we won't play any more chess, it's obviously too much of a strain for you. Bye.'

The door slammed behind him and there was a silence in the hospital room. Then, 'Well, Miss Price?' said Whitaker.

'Well, Mr Whitaker,' said Miss Price. She opened the briefcase and began to take out files and papers.

At Bamburgh the following weekend Billy stood in a freezing wind at the edge of an angry grey sea whose waves rose and sank back before him like jaws opening and then falling shut. '*He's all right*!' he yelled into the spray. '*He's all right*!'

Chapter Fourteen

Whitaker continued to make steady progress and to regain control over his left arm, but the doctor frowned at the mention of a trip to Austria and Miss Price became, if possible, even more stern than usual. 'You can hardly hope to offer moral support to Billy if you wear yourself out and make yourself ill again,' she said. So, with the utmost reluctance, he allowed himself to be persuaded to stay behind while Dr Jolland and Billy flew to Salzburg together.

The first audition for the three coveted scholarships to the Zuckmayer Academy of Music was held in the afternoon. Billy, who had only arrived that morning, went through his paces in a daze, just one of forty hopeful applicants from Europe and America. He hardly reacted when he was told he was among ten who had been shortlisted and should return next day. The

Academy, which was proud of its scholarship scheme, had arranged a buffet supper for the ten young people and their sponsors, and a minor press conference at which photographs were taken for the local paper and for the specialist music press of Europe. Throughout this, Billy still felt a sense of unreality. But the following morning, sitting once more in the ante-room to the Academy's Concert Hall with only eight other applicants, the situation suddenly snapped into sharp focus and he remembered how much he wanted to be accepted. The candidates sat on chairs about two feet apart, avoiding each other's eyes and listening to the efforts of the horn player which came to them from behind the high, closed doors to the concert hall. The horn solo came to an end. The player was ushered out through some other door which gave those in the ante-room the eerie feeling that he had simply disappeared. The long polished doors opened to reveal a neat efficient woman, the Academy secretary.

'Vilhelm Toth?' she said.

Billy stood up, gripping the flute case.

The secretary managed a slight smile. 'It is your time,' she said. 'Herr Zuckmayer is waiting.'

The pretty, dark-haired American girl, Julie, muttered something as he moved towards the door. 'What?' he said, pausing.

She looked up and he saw his own fear written all over her face. 'Just . . . good luck,' she said.

'Oh. Yes. Thank you,' said Billy embarrassed. He followed the secretary into the immense ornate concert hall from which all seating had been removed apart from a group of six chairs at a table two-thirds of the way down. He had to walk the whole length of the room, across its echoing polished boards, to the stage at the far end. High windows curved around its back and threw clear light onto the faces of Karl Zuckmayer and four members of his staff. The secretary took her place on a chair just behind them and, before nerves could silence him forever, Billy began to play, his eyes closed against the formidable group of listeners.

When he had finished he lowered the flute and opened his eyes to see Zuckmayer and his staff conferring, leaning towards each other along the table. At last Zuckmayer sat back and looked at Billy. He was an imposing figure, a man of perhaps fifty with a great stillness about him. His face was quite gentle, his expression mild, yet he made Billy more nervous than anyone he had yet encountered.

'What else have you for us?' said Zuckmayer.

Billy cleared his throat. 'Mozart?' he said.

Zuckmayer smiled. 'Why not? He sounds good in Salzburg.'

While Billy played, the staff made copious notes, but Zuckmayer only listened. Before the piece was finished he clapped his hands, once, to stop the music. Billy stood silent, dwarfed by the massive hall.

'Good,' said Zuckmayer. 'Thank you...' he consulted his notes, '...Mr Toth. That is not a very English name?'

'My father was Hungarian.'

'Ah. And why do you want to play the flute?'

Billy was totally unprepared for the question. 'It's the only thing I'm any good at,' he said.

Zuckmayer bellowed with laughter, and his staff smiled with him. 'Well,' he said, 'you're not bad. Who is your teacher?'

'Ernest Jolland.'

'Who?'

'Dr Jolland.'

'Oh, a doctor,' said Zuckmayer. 'I hope he is not a surgeon as well?' The staff, who seemed faceless beside the Maestro, laughed and Billy shifted his weight from one foot to the other. 'All right, Mr Toth,' said Zuckmayer, more gently. 'Is there anything else you want to tell me?'

'My mother played the flute,' said Billy.

'Hm,' said Zuckmayer. 'And mine took in washing. Would I have heard of her?'

'Tania Szabo,' said Billy. 'Her father was the conductor.'

'Szabo?' said Zuckmayer thoughtfully. '*The* Szabo?'

'Yes.'

Zuckmayer nodded. 'He was a fine musician. But you must understand that in the Zuckmayer School having famous forebears does not help you. You get in on your own ability...or not at all.'

'Oh no,' said Billy, confused. 'I didn't mean...'

Zuckmayer silenced him with a gesture. 'What we have to decide is whether you have any ability or whether you are just wasting our time,' he said. 'Come back this evening at six. Give your name to the secretary.'

Billy began the long walk to the door. The secretary rose and accompanied him. Unlike the horn player he was shown back into the ante-room. As he reached the door he heard Zuckmayer's voice behind him, *'Der Nächste!'*

The next was Julie. 'Oh my God!' she said, struggling to her feet, almost dropping her flute. She looked at Billy with wild eyes. 'You can't play the flute if you're being sick, can you?' she said, 'and I feel *so sick.'*

'Good luck,' said Billy.

'Will you wait for me?' she said.

'I have to meet my teacher, in the Tomaselli.'

'Miss Underwood,' said the secretary in a voice of ice. 'It is not a good idea to keep the maestro waiting.'

'I'm coming, I'm coming,' said Julie and followed the secretary into the concert hall, pulling a hideous face at her back for Billy's benefit. Billy laughed, feeling his tension begin to disperse as he did so.

Dr Jolland was sitting on the verandah of the Tomaselli, in the mild spring sunshine. Three empty Knickerbocker Glory glasses, scraped entirely clean, cluttered the small white table in front of him and he was about to plunge his spoon into a fourth garish concoction when he caught sight of Billy in the street below. He stood up and called to him, waving his spoon in nervous greeting. Billy ran up the stairs, threaded his way through the small tables and flopped down in a chair opposite.

'Well?' said Dr Jolland, his white hair looking somewhat wilder than usual in the anxiety of the moment. 'How did you play?'

'I don't know.'

'You *must* know. A professional always knows. Have an ice cream.'

'No, thank you,' said Billy, trying to avoid looking at the sickly mixture in the glass at the other side of the table.

'When I'm nervous,' said Dr Jolland, apologetically, 'I always want sweet things. I couldn't face another Sachertorte and the Strudels,' he burped discreetly, 'lie heavy. What did he say to you?'

'I have to go back at six.'

'Did you mention my name?'

'Yes,' said Billy uncomfortably.

'Good, Good. What did you play?'

'Pergolesi and Mozart.'

'Why choose the Pergolesi?' said Dr Jolland. 'You know

you're always too slow in the Pergolesi.'

'Can I have a coffee?' said Billy.

'Yes. Wave your arm. The Pergolesi I would not have chosen. I told you ... you're always too slow.'

'Well, it's too late now,' said Billy irritably. The waiter came up to the table and he ordered his coffee.

'You said you had been taught by Ernest Jolland?' persisted the old man. 'He will remember me. You said that?'

'Yes.'

'And?'

'He... he was very impressed,' said Billy helplessly.

'Of course, a good teacher doesn't necessarily have good pupils,' said Dr Jolland, hiding his pleasure as much as he could. 'How many others were there?'

'Ten, I think,' said Billy. His coffee was placed in front of him. 'Thank you.'

'And there were forty yesterday,' said Dr Jolland, gripping the table edge. 'You see? You do well.'

'And there are three places going,' said Billy. 'Fantastic odds.'

'I'm not a betting man.'

'You don't have to be a betting man to see how unlikely it is that I'll be chosen.' He looked over the verandah rail at the square below. 'I wish Mr Whitaker was here.' At that moment he caught sight of Julie and stood up to call her. Dr Jolland, who had done exactly the same thing minutes earlier, glowered at him. Julie scampered up the stairs and flung herself into a chair between them. Dr Jolland eyed her suspiciously. 'Oh my!' she said. 'Wasn't that awful? Wasn't that just *terrible?* Is this anyone's Knickerbocker Glory?' Without waiting for an answer she snatched up the nearest spoon and began to eat.

'It's mine, young lady,' said Dr Jolland, his white eyebrows bristling with indignation.

'Oh my God,' said Julie, pushing it from her in genuine embarrassment. 'I always eat when I'm nervous. Here — I only took a little.'

'Is this young lady anything to do with you, Stanyon?' said Dr Jolland.

'She and I...' Billy began, trying not to laugh.

'....were both Christians in the lion's den,' Julie finished for him. 'I'm Julie Underwood.'

'This is Dr Jolland, my teacher,' said Billy.

'Hey, you must be a great teacher,' said Julie. 'He's fantastic.' Dr Jolland's expression was transformed into one of avuncular benevolence. She turned to Billy. 'Why does he call you Stanyon? That's not the name you used in there.'

'I used my real father's name — Toth. Stanyon is the name of my adopted parents.'

'So what did they do wrong?' said Julie. 'Why don't you want to use their name?'

'I just thought . . . William Toth was a good name.'

'For heaven's sakes,' said Julie. 'You're Billy Stanyon, why try to be anything else?'

'What a sensible colonist,' said Dr Jolland, leaning forward to pat her hand approvingly. 'Let me buy you an ice cream.'

'Thanks,' said Julie. 'My mother is somewhere,' she shrugged, 'but she'll find me. She usually does.' She looked at Billy. 'You got to go back at six?'

'Yes.'

'That's good. If they're not interested at all they tell you. The horn player got the boot. I don't mind. He looked kinda tacky.'

'What's it matter what he looks like,' said Billy, beginning to laugh again. 'Can he play the horn?'

'Obviously not,' said Julie, 'or he wouldn't have got the boot.' She looked back at Dr Jolland. 'Did you say you were going to buy me an ice cream?' and then, even as he smilingly raised his arm to call the waiter, she changed her mood again, 'I'm so *sorry,*' she said contritely. 'I always come on strong when I'm terrified.'

'You?' said Billy, laughing outright now. 'Terrified!' He was far too intent on Julie to notice the woman who sat at a table outside the café opposite, and who had not taken her eyes off him since first he crossed the square towards the Tomaselli.

After a while, Dr Jolland set out for his hotel, to sleep off his pastries and ice creams, and Billy and Julie strolled together around the old town. Still Billy was unaware of the one woman in the crowd who kept him always in view. They looked at fountains, at souvenir stalls under brilliantly striped umbrellas, they even found a small gallery full of modern art. Both were keyed up about the final part of the audition. 'I know you're supposed to have a burning deep need,' Julie said, 'But I haven't. I just enjoy playing.'

'Maybe that's better. Did you tell that to Zuckmayer?'

She shook her head. 'I told him I had a burning deep need. I don't think he believed me for a minute. Why *did* you change your name?'

'My adopted parents are both dead,' said Billy. 'The only person alive is my father. I've been trying to find him. I thought that if I used his name... he might find me.'

Julie gazed up at him, her eyes enormous. 'That is *incredibly* romantic!' she said.

They had worked their way back to the square from which they had started, one square back from the Cathedral, the Dom, whose great bells were just beginning to ring. 'I must go to the hotel and collect Dr Jolland,' said Billy. 'Are you aware,' said Julie dreamily, 'That we're being followed?'

'Followed?' said Billy blankly.

He looked where she indicated, and suddenly he saw her, standing quite still on the other side of the square, her hands in the pockets of her mackintosh, buffeted slightly by the milling tourists—Hilde Gruber.

The moment he saw her, she turned on her heel and disappeared down a narrow, cobbled side street. Billy began to run after her, ignoring Julie's cry of 'Billy! Hey, Billy!' By the time he was in the side street, there was no sign of her. He ran to the end and looked both ways. Behind him, Hilde stood in the deep shadow of a doorway, staring at his back. Slowly she began to withdraw one hand from her raincoat pocket. It held a small, black hand-gun. Suddenly two drunken men in Tyrolean hats lurched up the street in the opposite direction, knocking into Billy, who gave up his fruitless search and allowed himself to be driven ahead of them, back the way he had run. Hilde returned the gun to her pocket and merged into the shadows as they passed.

A few minutes later, when Billy had finally decided to return to the hotel, he glimpsed her once more, over towards the Domplatz. Again, she moved off the moment he saw her, but this time it seemed that she was trying not so much to escape him as to lead him. But she had a good start and though he ran as fast as he could, dodging pedestrians, skirting a pony and trap on a sight-seeing mission, sending a cloud of doves exploding into the air in the Domplatz itself, he soon realized he had lost her. He slowed, stopped, then wandered into the little graveyard of St Peter's church, for which it had seemed she was making. There wasn't anyone there. A movement made him look up. He found himself staring right across the churchyard at the car of the funicular which was crawling up the rockface towards the Hohensalzburg, the great fortress that towered rather grimly over the old town. There was only one passenger in the car, standing at the back and looking down. Even from that distance, he recognized her instantly.

It was not immediately obvious to him how to find the station, and he wasted minutes running to and fro, too impatient to ask directions. His car, when he got into it, seemed to crawl unbearably slowly. When he climbed out at the top he found himself right within the ramparts of the castle. It was immense. It was like a small town with wide gravel streets and buildings and courtyards. He began to run, at random, and came out through a narrow opening on to a wide terrace with a view over the whole of Salzburg. As he walked towards the safety rail at the terrace-edge, he was aware of someone behind him. He turned.

'Hallo, Hilde,' he said. 'I'm sorry. I don't speak German.'

'I'm supposed to kill you, Billy Toth,' said Hilde, with no emotion in her voice at all.

'You do speak English,' said Billy. 'Of course. I should have thought of that.'

'I have a gun,' said Hilde, almost wonderingly. 'Look.' She took it out of her pocket and showed it to him, lying on the flat of her hand.

Billy stood quite still, facing her, his back to the view. 'Yes,' he said. 'From my father.'

She did not point the gun at him. She looked puzzled.

'I've been such a fool,' said Billy. 'He doesn't want me, does he? Of course he doesn't. Just because he's my father, I made him into a hero. Are you going to shoot me? It all seems a bit unreal.'

Hilde stared at him. Then she crossed to the edge of the terrace and dropped the gun over it, into a tangle of trees and undergrowth on the cliff face. There was a silence between them. At length Billy said, 'I was sorry about Elsa. I didn't think her the type. Is there one? For suicide?' His voice cracked. 'Why does my father hate me? Just tell me that.'

'He's dead, Billy,' said Hilde. 'Dead with your mother in that car crash.'

Suddenly Billy understood. 'Kurt!' he said. 'Kurt Gruber!'

'My husband always survives,' said Hilde quietly. 'He killed an

Austrian border guard. They hunted him...he had to get away...'

'Where is he?'

Her voice became harder. 'He wants you dead, Billy Toth,' she said. 'You are a threat to him. You didn't believe my mother-in-law, you must believe me.'

'Why are you telling me?'

Hilde turned away and looked out across the town and the river. 'I belong to an ordinary world,' she said. 'I wanted nothing more than...children and a small allotment. I am carrying a gun to kill a young man because my husband is threatened. Where is the ordinary world now?'

Billy watched her. 'You could turn him in,' he said.

'Yes,' said Hilde.

'But you won't?'

'His mother wanted to...' said Hilde.

'But she didn't.'

She shrugged. 'When your father was killed in the crash it was the perfect opportunity for him...'

'Killed by whom, Hilde?'

'It was an accident.'

'A convenient one,' said Billy. 'Will you tell him I was only ever looking for my father. I was a bit lost...I don't give a damn about his squalid little life. Will you tell him that?'

'I never see...' Hilde began, but Billy cut in. 'And add something else,' he said, quite loudly. 'If he wants to get rid of me, he should do it himself!' He turned and walked away, leaving Hilde alone on the ramparts of the old dead fortress.

He sat for a long time in the little churchyard at the foot of the great rock, below the ancient catacombs cut into the rock's dark face. The image of the crash came to him again—but this time there was more to it. A border post on a misty night. A car racing for the barrier, breaking through it, splinters flying high. Border guards leaping clear, recovering, firing. The car door opening and a man's figure half-falling, half-jumping out. Rolling. Crouching into the undergrowth unseen. The car skidding, crashing, exploding into an orange flower of flame, burning vividly against the grey night. The hidden man, still crouching low, limping away unnoticed.

Kurt Gruber had survived.

And still he sat, on a wooden bench, among graves which

seemed to live, so many bore fresh flowers and candles which glimmered behind glass shades. That was where Julie found him.

'Oh, Billy,' she said. 'People have been looking all over for you. You didn't go to the Academy.' She sat down on the bench beside him. She had obviously been crying.

'I was busy,' said Billy quietly.

'There's an old guy looking for you, too,' said Julie. 'He's just arrived. Your guardian?'

'Vincent?' said Billy brightening.

'I don't know...'

'Mr Whitaker?'

'I guess so.'

'Well, where is he?' said Billy, jumping to his feet.

'At the hotel,' said Julie. 'Like I say, everyone is going spare, trying to find you.'

Billy was already hurrying towards the hotel. Julie had to run to keep up with him. 'Don't you want to know what happened?' she said. But it was plain that Billy wasn't listening. She stopped and let him go on. He didn't seem to notice. 'Billy!' she called after him. 'You've won a scholarship to the Zuckmayer Studio...' He was already out of earshot. 'Congratulations, Billy,' said Julie quietly. She turned and walked away in the other direction.

Whitaker looked a little tired, but reassuringly himself. He even showed an interest in taking an extremely leisurely stroll by the river, while he listened carefully as Billy gave him a censored version of the afternoon's events, omitting any mention of the gun and the threats. 'He's dead, Vincent,' said Billy at its end. 'He's dead and I don't feel...anything. I'm free. I don't have to go on looking.'

They walked on in silence for a few moments. 'I *am* so glad to see you,' said Billy. 'How did you get here?'

'On a wing and a prayer,' said Whitaker. 'And Gunter met me at the airport. I should never have listened to them all in the first place. I couldn't miss you making a fool of yourself.'

'What?'

'Didn't anyone tell you? You have a scholarship, Billy.'

'But I wasn't even there,' said Billy, beginning to laugh.

'It was, I understand, noted,' said Whitaker. 'Jolland is hopping mad! Dear boy, I'm so relieved. Perhaps now I will be spared that infernal instrument morning, noon and night. Do you realize I have spent the whole day travelling—you'd better be good tonight.'

'Tonight?' said Billy, who was still absorbing the first piece of news.

'Am I not right?' said Whitaker. 'You are expected to perform for your new master? I hear that Maestro Zuckmayer is even more frightening than Jolly Jolland!'

The next time Billy and Julie met they were once again in the ante-room, both dressed for the short concert to be given by the three scholarship winners, Julie in a long red evening dress which set off her vivid dark prettiness and Billy in a hired dinner jacket.

'Oh, Billy,' said Julie. 'You look like a penguin!'

'I'm sorry I kept rushing off. I will explain,' said Billy. 'And I'm sorry you didn't get through.'

She shrugged. 'It's OK. You know what he said about you?' She attempted Zuckmayer's accent. 'That your absence did not auger vell for ze future!'

'I wish you'd won,' said Billy, laughing at the imitation. 'I'd like to think you were going to be here with me.'

Julie looked at him for a moment, then she smiled. 'Well,' she said, 'there is a place for me. He just couldn't offer me a scholarship.'

'But could you afford...?'

She winked. 'Mother rather likes Salzburg,' she said.

Their conversation was interupted by the secretary, this time in a short black evening dress. Like a sophisticated sheepdog she separated the three finalists from those who were to sit in the audience and ushered them in their separate directions.

'Good luck, Billy,' said Julie. She stood on tiptoe and kissed him briefly on the cheek, then fled to join her formidably glamorous mother.

When Billy followed the other two contestants onto the stage he was quite shaken by the transformation which had been wrought upon the concert hall. The great curved windows were now covered by long red velvet curtains, the immense central chandelier glittered with light, and seating filled the auditorium. Karl Zuckmayer sat in the centre of the front row, flanked by his staff, and the twenty or so rows behind him were taken by the failed candidates and their friends and families. As his name was announced, Billy picked out Julie's bright-eyed face. Two rows in front of her he saw Dr Jolland, beaming with pride through his half spectacles, Gunter Walser grinning and clapping with the rest and, between them, Whitaker, smiling, clapping and nodding encouragement.

Zuckmayer rose to his feet and the applause died respectfully away. 'Delighted you could make it, Herr Toth,' he said, in a voice that carried easily throughout the hall. 'Have you any explanation for your earlier non-attendance?'

'No, Maestro,' said Billy softly.

'Maestro, no less!' said Zuckmayer, relenting a little. 'You have a talent, Herr Toth. But talent is like a garden. It needs weeding and fertilising and work, work, WORK!'

'Yes, Maestro.'

'All right,' said Zuckmayer, sitting down. 'Perhaps you will play something for us.'

The other two contestants sat on the chairs provided, to await their turn, and Billy passed his music to the pianist. He turned to face the audience once more, but before raising the flute he said, in a quiet but entirely audible voice, 'I would like to say thank you to my teacher, Dr Jolland, for getting me here... and most of all... to my dear friend Vincent Whitaker, thank you for... just... thanks.'

'Yes, yes,' said Zuckmayer irritably. 'Very pretty, but you haven't got anywhere yet. You are only starting, and really the sooner you do so the better.'

In the audience Dr Jolland beamed, Gunter turned his head to smile at Whitaker, and Whitaker himself nodded just once, almost imperceptibly, to Billy. His eyes were perhaps rather brighter than usual.

Billy raised the flute and began to play.

Chapter Fifteen

Life in Salzburg was very pleasant and offered a kind of freedom Billy had never known before. Gunter, it transpired, had a girlfriend, Anna, who lived and worked there, illustrating books in the studio of her flat at the top of a block in the old part. She was happy for Billy to move into her attic room, at a very modest rent, and was easy-going about when he ate, and even whether he ate in or out. Gunter, whose Munich flat was only about fifty miles away, was a regular visitor, so Billy felt none of the usual loneliness of a new environment. Despite the medieval atmosphere of the narrow cobbled streets, the market squares, the pony and traps and the many, many churches, it was a youthful town, full of students and young tourists who ski-ied in the nearby mountains when the snow was right, and congregated in pavement cafés when the air was warm. It was a town rich in concerts and music festivals, Mozart and Gregorian chant, church organs, and the ghostly sound of glockenspiel like memories of past bells. And there was Julie. She and Billy were rarely out of each other's company, enjoying the same relaxed life-style, laughing at the same jokes. It seemed too good to last, and in a way it was. There was so much to do that it was simply not possible to do everything. Something had to suffer. And Julie, it soon became apparent, was not happy to be left on her own, even in favour of a compulsory tutorial.

'Who do you love the most?' she said one afternoon when they were walking at the snowline in the hills behind the town. 'Me or that goddamn flute?'

Billy kissed her. 'Come on,' he said, 'I'll be late back as it is.'

He kissed her again, but she was barely mollified. 'There's always something in the way,' she said, pulling back against his hand as he led her down the white slope.

This time neither of them was aware of being watched. The man with the binoculars did not intend to be seen. He stood well back among the trees, and in any case they were too wrapped up in each other to notice anything else.

Billy was right, he was late for his tutorial, but that was not the only problem. There was also the fact that he had not once practised the piece he had been set. His tutor, Herr Greisinger, listened sourly for a few moments and then clapped his hands together once. Obediently, Billy stopped playing and lowered the flute.

'You keep me waiting for three-quarters of an hour,' said Herr Greisinger, 'and then you play like... that? You breathe like an athlete after running the Marathon. You gulp and heave and PANT.'

'I was nervous,' said Billy. 'I'm sorry.'

'Nervous?' said Herr Greisinger. 'You have reason to be

nervous. I cannot have my time wasted, Herr Toth. I will give you all my time, every minute of it, but you *must* give me something back.' He waited for some response but Billy just stood, staring at the floor. 'Billy,' said Herr Greisinger, more gently, 'you have such a talent. You are going to throw it away? Discard it? Turn your back on it?' He shook his head. 'A crime! The Maestro, Herr Zuckmayer, is not as patient as I am, and even my patience is near its end.'

Billy looked up from the floor. 'Shall I do it again?' he said.

'No point,' said Herr Greisinger. 'It will not improve without work. You seem not to want to work.' He waved his hand in a dismissing gesture. 'Go now.'

Billy chewed at his lip. He turned from the music stand and made for the door. Behind him he heard Herr Greisinger's voice, 'I am *bitterly* disappointed.'

Billy went out and closed the door quietly behind him.

On the same afternoon, Dr Jolland was pacing and puffing in Whitaker's office, periodically pausing to glare at Whitaker himself who was sitting behind his desk and reading a letter with great thoroughness.

'Well?' demanded Dr Jolland, who had not even bothered to remove his coat and hat.

'I haven't finished yet,' said Whitaker, with an almost visible effort to remain calm.

'For heaven's sake!' Jolland spluttered, resting his knuckles on the desk top and glowering at him like an angry white bear.

Whitaker finished the letter and put it down. 'I see,' he said.

'You see?' said Dr Jolland. 'That boy is going to lose his place at the Academy and all you can say is "I see"?'

'I wonder why they wrote to you,' said Whitaker. 'You haven't previously heard from the Academy?'

'They wrote to me,' said Dr Jolland, 'because he is my creation. Because I got him to Salzburg. What does it *matter* why they wrote to me? The fact is they have, and now it is up to us to act.'

'Act?' said Whitaker, trapped behind his desk by the wrath of the doctor.

'We must go to Salzburg,' said Dr Jolland.

'Both of us?'

'At once! If he doesn't pull his socks up, he won't have a scholarship, he won't even have a place there. Then what'll he do? Come back to Newcastle? Take his old job in the bookshop, *if* it is still waiting for him? Play amateur in the evenings?' His lip curled in distaste, '"The Desert Song?"' he said. '"The Noise of Music?"'

'I always rather liked "The Desert Song,"' said Whitaker mildly.

'It is no score for the flute,' snapped Dr Jolland, striding to the door. He flung it open and bellowed into Miss Price's room, *'Secretary!'*

Whitaker cowered back in his chair in horror. 'What in heaven's name are you doing?' he said.

'You do have a secretary, I suppose?' said Dr Jolland, returning to the middle of the room.

'Indeed I do!' said Whitaker.

After a moment Miss Price walked with slow dignity into the office. 'Was that you shouting?' she said to Dr Jolland.

'It was.'

'Where,' said Miss Price, 'is the fire?'

'We need return tickets to Salzburg,' said Dr Jolland, with slightly less aggression in his voice.

'Dr Jolland,' said Miss Price calmly, 'you are standing in the offices of Whitaker and Belton. This is not Thomas Cook. I am not a courier, nor am I a booking clerk.' She stared pointedly at Dr Jolland's hat. Quelled by her look, he removed it. She turned to Whitaker. 'You have an appointment at eleven-thirty,' she said. 'It is now twenty to twelve.'

Dr Jolland sank into the chair in front of Whitaker's desk. 'But this is a matter of extreme urgency,' he said desperately. 'Billy was to be my final achievement, my immortality.'

Miss Price continued to look at Whitaker. 'Billy?' she said.

Whitaker handed her the letter. 'Apparently he has hardly attended the Academy all this term,' he said, 'done no work...'

Miss Price read the letter.

'Naturally,' Whitaker went on, 'they point out that there are other students anxious for the opportunity he has been given.'

'So unlike Billy,' said Miss Price, returning the letter. 'You don't suppose he's ill?'

'Dear lady,' said Dr Jolland, pleadingly, 'there is only one way to find out...'

At 5.30 that afternoon, Whitaker sat alone at last by the fire in his living-room, a liberal glass of Scotch in his hand, enjoying the undemanding sound of the flames. The front door opened and closed, and quickly he put his glass down on the floor, under his chair.

Miss Price came into the room from the hall. She had her coat on and her handbag was over her arm. 'Everything is locked up,' she said.

'Thank you, Pricey,' said Whitaker. 'Ridiculous to be so senile that I can't lock up for myself.'

'You're not,' said Miss Price. 'You felt tired. We all do.'

Whitaker looked across at her and smiled. 'He is a *terrible* man,' he said. 'Ernest Jolland.'

'Rude,' said Miss Price. 'I can forgive most things, but never that. Rita will collect your tickets in the morning. You're flying out on Friday and back on Monday.'

'Do you suppose we're all over-reacting?' said Whitaker.

Miss Price began to button up her coat. 'Difficult to tell,' she said. 'Billy was never a letter writer. But this term there have been none. I know I'm not allowed to speak ill of him, but I do think he's rather ungrateful.'

'Why should he be grateful? He's young, Pricey.'

'Yes,' said Miss Price. 'That is the most worn out excuse in the book.'

Whitaker snorted. 'What about "he's getting on, you know"?' An expression of anguish crossed his face. 'Oh!' he said, 'the thought of a weekend with Jolland in Salzburg!'

'I envy you the trip.'

'I wish you could come.'

Miss Price gave a slight, distant smile. 'But you know I can't,' she said. 'Who would look after mother?' She turned to go, but paused at the door. 'I don't know why you leave your whisky on the floor,' she said. 'It'll get dusty down there. Goodnight, Mr Whitaker.'

In Salzburg, pressure of a different kind was beginning to build up for Billy. He was sitting in a café he visited often, the Salz, all dark wood and low ceilings on one of the oldest streets in the town, staring gloomily at the last two inches of beer in his glass and waiting for Julie. It was early in the evening and the café was not crowded. Eventually he became aware that the middle-aged man, who so often sat at the small table next to the counter, had lowered his paper and was watching him. Billy met his look. '*Guten Abend,*' said the man, smiling at him.

'Hallo,' said Billy.

'Your girlfriend stood you up?' said the man sympathetically, speaking with a strong German accent.

'No,' said Billy. 'She should be along soon.'

He looked back into his glass, but the man continued to watch him. 'Come on!' he said at last. 'Cheer up. It may never take place.'

'What?' said Billy.

'Whatever is making you so down,' said the other man. He reached up to rap on the high counter, to attract the waiter's attention. 'Hans,' he said, and then, in English for Billy's benefit, 'a beer for my young friend.'

'*Ja,* Herr Spetz,' said Hans.

'No, I'm fine. Really,' said Billy.

'Yes, yes,' said Konrad Spetz, 'you're fine. But a beer will make you finer.'

Billy gave way with good grace. When Hans brought the full glass he raised it to Herr Spetz and said, 'Next time it must be my turn.'

'Why for?' said the German, waving this aside. 'I have money. You are a student.'

The door opened and Julie came in, looking rather small and huddled in her anorak. She hurried over to Billy's table and sat down. 'I'm sorry I'm late,' she said.

'I thought you weren't coming,' said Billy.

'Mother is on her third Vodka Martini!'

'You want a beer, or coffee?'

She shook her head. 'Billy, what are we going to do?' She was nearly in tears and her hands were clenched on the table top.

'I don't know,' said Billy.

'You must start knowing,' said Julie, urgently. 'The term ends soon — then what?'

Billy made a face. 'The rate I'm going,' he said, 'I'll be out on my neck.'

'No,' said Julie impatiently. 'I mean about me. About us.' She searched his face. 'I know all the signs, Billy. She's bored with Salzburg now. Two terms! We've lasted longer than I've ever known. We'll go back to New York and move in on Daddy again. Demand our rights!' She was sitting on the edge of her chair, tipping it forward towards him. 'I can't,' she said. 'I want to get away.'

Billy took her hands in his. 'I know, I know,' he said gently.

'Let me stay with you,' said Julie. 'Please, Billy.'

'But how?'

'We could go to England,' she said brightening. 'You could get a job. We could both get jobs. You've got money, Billy, and a house we could be living in. Our own place...'

Billy drew a deep breath. 'Julie,' he said carefully. 'I've got *three years* at the Academy.'

She stared at him in silence. Then she pulled her hands free of his. 'Yeah, well, there you go,' she said. She gave him a twisted little smile. 'You can't win 'em all.' She started to get up. 'So long, Toth.'

He reached across the table, caught her arm and pushed her down into her chair again. 'We'll work something out,' he said, trying to keep his voice down, aware that one or two customers were enjoying the drama. 'Just give me time.'

'We don't have time,' said Julie. 'I'm telling you. We don't have that long.' She shrugged. 'I must get back to mother.'

Billy stood up. 'I'll walk you home.'

'Terrific,' said Julie flatly.

As they crossed the café to the door, Herr Spetz called out, 'Good night.'

'Good night,' said Billy, turning and smiling at him as he held the door for Julie. 'Who was that?' she said as they went into the cold street.

'I don't know,' said Billy. 'He's often in there. I sometimes talk to him.'

Julie put her arm round him and gave him a hug. 'You're such a friendly guy, Toth,' she said. 'I like that.'

Billy put his arm around her. 'I love you,' he said.

She looked up at him in the light from the street lamp. 'Prove it,' she said, half-joking; but only half.

Billy walked her back to the hotel where she and her mother had a suite and then made his way to Anna's. He tried to go into the flat quietly, knowing that she would probably be working, but she heard him anyway and called out to him from her studio. He went to stand in the doorway, looking at her where she sat at her drawing board, her blonde head bent over a large illustration which she seemed to be finishing off. 'Sorry,' he said. 'I didn't mean to disturb you.'

'I was listening for you,' said Anna, without looking up.

'How's it going?'

'Slowly! I hate fairy stories! I hate publishers! I hate books! And most of all I hate commissioned work!'

Billy grinned. 'That make you feel better?'

'Look at it!' said Anna, leaning back so that he could see. 'Ugh! Do you know what the title is? *The slipper fits.* I ask you! You shouldn't have asked how it's going. It's going rotten.' She raised her eyes from the drawing board and looked at him for the first time. 'Oh,' she said. 'Not so good with you either, hm?'

'Not very.'

'Then I think I am the bearer of bad tidings.'

'I'd welcome World War Three,' said Billy, 'if that's what you're going to say.'

'How about—Vincent Whitaker and . . . someone . . . are arriving on Friday?'

'What!' said Billy horrified.

'He telephoned about an hour ago,' said Anna. 'Did Julie give you a bad time?'

'No!'

'All right,' said Anna, gently. 'I didn't ask.'

'You don't like her, do you?'

'Julie?' She shrugged. 'I don't like most women.' She turned to a pile of discarded sketches at her side and selected a tiny scrap of paper from among them. 'He's arriving at 3.30,' she read, 'with Dr Jolland.'

''Oh, my God!' said Billy.

'What is it for? You know?'

'I've a pretty good idea.'

Anna looked at him for a moment, then got up from the drawing board and stretched. 'Come,' she said, 'let's make some coffee. I've been working too long anyway.'

Billy followed her through into the small neat kitchen. He hitched himself onto a stool and watched as she put on the kettle. 'Why haven't you and Gunter ever got married?' he said.

'Aha!' said Anna, lighting a cigarette while she waited for the water to boil. 'We're not talking about me.'

'You're the nicest people I know,' said Billy wistfully.

'Well maybe if we got married we wouldn't be so nice anymore. Besides, I thought Vincent Whitaker was your favourite nice person!'

'Vincent?' said Billy. 'I hardly see him now. Oh God, I wish he wasn't coming.'

'Why is he?'

Billy scuffed his shoes on the bar at the bottom of the stool. 'I'm going to be kicked out of the Academy,' he said. 'They'll have informed Dr Jolland.'

'Are you sure of this?' said Anna. Billy nodded without looking at her. 'But I thought you were good.'

'Of course I'm good,' said Billy angrily. 'I'm the best. I could be the very best.'

'So?'

His anger subsided. 'I haven't done any work for weeks, Anna. I've broken every rule in the book.'

Anna put her cigarette down on the edge of an ashtray and began to pour boiling water onto the coffee granules in two mugs. 'Why, I wonder,' she said. It didn't sound like a question. 'There's the coffee. Help yourself to milk.'

'She wants us to go away,' said Billy quietly. 'Live together.'

There was a moment's pause. 'And you?' said Anna.

Billy slid off the stool and picked up one of the mugs. 'I don't want to lose her,' he said. 'I'll go up to my room if you don't mind.' He carried the coffee across to the door.

'And the flute?' said Anna. 'Your music?'

Billy didn't look back. 'I just don't want to be on my own any more,' he said. He pulled the door shut behind him.

He was not at the airport on Friday. He knew he couldn't avoid the confrontation but he had no urge to hurry into it. On Friday evening Whitaker telephoned him at Anna's and they agreed to meet the following day. Billy suggested the Winkler café. It was less personal to his life than the dark, crowded Salz and did not have the Tomaselli's dubious associations with the scholarship auditions. Also, its staggering views over Salzburg might prove a welcome distraction.

On the enclosed terrace of the Winkler, Whitaker drank a single coffee while Dr Jolland downed two slices of Torte and two iced coffees with cream. When he ordered the same again, Whitaker rose from the table and stood with his back to it, looking out of the window.

'I suppose he will turn up,' said Dr Jolland, his mouth full.

'If he said so.'

'What a touching faith you have in him!'

'Yes.'

Dr Jolland glared at Whitaker's back. 'His tutor was most distressed,' he said.

'So you said.'

'A charming man, Herr Greisinger,' said Dr Jolland. 'I spent most of last evening with him. He said to me, "We will fight for him together," but will it do any good?' Whitaker continued to inspect the view, his hands clasped rather tensely behind him. 'Damn it, Whitaker,' said Dr Jolland, 'He has talent and he's throwing it away. He hasn't even completed two terms before this happens.'

Whitaker turned wearily to face him. 'If you shout and rant at him it'll do no good,' he said.

'He isn't here, is he? I'm shouting and ranting at you.'

Billy appeared at the far side of the café. He saw Whitaker first and walked over to greet him. They smiled rather warily at each other, then Whitaker inclined his head towards the large figure which sat at the table. Billy looked down at the frowning face. 'Hallo sir,' he said.

Dr Jolland pointed at the chair opposite him and Billy sat down. Whitaker remained standing between them, like an anxious heron. 'I have seen your tutor, Herr Greisinger,' said Dr Jolland. 'He is good?'

'The best,' said Billy, adding hastily, 'in Salzburg.'

'I know he's better than I am, boy. He is a tutor at the Zuckmayer Academy. You could not get a better teacher.'

'No.'

'Then why in the name of sanity are you behaving like a little idiot? You are going to lose your place. He wrote to me! "Can you talk some sense into the child?"' He leaned forward across his empty plate. 'Well, can I? There are four thousand flautists waiting for your chance.'

Billy drew a deep breath. 'Then one of them ought to be given it,' he said.

'What!' said Dr Jolland. Whitaker winced. Dr Jolland fought his chair back from the table and rose to his feet. His voice grew louder and louder and people at nearby tables watched unashamedly. 'Pay the bill, Whitaker,' he roared. 'I have no desire to stay in this company. You're a fraud, boy. That's what you are. This whole trip has been a waste of my time and effort.'

He strode across the café and slammed out of the door. Whitaker sank down into the chair he had just vacated. 'Now look what you've been and gone and done,' he whispered.

'I'm sorry,' said Billy. 'Do you think he's really gone?'

'Only temporarily, I'm afraid.'

'It was the last straw when I heard he was coming.'

'What's gone wrong, Billy?' said Whitaker gently. Billy looked down at the table top. Whitaker waited, but there was no answer. 'You're going to be kicked out of a school you worked your socks off to get to,' he said. 'You haven't written to us once this term. Pricey has been all for suing the Post Office for non-delivery of mail. And now that I'm here where I can see you, you look on the defensive.' Billy turned his chair sideways to the table and looked silently out of the window, screwing up his eyes against the light. 'We've been through a lot together,' said Whitaker. 'Shouldn't we at least try to get through this?'

'There's this girl, Julie,' said Billy at last. 'You met her at the Scholarship concert.'

'I remember,' Whitaker nodded. 'Little American girl.'

'We've been seeing a lot of each other.'

'Not surprising, if she's also at the Academy.'

'She's leaving. Her mother and she are going back to the States.' He watched Whitaker's face. 'I'm in love with her.'

Whitaker avoided his eye.

'I knew you wouldn't understand,' said Billy.

Whitaker met his eye. 'Make me!' he said.

Billy began to fiddle with the used crockery on the table. 'While I was looking for...I don't even know how to say it any more...for Jerri...it helped me not to mind about...mother and father. But now...I'm lonely, Vincent. I'm sorry.'

'Yes,' said Whitaker quietly. 'And Julie? She loves you?'

'I don't know,' said Billy. 'I think so. But I don't want to go on being alone.'

'How will you live?'

'I'll get a job.'

'As what?'

'I don't know,' said Billy. 'But we'll be together.'

Whitaker watched him. 'I hope to goodness that'll be enough for you,' he said.

'I want to take her to Bamburgh.'

'Then take her to Bamburgh,' said Whitaker. 'You have the holidays coming up in a few weeks.'

'You're not shocked?'

'Shocked?' said Whitaker, suddenly angry. 'You silly child. You don't begin to know me. Yes, I am shocked, but you will never understand why. Take her to Bamburgh for the holidays. Unless... isn't her mother going to object?'

'She's nearly twenty-one.'

'Oh. A great age.'

'Would you see her mother for us?'

'No,' said Whitaker, sharply. 'For what reason? As your solicitor? There is no legal problem. As your guardian? I ceased to be that on your eighteenth birthday.'

Billy hesitated. 'As my friend?' he said.

'No,' said Whitaker. 'You don't need me or my advice. Your mind's made up.'

Billy stood up. 'Thanks,' he said bitterly. He walked away from the table. Behind him Whitaker said, to himself, 'What else could you expect?'

Whitaker took temporary refuge at Anna's. Billy was not there, but Gunter was. 'We feel responsible, Vincent,' he said, putting a large and most welcome glass of whisky into Whitaker's hand. 'Billy was in our care.'

Whitaker looked wistfully into the glass. 'I've lost Billy,' he said. 'All birds must fly the nest.'

Anna lit a cigarette. 'Billy is confused because he's being pulled two ways,' she said. 'The girl will win. She's more determined.'

'Will that be such a bad thing?' said Whitaker.

'It won't last,' said Anna. 'And he will have made a mess of everything.'

'Then he'll have to begin again,' said Whitaker. 'He's used to that.'

'With your help?' said Anna.

Whitaker paused. 'He knows where to find me,' he said.

Anna sat forward on her chair. 'But maybe just once he needs someone to find him,' she said. 'Maybe he needs you to fight him. Maybe he wants your guidance.'

'I can't, do you see?' said Whitaker unhappily. 'I will not interfere.'

'Poor Billy,' said Anna.

'Anna!' said Gunter, shushing her.

'She's right, Gunter,' said Whitaker. 'Everything tells me he should stay here, but it isn't telling him. How do you change someone's mind? By imposing your will on them? I don't think so. By example? Perhaps. But we all have different experiences.'

'But would you not stop him, for instance, robbing a bank?' said Gunter.

'If that was what he wanted, he'd do it while I wasn't looking.'

'Or killing a man?'

There was a long pause. Whitaker inspected his whisky and then drank a little. 'He'd have to stop himself doing that,' he said.

'And if he couldn't stop himself?' said Anna.

'Then I hope he would look for me.'

Anna shuddered suddenly. 'I don't like this talk,' she said.

'I doubt it'll ever come to that,' said Gunter, lightly. 'By the way, Vincent, did Billy tell you I heard from a friend at the UN? The strangest thing...he'd seen a report of a trial in Turkey, some man on a drug-smuggling rap. The man said he was doing the job for "Jerri Toth, the Hungarian".'

'What did Billy make of that?' said Whitaker.

Gunter shrugged. 'He just said the name Toth is as common in Hungary as Smith is in England.'

Whitaker laughed. 'God bless the boy,' he said. 'He still has some sense in him.'

'I was disappointed,' said Gunter. 'I rather enjoyed our adventures.'

Billy and Julie stood on one of the footbridges over the Salzach, Billy watching the fast flowing water and Julie looking at the familiar skyline of castle and domes. 'I love this town,' she said. 'I'll be sorry to leave.'

'But you'll like Bamburgh as well,' said Billy.

'All right, Toth!' said Julie. 'So long as you're there.'

'You really mean that?' he said urgently. He turned her to face him.

She grinned up at him. 'I think I do,' she said. 'Yes.'

Billy pulled her into his arms and kissed her. A figure passed across the bridge behind them, Whitaker on his way from Anna's flat to rejoin Dr Jolland at the hotel. He saw them and hesitated—then he passed quickly by and hurried on his way.

Chapter Sixteen

The contrast between life in Salzburg and life in Bamburgh could hardly have been more extreme. Salzburg had cafés, concerts, friends and unremitting activity; Bamburgh had the sands, the sea and the small castle. Salzburg had bells and choirs and orchestras and voices, the clatter of pony and traps and the sudden zipping roar of motor-scooters; Bamburgh had the sound of the waves and the wind and the purring of an open fire. Bamburgh's special qualities, its ever-changing yet unchanging sea and sky, its peace, were not always apparent to everyone.

Julie walked along the edge of the sea, her jacket pulled tightly around her, her long dark hair whipping against her face in the stiff breeze that so often came off the water. Her jeans were tucked into short seaboots and from time to time she kicked a pebble irritably towards the incoming tide. Billy walked with her, but slightly behind, watching her, wary of her mood.

They both saw the car at the same moment, when it was still not much more than a blob in the distance. It was being driven fast across the beach towards them, along the line where water met sand. As it came nearer they could see it was a Beach-buggy whosc lonc driver was swinging the wheel to right and left, sending the car in and out of the shallows, so that the spray arched high and glittering into the air.

Julie started to laugh. She ran towards the oncoming car, then stopped, her seaboots planted firmly in the sand. The driver saw her, turned the wheel and drove straight at her. Billy, panicking, yelled 'Julie!' but she stood her ground and at the last moment the car spun aside into the water. A great fan of spray shot out from the wheels and drenched Julie in a gaspingly cold shower. She shrieked. The car pulled out of the water and stopped and the driver, a tall dark young man in his early twenties, climbed out. 'I say,' he said, in a soft Irish accent, 'I'm terribly sorry.'

Billy, who had caught up with Julie and was holding her, glared at him. 'Lunatic!' he said. 'What the hell d'you think you were doing?'

The young man spread out his hands. He had a charming smile. 'What can I say?' he said.

Julie shook herself free of Billy. 'You could start by pleading for mercy,' she said. 'I'm soaked!'

He looked from one to the other and then advanced towards Julie, holding out his right hand. 'Michael O'Connell,' he said, 'and I really am *very* sorry.'

Julie ignored the hand. 'I should warn you,' she said, 'I will not rest easy until you are so wet you're almost drowned.'

Michael raised his eyebrows and smiled at her. Then he gave a huge, shrugging gesture of surrender, turned, and walked unhesitatingly into the sea. He walked until the water reached his knees and then, quite calmly, lay down and sank out of sight. Billy and Julie watched, wide-eyed. 'He's crazy!' said Julie, beginning to laugh. 'Who is he?'

'Never seen him before,' said Billy.

'Things are looking up,' said Julie, half to herself. Billy glanced at her. Michael rose from the sea, his dark shirt and trousers blacker now that they were wet, his dark hair glued to his head, water streaming down his face. He stood there, knee-deep in small waves, and looked at them.

'*I* want to soak you,' Julie shouted to him. 'What you do to yourself is your own affair.'

'Be my guest,' said Michael resignedly.

Julie ran out to join him, leaping through the slight swell, and began to dance around him, kicking water up at him, although it was utterly impossible for him to be made any wetter than he was already.

'Julie!' said Billy.

'Do join in if you feel you want to,' Michael called to him.

'No thanks,' said Billy.

'Oh, come on, Toth,' Julie shouted, kicking and splashing, kicking and splashing, 'Act crazy!'

'Have you had enough now?' said Michael, most politely. 'Only I'm getting a tiny bit chilled.'

'Me too,' said Julie. She turned and ran through the sea towards the car. 'Can I drive?'

'If you like,' said Michael, following her. 'Only where are we going?'

Julie got into the driving seat. 'I'm going back to the cottage to dry off,' she said. 'You please yourself.' She looked up at Billy, who was standing beside the car. 'You can borrow some of Billy's clothes,' she said.

Billy and Michael eyed each other warily. 'They won't fit you,' said Billy.

Michael shrugged. 'I have a change in the car.'

'Don't argue,' said Julie. She started the engine. 'Let's go or I'll catch pneumonia.' She rammed the car into gear and drove off across the sands. Her voice came back to them above the sound of the engine, 'And that'll be murder!' The car roared towards the dunes, swerving crazily.

'Can she drive?' said Michael.

Billy began to laugh. 'That remains to be seen,' he said. They looked at each other, then took to their heels and ran in pursuit of the Beach-buggy.

Billy had left the fire alight in the cottage and when Michael and Julie had changed, they draped their wet clothes over the backs of chairs near the hearth. Michael had put on an expensive-looking shirt and another pair of trousers. Julie wore Billy's short dressing-gown. She made them mugs of hot coffee and they settled around the fire in a semi-circle in the slightly steamy atmosphere of the drying clothes.

'He could always stay the night here, couldn't he?' said Julie to Billy. 'Set off fresh in the morning.'

'Now, I didn't mean to invite myself,' said Michael.

'You didn't,' said Julie. 'I did. But you must wait for my Lord and Master...'

'Sure,' said Billy after an almost imperceptible pause. 'Why not.'

'Right,' said Julie. 'If you want to eat, we have sausages and potatoes. We're on a limited budget.' She got up, pulling the short dressing-gown around her. 'I should go and dress.'

'I tell you what,' said Michael. 'Let's eat on the beach!'

'It'll be cold,' said Billy.

'No, it won't,' said Julie, stopping in the doorway.

'We could build a big fire,' said Michael. 'The sausages and potatoes could do in the ashes.'

'A barbecue!' said Julie, exaggerating her American accent in her excitement. 'Why not! Then we can limbo 'til dawn! I'll go and dress.'

'Wear something warm,' said Michael, in his gentle Irish brogue. For a moment he and Julie looked at each other, then she went out of the room and they heard her footsteps scampering up the stairs.

A silence fell on the room behind her. Then, 'Look—if I'm in the way...' said Michael.

'Of course you're not,' said Billy.

'She seems very nice,' said Michael. 'Comes on a bit strong, maybe...'

'No,' said Billy, curtly. 'She doesn't, actually.'

'I didn't mean to criticize. Is it serious, between the two of you?'

'Yes.'

'Then I'm in the way.' He looked round the cosy sitting-room. 'It's a nice place.'

'It was my parents...' said Billy, needing to explain.

'Toth doesn't sound a very Geordie name!'

Billy shook his head. 'They aren't Geordies up here. Anyway, Toth was the name of my real parents. They were killed getting out of Hungary. This place belonged to my adopted parents.'

'And where are they?'

'They were drowned in a sailing accident.'

'Jeeze!' said Michael, laughing. 'You lose parents like some people lose biros!' He clamped his hand over his mouth in comic horror. 'Sorry. That was hardly polite considering we've only just met. Still, maybe you could teach me your trick. I've been trying to lose mine for years. I have a stepmother that makes Snow White's sound ginger-peachey. My father must be insane!'

Billy laughed despite himself. 'And your mother?' he said.

'Ah, now, she's very dead,' said Michael. 'Which is a pity because she was one wonderful lady. She was also one very rich lady who thought her son should inherit—which means that I am now one very rich lay-about who travels the country soaking young girls.'

'I wonder how much of all that is true,' said Billy, amused.

'It's no more far-fetched than your little epic.'

'Touché!'

Michael threw up his hands. 'French already!' he said. 'You're so cosmopolitan up here. You should have been in the pub at lunchtime, there was a German in there. They fascinate me, you know, because they used to be the baddies...and now the Irish are. I only have to open my mouth and people check my underwear for bombs.' He jumped to his feet. 'Talking of the pub,' he said, 'why don't I nip along and get a couple of bottles of wine, for the picnic?'

'OK,' said Billy, 'Thanks. I'll hurry Julie.'

Michael let himself out of the front door and Billy ran upstairs to find Julie in jeans and sweater, combing her hair at the small mirror on the bedroom wall. 'OK?' he said.

'Terrific,' said Julie, without much expression in her voice.

He went up behind her and put his arms round her. 'You're sure?'

She turned round in his arms and looked up at him rather sadly. 'Oh, Toth,' she said. 'You're such a nice guy.'

'"Nice guy" sounds rather dull,' said Billy.

Julie kissed him briefly. 'Let's get rid of him,' she whispered.

'But you asked him to stay,' said Billy, surprised. 'I thought you wanted this picnic.'

She turned her back again and went on combing her hair. 'Yes,' she said. 'It'll make a change from sitting in this damn cottage for another night.'

'Hey,' said Billy. 'You like it here. Remember?'

'Sure,' said Julie, 'but everyone needs a change from time to time.' As she went out of the bedroom, Billy caught at her arm and said, 'Love you.' She gave him a bright smile. 'Terrific!' she said. She ran on down the stairs. Billy looked after her. 'Yeah!' he said to himself. 'Terrific.'

He opened a drawer in the chest and dragged out a thick sweater. Under the sweater lay the flute case. He dropped the sweater on the floor and opened the case; took out the flute and slowly fitted it together. He crouched there, on the floor by the open drawer, staring into space. Then he raised the flute to his mouth and began to play.

Downstairs, Michael slipped back in at the front door, with two large bottles of wine in a paper bag. He walked through to the foot of the stairs and stood for a moment watching Julie as she collected together the sausages, the potatoes and plates. Then he called up the stairs, 'Hurry up, Pied Piper. You're keeping the lady waiting.'

Julie turned and looked at him. 'Is it "Lady" that I'm after being now?' she said in a heavy Irish accent. Michael gave her a very slow thoughtful smile. Julie stared back at him. 'I don't know you...' she said softly. 'No,' said Michael, still smiling. 'I mean, anything about you...' said Julie. Upstairs, the music stopped and a moment later Billy came down the stairs. They only looked away from each other as he came into the room.

There was plenty of driftwood on the beach and they built an enormous fire at the edge of which the sausages and potatoes cooked with satisfying speed. When the picnic was over, though the cold breeze which crossed the dark beach was beginning to make itself felt, they were reluctant to leave the dying fire. They fetched blankets from the cottage and sat as near the embers as they could, listening to the sea sounds and drinking Michael's wine. As the level in the bottles fell, Julie began to expound on her background. 'Daddy always goes for young girls,' she said. 'Not babies, but younger than mother. It makes her frantic.'

'Where is she now?' said Michael.

'New York. I had a letter—"Daddy and I are trying to make a go of it. Please come home, baby." Make a go of it! That poor man has been trying to get away since before I was born.' She shook her head dreamily. 'Imagine that!'

'And what will you do?' said Michael.

'Not go back, that's for sure.'

Michael knocked back his wine and poured himself some more. 'So you two will get married,' he said, 'and live happily ever after.'

'Married!' said Julie. 'Not ever! Not with Billy or anyone.'

'So?' said Michael.

Julie shrugged. 'What'll we do, Toth?' she said.

Billy said nothing. He sat still, watching her face in the flickering firelight.

'He's pining for his flute,' said Julie crossly. 'It wasn't my fault, I didn't drag you away from Salzburg you know.'

'It needs a particular character to be a success as a drop-out,' said Michael soothingly.

'A drop-out with a car like that ain't a drop-out,' said Julie.

Michael turned his broad smile upon her. 'I really cannot be blamed for being very rich,' he said.

'Very rich?' said Julie.

'Very, very rich.'

'How delicious,' said Julie. She held out her glass. 'More wine, please.'

'You've had enough,' said Billy, quite quietly.

'Enough!' said Julie. 'I haven't even started!'

Michael leaned forward and poured some wine into her glass.

'She's had enough, Michael,' said Billy.

Julie turned on him. 'God, you're so boring,' she said. 'You're so *dreary,* Toth.'

'Steady,' said Michael. 'Little birds in their nest must agree.'

'It gets hard when a cuckoo arrives,' said Billy sharply.

Julie stood up, letting the blanket fall to the ground behind her. She raised her glass to the skies and began to dance around the fire, chanting 'Cuckoo! Cuckoo!'

Billy got up and walked over to her. He took the glass from her hand and emptied out the wine. It sank into the sand leaving a red stain. 'You've had enough,' he said.

Julie stood quite still and stared at him. 'I haven't, you know,' she said, sounding entirely sober. 'It would be easier if I had.'

Michael appeared at her other side, holding a full glass. He passed it to her. 'You spilt your wine, Madam,' he said.

Julie took the glass from him and drained it. Then she flung it away from her, put her arms round Michael's neck and began to kiss him. Michael did not resist, but he didn't hold her, either; instead he raised his arms in the gesture of surrender he had used before. Billy took two steps towards them, grabbed Julie's arm and pulled her away from Michael so roughly that she fell. Then he turned and hit out at Michael, savagely and wildly. Michael dodged the worst of the impact, but instantly hit back and in a moment they were rolling on the ground in an ugly, thrashing, vicious fight.

Frightened, Julie tried to separate them, clawing at the two figures as they struggled on the sand, screaming at them to stop. But it had gone too far. The fight moved beyond the glow of the dying fire, out into the windy dark, by the white rim of the black sea. Julie ran up the beach away from it and huddled, crying, in the shelter of a sand dune.

Sheer exhaustion finally put an end to it. The two figures crawled apart and sat for a moment or two in silence on cold, wet sand.

'What are we doing?' said Billy in a muffled voice.

'Not being very civilized, that's for sure,' said Michael.

Billy got to his feet. He staggered for a moment, then righted himself. 'Julie?' he called. He limped back to the fire. 'Julie?' He started to run.

He found her, crouching behind the arm of the dune. He knelt down beside her. 'My fault, Toth,' she said, very softly. 'I was bored, you see.'

'Come back to the cottage,' said Billy. 'He'll go.'

Julie looked at him and the tears welled up and flowed down her face. 'I'm not cut out for love in a cottage, Billy,' she said. 'No more are you. Oh, Billy, I'm sorry. I'm sorry.'

Billy put his arms round her and rocked her gently. 'It's OK,' he said, 'It's all right.'

'You haven't once played the flute till tonight,' said Julie. 'Why tonight?'

Billy stood up and pulled her to her feet. 'I just saw it there,' he said. He led her back to the remains of the fire. Michael, very subdued, was making an attempt to gather the picnic things together. 'I'm off, then,' he said, without looking at them.

'Take me with you,' said Julie.

'What?' said Billy, shaken.

'I have a first-class ticket to New York,' said Julie. 'Daddy believes in doing things in style.'

Michael ran his hands through his hair. 'This really isn't my scene, you know,' he said. 'I'm the happy-go-lucky carefree type. I'll be at the cottage, collecting my things. If you want a lift I'll be off in twenty minutes.' He held his hand out to Billy, who ignored it. 'I'm sorry,' he said, quite sincerely, 'I was just passing through.' He turned and walked away.

'Don't go without me,' Julie called.

'Twenty minutes,' came Michael's voice out of the darkness.

Julie moved to Billy and kissed him. 'It was nice while it lasted,' she whispered.

'Then let it go on.'

'Goodbye, Billy.'

'Why? Why, Julie? What have I done?'

'I can't help it,' said Julie. She was crying again. 'I don't feel anything any more... I'm not going to live lies like my mother and father. I can't. Goodbye Billy.'

She turned and began to walk into the dark, the way Michael had gone.

'But you don't even know him,' Billy shouted after her.

'I don't have to,' she shouted back. 'I'm only hitching a lift.'

'But what about me?' There was no answer. There was no longer anyone else on the beach. He crouched down on his haunches and began to throw handfuls of sand onto the ashes and embers of the picnic fire. 'God Almighty! What about me!'

In Newcastle on the same evening a very different supper party was taking place. Gunter Walser was in England, researching for an article on the British attitude to the Common Market. He had asked Whitaker if he might stay for the night, and Whitaker invited Miss Price to join them for the evening meal. She neatly evaded his heavy hints that she should actually cook it. 'Don't tell me what we're having! Surprise me!' she said. 'Oh, well, it'll be *stew* then,' said Whitaker crossly. 'Delicious,' said Miss Price, smiling maddeningly. 'Shall I come at seven? For cocktails?'

Gunter was already there when she arrived and Whitaker, having handed out drinks, left them in each other's company while he went to check progress in the kitchen. As soon as he was out of the room Gunter said, 'Miss Price, what's happened to him? He hasn't had another stroke?'

Miss Price shook her head. She got up and closed the door, quietly.

'Then what?' said Gunter. 'He's become an old man.'

'He *is* an old man,' said Miss Price.

'But so sudden.'

'Perhaps that's what happens. You just give up.'

'No, not Vincent,' said Gunter.

Miss Price made a face. 'He's missing Billy.'

'Yes,' said Gunter. 'I didn't like to ask. What has happened?'

'I expect you know as much as any of us do,' said Miss Price. 'Billy and that girl are living together at the cottage in Bamburgh.'

'On what? Has he a job?'

'You must ask Mr Whitaker,' said Miss Price, just as Whitaker came back into the room.

'Ask me what?' said Whitaker. 'Don't look so guilty both of you. I knew there were secrets as soon as I saw the door was shut.'

'We were discussing Billy,' said Miss Price.

Whitaker's face hardened. 'Then it must have been a very brief discussion,' he said. 'After all, there is nothing new to say is there? Your supper is ready. I hesitate to call it dinner. Shall we go in?' He led the way into the dining-room where the table was neatly laid for three. 'He refuses even to talk about him,' said Miss Price as she and Gunter followed.

'I don't refuse,' said Whitaker, 'but there is nothing to talk about.' He indicated the chairs where they were to sit and then stood at the head of the table and began to ladle out the stew.

'Actually, I have some news,' said Gunter.

Whitaker ignored him. 'Help yourself to vegetables, Pricey,' he said, passing her plate to her, 'and Gunter, be a good fellow and pour the wine. You're all family. No point in ceremony.'

'Mm, it smells very good,' said Miss Price.

Gunter waited until everyone was served and then, 'I said I had some news,' he repeated.

'About Billy?' said Miss Price. 'One rather dreads that at the moment.'

'No,' said Gunter. '*For* Billy, really.'

'Then I'm afraid you've come to the wrong house,' said Whitaker curtly.

'Hilde Gruber is dead,' said Gunter.

Whitaker looked up from his stew, fork poised. 'But she was quite a young woman,' he said.

'She was killed. I saw a mention in the paper. And this is the strangest part... the car she was driving went off the road, and blew up.'

Whitaker ate his forkful of stew thoughtfully. 'Now isn't that odd,' he said when he had finished.

'Why?' said Pricey.

'Because,' said Whitaker, 'that's how Jerri and Tania Toth were killed.'

'And Hilde is...'

'The wife of the man who was helping the Toths to get Tania's father out of Hungary,' said Gunter.

'Of course,' said Miss Price. 'You met her and the man's mother... Elsa?'

'That's right,' said Gunter. 'Elsa Gruber committed suicide.'

A silence fell over the table. At last Whitaker said, 'It could all be coincidence, couldn't it?'

'Apart from one thing,' said Gunter. 'I have been spending a lot of time at Anna's flat in Salzburg recently, so I have a telephone answering machine for the Munich flat. About three weeks ago I returned to find a message from Hilde Gruber. She said it was urgent she should see me and she would telephone again. But she never did. The "accident" was the following night.'

Whitaker whistled softly.

Miss Price put down her fork. 'But Billy had no connection with any of them,' she said, anxiously. 'He was simply looking for his parents, who are dead.'

'I know, Pricey,' said Gunter. 'But why was Hilde ringing me? And, you remember Vincent, Jerri Toth's name came up quite recently.'

Whitaker studied Gunter. 'Have you some free time tomorrow?' he said. 'Could you come up to Bamburgh with me?' He sounded almost light-hearted. 'We must see Billy.' He turned quickly to Miss Price. 'I think I should go, don't you? It wouldn't be intruding?'

'Heavens no,' said Miss Price, picking up her fork again. 'So long as you knock before entering! Your stew will be cold.'

Whitaker lifted his wine glass. 'Cheers,' he said, and smiled.

Gunter and Whitaker set out early the next day and arrived at Bamburgh at about 9.30, but they found the cottage empty, though the door was unlocked. Whitaker drew back the sitting-room curtains, letting in the day. As the light washed around the room Gunter noticed something on the table. He walked over to look at it, then caught Whitaker's eye and pointed to it. It was Billy's flute, and propped against it was a scribbled note which read, 'I'm sorry. Mozart never lets you down.' It was not signed.

'We'd better find him,' said Gunter.

Whitaker nodded. 'The beach, I expect,' he said.

They saw the remains of the fire first. Then they saw the figure that stood at the edge of the sea, wrapped in a grey blanket which flapped in the wind. Whitaker hung back. Gunter touched his arm gently, then walked on down the beach until he stood behind Billy. 'Excuse me,' he said, 'Can you tell me the right direction for Salzburg?'

Billy turned to face him. His right eye was so swollen it was barely open and dark bruises were beginning to show around his jawline and on his left cheekbone.

'Hey!' said Gunter. 'What happened to you?'

'It's a long story,' said Billy. 'What are you doing here?'

'A long story,' said Gunter.

Suddenly Billy grinned. 'It's good to see you,' he said.

'I'm not alone,' said Gunter. Billy looked past him to where Whitaker stood, leaning on his stick. 'Hallo,' he said.

'Hallo, Billy,' said Whitaker, walking slowly towards him. 'You look as if you've been in the wars.'

'A bit. Did you go to the cottage?'

'Yes.'

'Was there . . ?' he stopped as if he didn't know how to ask.

'There was no one there,' said Whitaker.

Billy nodded. 'I spent the night on the beach,' he said. 'I've never done that before. Why are you here?'

Whitaker prodded at the sand with his stick. 'I just thought it would be nice to see you,' he said. 'Then Gunter gave me the excuse.'

'You chose rather a good day to come,' said Billy quietly.

A rather sad silence fell and Gunter braced himself. 'I think a coffee would be welcome,' he said cheerfully.

'Yes,' said Billy. 'I'll just collect the junk.' He took off the blanket and rolled it up, walking towards the pile of plates and glasses. He stooped, rather painfully, and began to push things into a shopping basket and a plastic carrier bag that lay among the rest of the equipment.

Whitaker and Gunter watched him from a few paces away. 'You know,' said Whitaker, speaking softly so that his voice would not carry up the beach towards Billy, 'he looks as though he's had enough for one day. I'll tell him your story at a more opportune moment.'

'There's no rush,' agreed Gunter. 'After all, it doesn't exactly add up to anything.'

He moved over and took the basket from Billy. Whitaker plodded up on the other side and took the carrier bag. Billy gathered up the rugs. Together they trudged up the beach, back towards the cottage.

Up on the ramparts of the castle, some way behind them, the watery sun glinted on glass. A middle-aged man stood watching them through a pair of powerful binoculars, just as he had watched Billy and Julie at the snowline outside Salzburg. As they moved out of sight through the dunes he lowered the glasses and stood looking after them. He made no attempt at concealment—because even if Billy had turned around he would have been too far away to recognize him as Konrad Spetz.

Chapter Seventeen

Billy seemed to be in a kind of daze. He wouldn't talk about Julie, wouldn't talk about Salzburg or his music, didn't want to leave Bamburgh. Concerned, but unwilling to interfere, Whitaker moved into the cottage with him, as a temporary measure, and waited patiently for him to sort himself out.

Although he wasn't rich, Billy still had money from his parents' estate and he bought himself a second-hand racing dinghy, christened her *The Amadeus,* and rented a mooring at Seahouses, just down the coast from Bamburgh. He rode over most days on the motorbike and collected the outboard motor from the shed behind the fishmongers on the quay. He only used the motor to get himself clear of the harbour. Once at sea, he pulled it in and went on under sail. Three of the young locals, all out of work and with nothing to do but lounge against the harbour wall, watched his comings and goings with undisguised envy. Konrad Spetz, who kept himself well out of sight on the far side of the harbour, watched him with a different emotion, though none showed on his face.

On early closing day, Spetz watched through binoculars as Billy brought *The Amadeus* in, moored her, returned the outboard motor to the fishmonger's shed and set off on his motorbike. He watched as the fishmonger locked up and walked off home for his lunch, shooing away the three lounging youngsters as he went. Then he made his way round the back of the shop to the shed, forced the door easily enough with a penknife, and crouched down by the motor, examining it intently.

Billy rode back to Bamburgh at speed. Miss Price was due to arrive on the Newcastle train, to keep Whitaker up to date with the office, and Billy had promised to meet her at Berwick in the Rover. But bringing the boat in had taken him longer than he had expected and he was very late. When he arrived at the cottage he saw that the car had gone; Whitaker, who was not supposed to be driving yet, was meeting the train himself. Billy went into the cottage and began to prepare crab salad for lunch. He had just finished setting the table when he heard the car draw up outside and the doors close one after the other. He hurried out of the cottage and greeted Miss Price with a hug. 'Lovely to see you, Pricey,' he said.

Whitaker walked past them and indoors. 'If you'd collected her as arranged you could have seen her for longer,' he said tartly.

'I'm cross with you, Billy,' said Miss Price, though she returned his hug. 'You know I don't like him driving.'

They followed Whitaker and found him in the living-room, pouring himself a glass of whisky.

'We *are* on holiday,' said Miss Price.

'It's after twelve,' said Whitaker. 'Sherry, Pricey?'

'No, thank you,' said Miss Price. She put her coat over a chair at the back of the room and settled herself down on the sofa with a large brief-case on her lap. 'I want to be coherent when you start quizzing me.'

'You're not here to work,' said Whitaker, still at the sideboard, pouring.

'I most certainly am,' said Miss Price. 'I'm charging the fare to the firm!' She looked approvingly round the room, which she had not seen before. 'It all looks very nice, Billy.'

'Look, I'm sorry,' said Billy, standing behind the sofa, between them. 'I was sailing and I didn't realize time was passing. I've no excuse.'

'In that case,' said Whitaker, grudgingly, 'I absolve you. But Pricey never will.' He crossed the room and placed a glass of sherry in her hand. 'She doesn't like me driving her.'

Miss Price took the sherry. 'To tell the truth,' she said, 'I've never been driven by Billy.' She took a sip of sherry. 'Very nice,' she said appreciatively.

'Cheers!' said Whitaker, settling into his chair with his drink.

'Oh, look,' said Miss Price, staring at the glass in her hand. 'I didn't mean to.' She shrugged. 'Oh well, it's done now. Cheers.' She took another, larger, mouthful, and set the glass down. 'There are two letters for you Billy. And a whole stack for you,' she said to Whitaker, rummaging in her brief-case, 'but I've dealt with the important stuff.'

'You have a genius for making a chap feel wanted,' said Whitaker. 'Can't all this wait?'

'Sooner it's over, the sooner we can forget about it,' said Miss Price. 'I want to go on the beach this afternoon.' She handed two letters over her shoulder to Billy and then a stack of papers to Whitaker.

'Ugh,' said Billy, still standing behind the sofa, 'one's from the Academy. I think it can wait until we've eaten.'

'I wish people would realize paper costs trees,' said Whitaker irritably, dropping page after page of circulars and advertisements into the wastepaper basket beside the fireplace. 'All rubbish, this.'

'I told you,' said Miss Price complacently. 'There are cheques to be signed. Don't let me forget.'

'I don't know who this is from,' said Billy, examining the second letter. 'It was addressed to me at the Academy and forwarded.'

'He is infuriating with letters,' said Whitaker. 'Open it... don't speculate.'

Billy tore the envelope open. Whitaker was glancing through the few letters he had not discarded and Miss Price was once more sipping her sherry.

'Good God,' said Billy, quite quietly.

They both looked up at him. 'What, Billy?' said Whitaker.

'From Hilde Gruber,' said Billy.

'But she's dead,' said Whitaker. 'I told you.'

'Yes,' said Billy, still looking at the piece of paper in his hand. 'Must have been written before.'

'What does she say?' said Miss Price.

'Not a lot.'

Whitaker stretched out his hand. 'May I?' he said. Billy handed him the letter. '"It is not safe for you,"' Whitaker read aloud. '"I am sorry. He knows. I am sorry."' He looked up at Billy again. 'It isn't signed. How do you know it's from Hilde?'

'I think I've been expecting it,' said Billy. 'Let's have lunch.'

Whitaker got to his feet and made his way over to the table. Miss Price got up, too, but stood where she was. 'No,' she said. 'You cannot pretend nothing has happened. I must know. I shall worry all the more if I don't.'

Billy drew out a dining chair for Miss Price and she allowed herself to be persuaded into it. 'I can't really tell you very much,' said Billy.

'Try,' said Whitaker, sitting down opposite Miss Price.

Billy still stood, looking down at the table. He seemed to be checking that he had laid it properly and when he spoke he sounded preoccupied. 'When I saw Hilde in Salzburg,' he said. 'When she told me my mother and father were both dead...' His voice tailed off.

'Yes,' said Whitaker impatiently.

Billy woke out of his trance. 'Kurt Gruber isn't dead, Mr Whitaker.'

'What!' said Whitaker.

'Not if his wife was telling the truth. Jerri and my mother are dead, but not Kurt Gruber. And he wants me dead. She told me. I don't know why. But that's what she said.'

Miss Price sat looking at the two dressed crabs. 'Then . . . you must go to the police,' she said.

'And tell them what?' said Billy. 'Kurt Gruber is officially dead. He died in the car crash on the Hungarian border in 1963.'

'But why should you be in danger,' said Miss Price fearfully. 'What difference do you make to this terrible man?'

'I don't know,' said Billy.

Whitaker read the letter out again. 'It is not safe for you. I am sorry. He knows.' He looked up at Billy. 'Knows what?'

'I don't know,' said Billy again.

'You should have told us all this at the time,' said Whitaker crossly.

'Yes,' said Billy, 'but . . . I'd just got the scholarship . . . you were just recovering from your stroke . . .'

'My miserable little stroke is used for far too many excuses.'

'And then of course, Julie and me . . . I wasn't really bothering about the past so much.'

'And quite right, too,' said Miss Price briskly, to cover his embarrassment.

'We can't leave it at that,' said Whitaker, 'but I suppose it's the concern of the Austrian authorities, really. I mean . . . it all belongs over there.'

'Well, thank goodness you're in England,' said Miss Price with feeling.

'Maybe . . . if I told Gunter?' said Billy dubiously, looking at Whitaker.

'We'll talk about it later,' said Whitaker, with sudden resolution. 'Do we get to eat or not?'

Billy nodded. 'I'll get the bread,' he said. He went into the kitchen. Whitaker called after him, 'And there's a bottle of white wine in the fridge.'

'What a stupid letter,' said Miss Price, as soon as Billy was out of earshot. 'Why didn't the wretched woman write more?

It's worse than useless. She might just as well not have sent it.'

Billy came back into the room with the wine and bread. He was obviously making a positive attempt at being cheerful. 'Lunch is served!' he said. 'Don't worry, Pricey. Nothing will happen.'

After lunch Whitaker was disinclined to do anything but doze in his chair, so Billy took Miss Price for a walk along the beach. She seemed to be revelling in her day away from the office and her mother, sniffing at the fresh breeze and smiling out across the wide expanse of sea. Their route took them to the castle. They wandered past the ruined keep, on velvety Ministry of Works grass, and out onto the ramparts with their splendid views.

'I was sorry,' said Miss Price, 'about you and Julie.'

'Sorry?' said Billy. 'I thought you'd be pleased. Not the done thing, surely, shacking up with someone at my age?'

'I said "sorry",' said Miss Price, 'because I didn't want you to be hurt.' Billy said nothing. She looked at him. 'Were you?' she said.

'Hurt? I don't know. No, not really. I should have guessed. She and Michael will make a lovely couple—for a week or so.'

Miss Price linked her arm in his and they walked slowly on. 'I know it never helps to say this, but it will get better.' She jammed her small hat further down on her head, to defeat the wind's efforts to remove it. 'Perhaps you'd rather not talk about it.'

'Is that why you came?' said Billy. 'To get Billy to talk?'

'No,' said Miss Price in matter-of-fact tones. 'I came to bring Mr Whitaker the week's cheques to be signed.'

'I'm choked, if you must know,' said Billy. 'I feel a fool.'

'Yes,' said Miss Price.

'Oh, Pricey,' said Billy. 'You don't know what I'm talking about, do you? You've led such an ordered little life. I'm sorry, I don't mean to be unkind, but—honestly! I don't want to talk about the fiasco of Julie and me. She walked out on me. I bored her.' Miss Price made no comment. 'We didn't give each other a chance. It was my fault. I was worried about the Academy. I didn't give that a chance, either.'

'You didn't open the other letter,' said Miss Price.

'I know what it says.' He put on his best Zuckmayer accent. 'Ve are sorry, Herr Toth, but your scholarship is needed by more dedicated students. And of course they're right.'

'Then you'll have to pay to go,' said Miss Price resolutely.

'One hell of a lot of money!'

'It's only money. That can always be found.'

'Oh yes!' said Billy sarcastically. 'No, I've screwed it up. I can't go back.'

'If you don't,' said Miss Price, 'then you will regret it for ever.'

'Dear Pricey,' said Billy, hugging the arm that was linked through his. 'I'm very fond of you.'

They had wandered as far round the edges of the castle as they could. They began to make their way back to its centre again. 'I wish you'd introduced me to Julie,' said Miss Price. 'I'll never know what she looked like.'

'I couldn't, Pricey,' said Billy. 'I didn't want to risk your disapproval.'

'No,' said Miss Price. 'And I would have. Disapproved.'

'Well . . . there you are . . . ' said Billy at a loss.

Miss Price shook her head. 'Lovely air,' she said dreamily.

'Pricey?'

'Memories, Billy. Yes, I'd have disapproved of you and Julie "shacking up". Is that what you call it? Such an old-fashioned phrase! Not my style at all. I wouldn't do such a thing. Not in my "quiet little life".'

'Ordered,' corrected Billy.

'Ordered.' She sat down abruptly on a wooden seat, her handbag on her lap and her hands folded on it. She looked straight ahead, ignoring Billy who leaned on the back of the seat. 'His name was Gerald,' she said. 'He wanted me to go away with him to a hotel in Mousehole in Cornwall. I got as far as Paddington Station. Of course the war was coming, we all knew that. It was an excuse for us.' She drew a surprisingly deep sigh. 'I had a sort of cherry-coloured coat. I saw him standing at the barrier. He looked so young. His face was shiny, as though it had been polished.' She shook her head. 'I didn't dare,' she said. 'Didn't have the guts. Oh, it wasn't morality, or religion, or even what the family would think. I just didn't dare.' She looked briefly over her shoulder at Billy. 'I'd like to have met Julie.' She looked away again. 'He was killed in North Africa,' she said, 'but the last time I saw him he was standing at the barrier at Paddington Station. Eager and waiting.' A note of wonder came into her voice. 'For me.' She stood up and brushed down the back of her coat with one hand. 'I haven't thought of that for years,' she said. 'And you are the first person I've ever told.'

Billy straightened up and looked at her. 'Thank you,' he said.

Miss Price turned away and began to walk purposefully towards the road. 'My train is at five,' she said, 'and I shall expect you to drive me this time.'

That evening, Whitaker and Billy sat by the fire. Whitaker, who was taking noticeably more naps than he used to, was dozing. Billy was drinking coffee and staring moodily into the flames. Whitaker opened one eye, sighed, and opened the other.

'Did you open your letter?' he said.

'Yes.'

'And?'

Billy shrugged. 'The Academy regret... need I say more?'

'Go on,' said Whitaker.

Billy dragged the letter out of his back pocket and chucked it into Whitaker's lap. 'I've lost the scholarship,' he said. 'Read it for yourself.'

Whitaker picked the letter off his lap and put it on the table beside him, unread. 'I'm very glad,' he said.

'Well thanks!' said Billy bitterly.

'We never really appreciate something for nothing,' said Whitaker.

'I'm not going back there...'

'That's up to you, of course,' said Whitaker. 'But it should be possible. Anna's attic isn't expensive and you could get some sort of job to cover living expenses.'

'But the fees are astronomical.'

'You're not destitute. You have assets. This cottage, for example.'

Billy turned from the fire in horror. 'No!'

'Why not?' said Whitaker. 'Your money from the Newcastle house is tied up in trust until you're twenty-one.'

'Untie it,' said Billy, turning back to his contemplation of the flames.

'I have to ask myself what Alan and Marian would have wanted for you...'

'I won't sell this place.' It came out almost in a growl.

'Billy,' said Whitaker, as patiently as he could, 'this roof will be your downfall. You don't need safety and security. Not yet. Risk! That's what you need!' He grimaced rather sadly. 'I'm telling you what you need!' he said.

'Yes, tell me,' said Billy.

Whitaker got up and crossed over to the sideboard where the flute lay on top of its case. It was dusty. He picked it up and held it, rubbing at patches of dust with one finger. Billy watched him. 'I can't tell you,' said Whitaker. 'It's the flaw in my character. I can't tell you, you must work it out for yourself.'

Billy nodded, 'It's OK,' he said gently. 'Don't worry.'

Whitaker spun round from the sideboard, his face flushed with anger. 'I'm not worried, damn it!' he said. 'Don't talk to me like some senile old dotard. You've got a gift, boy. Do you know what that means? Have you the vaguest inkling of what a privilege that is? I haven't heard you play this *once* in all the time I've been here. *Shame* on you.' He was beginning to shout. 'Shame! Shame! Shame! There are people desperate for what you take for granted. I am so envious of your talent—so disappointed by your attitude—and do you know what hurts me most? Envy and disappointment are so alien to me.' In a sudden, uncharacteristic movement he flung the flute from him, across the room. It fell on the floor and skittered half way under the table. *'No!'* cried Billy, leaping to his feet. He gathered up the flute and stood holding it, staring down at it. There was a long, desperate silence.

At last, 'Is it damaged?' said Whitaker.

Billy raised the flute to his lips and played up the scale, then down again. 'No,' he said, almost fearfully.

There was another silence. 'I am *very* sorry,' said Whitaker.

Billy looked across at him. 'A whisky?' he said, trying to sound casual.

'No,' said Whitaker. 'I think I'll have an early night.'

'Mr Whitaker...'

'No, Billy. Too much emotion flying around. Wait until tomorrow.'

'Why are you so afraid of emotion?' said Billy.

'Am I?'

Billy stroked the flute. 'I'm going out in the boat tomorrow,' he said after a moment. 'Come with me.'

'Dear child!' said Whitaker. 'I'm very old.'

Billy smiled. 'So is *The Amadeus.*' He put the flute down carefully on the table. 'One day you and I must talk.'

'One day,' said Whitaker, with caution, 'when I know you a great deal better.'

'Come sailing!' said Billy. 'I've got a spare lifejacket!'

'Not a phrase to fill one with confidence,' said Whitaker.

Purged by his anger, he looked unexpectedly benevolent. 'I am trying very hard to allow you your youth,' he said, 'leave me my age.'

Billy grinned at him, unrelenting. 'You'll love it out on the water!' he said.

Stan the fishmonger helped Whitaker to disentangle the intricacies of the lifejacket. The two men stood on the quay together, watching as Billy fitted the motor to *The Amadeus,* Whitaker wearing his overcoat under the inflated orange contraption and leaning on his stick. 'You wouldn't get me out there,' said Stan, shaking his head slowly. 'Thank you very much!' said Whitaker. 'It's all right for them,' said Stan, jerking his head to indicate his stock which gaped in rows on the slabs. 'This vestment will be far from adequate,' said Whitaker in a voice of doom.

The three young locals were in their usual place, draped against the sea wall. As Billy walked up the ramp from the dinghy one of them called out to him, 'Sailing again!'

'Yeah,' said Billy, embarrassed. He hurried up to Whitaker, to check his lifejacket before fitting his own.

As soon as his attention was elsewhere, the boy who had spoken to him pushed himself free of the sea wall and began to run down the ramp towards the dinghy. The other boy just watched, but the girl called out 'Jim! No!' Billy looked round in time to see Jim climb aboard, take an oar and push off from the quay. 'Hey!' he called. *The Amadeus* slid several feet away from the quayside and Jim drew in the oar and bent over the outboard motor. He pulled the string, but the engine did not start. Billy ran to the edge of the quay and Whitaker walked slowly forwards behind him, watching.

Jim pulled the starting string again. The outboard motor exploded in an orange ball of flame and he toppled sideways and fell into the water.

Billy stood still for one second. 'No,' he said, almost like a prayer, 'No.' Then he dived into the water and began to swim towards the struggling figure.

'Oh dear lord,' said Whitaker, his voice barely more than a whisper.

From his unobtrusive place at the far side of the harbour, Konrad Spetz watched, his face impassive.

And *The Amadeus* turned slowly on the still surface of the harbour water, burning brightly.

Chapter Eighteen

Jim survived his experience with, as he put it, 'a bruised head and a burned bum'. *The Amadeus* was no longer seaworthy, but the flames had been expertly doused before they could go too far and she was not destroyed. In fact, the most powerful effect of the explosion was on Billy himself. It shook him awake.

The following day, he had the boat hauled out of the water and stored, upside down, in the shed behind the fishmonger's. Then he sought out Jim who, after a brief visit to the nearest casualty ward and a night's sleep was willing to talk, though he had no clear idea of what had happened. He stood on the quay with Billy and surveyed the quiet harbour.

'There's got to be more to life than this place,' he said.

'Oh, come on!' said Billy. 'It's beautiful.'

'Maybe,' said Jim. 'If you're a rich weekender. I hear you've been telling stories to the police. Thanks.'

Billy shrugged. He turned from the harbour view and strolled across the road to look at the stricken dinghy. Jim walked with him. 'What exactly did you tell 'em?' he said.

'That I had said you could use the boat. That I knew it was leaking petrol from the motor. And that you were smoking when you went on board.'

'I wasn't,' said Jim.

Billy grinned at him. 'What's one lie among three?'

'Why did you do that?' said Jim. 'I don't know you.'

'Tell me what really happened.'

'You tell me,' said Jim. He leaned on the open shed door, looking down at the blackened stern of the boat. 'The first time I pulled the starting cord I think I did it wrong. I pulled it up instead of across. And I noticed —what? I don't know. That it was sticking, I think. The next time I pulled it the right way... and *boom!* Serves me right. It's your toy, not mine.'

'You really resent that, don't you?' said Billy.

'If I had a boat,' said Jim, 'I'd sail out of that harbour mouth and never come back.'

'And go where?'

'Even Berwick-on-Tweed'd be a change.'

'There *are* buses,' said Billy.

'Oh sure,' said Jim. 'And trains. Fly Concorde to the States! Why not?'

'You could even hitch a lift.'

'You're not out of work, are you? What are you? A student?'

Billy pulled a face. 'I think so. If I haven't been chucked out.'

'Let's hope you haven't, then. It's cold out here.' He began to walk slowly around the boat, bending over her, sometimes tapping at the hull. 'My dad was a fisherman,' he said. 'Just didn't come back one morning. Whole crew went down. So fishing isn't for me. I've been out of work nearly two years.' He straightened up and looked across the quay to the water. 'I did get a job,' he said, 'soon as I left school. One of the lucky ones. Carpentry with a small builders. Too small—they went bust. You get bored sitting on this quay all day, if you haven't a toy boat to play with.' He seemed to be talking to himself as much as to Billy. 'Funny...' he said.

'It isn't funny,' said Billy.

Jim was looking across the harbour to the row of fisherman's cottages on the far side. 'No, I meant it's funny the Spy's gone,' he said.

'What?'

'There was a bloke with a red car.' He pointed. 'Over there near the end house. Here every morning with binoculars. We nicknamed him The Spy.'

'There must be other carpentry work you can get,' said Billy, frowning at him. 'You could set up on your own.'

'Oh sure. Even a screwdriver costs money, you know. Did you ever notice him?'

'Who?'

'The Spy. We thought he was something to do with you. He seemed to watch you as much as anyone. He was German.'

'How do you know that?' said Billy, suddenly interested.

'How do you think?'

'His car?'

'No,' said Jim. 'That was hired from Beales in Newcastle. Said so on the back window, didn't it? You have time to notice things when you're out of work. No, I spoke to him. Asked if I could borrow the binocs. I think he thought I was going to nick 'em.' He laughed. 'Some people have no trust! He had an accent you could cut with a knife.'

'What did he look like?'

'Oh, I don't know. Middle-aged. Dark hair. Medium height.'

'Hundreds of people look like that,' said Billy.

'Yes. He was sort of... ordinary. I don't think I'd know him again myself. Is it important?'

'It could be,' said Billy thoughtfully. He looked at his watch. 'Hey, I must go.'

'See you again?' said Jim.

'Well—we're going back to Newcastle this afternoon,' said Billy. 'But I'll be down next weekend.'

'What a nice life!'

'Yes,' said Billy. He closed the shed door on *The Amadeus* and locked it. 'I'll see you.'

'You know where to find me,' said Jim with a wry smile.

Whitaker drove back to Newcastle at a stately pace that infuriated Billy, who had left his bike in Bamburgh for the week for the sake of accompanying him. 'This is not a motor race,' he said, when Billy complained. 'I am driving an old car, and old cars must be respected.'

'I could walk there faster,' said Billy.

Whitaker accelerated very slightly. 'We are now going at forty-three miles per hour,' he said. 'Satisfied?'

'Steady,' said Billy, 'you'll be taking off next.'

They drove on in silence for a while, then Whitaker said, 'Why not tell me what's on your mind?'

'I have told you.'

'Yes,' said Whitaker, 'And we've agreed we'll call in at this car hire firm on the way home and make enquiries.'

'No,' said Billy, 'it isn't that. I was thinking about Jim. He's been out of work for *two years.* Just sitting around.'

'Not the best of times to be unemployed then, is it?' said Whitaker.

'Meaning?'

'I should have thought that self-evident. If you're lucky enough to have a place at the Zuckmayer Academy, with the possibility of a career to follow, it seems to me wilfulness to throw it away. Of course, it has nothing to do with me. You make your own mistakes.'

'I'm not talking about me,' said Billy, glaring out of the window.

'No. But I am,' said Whitaker, approaching Newcastle at his

relentlessly steady speed.

At the reception desk of Beales Car Hire they were faced with a pretty girl of about twenty, sitting behind a neat sign that read 'Miss Tomkins'. She was quite adamant about the rules of the firm. 'No,' she said to Whitaker, politely but most firmly, 'I am very sorry, but I can't give that sort of information.'

'But why not?' said Whitaker, 'Look my name is Vincent Whitaker. I am well known in Newcastle. I'm a solicitor. Damn it, I'm a respectable member of the community.'

'Yes,' said Miss Tomkins implacably, 'but I am not allowed to give that information.'

'But I'll get it in the end,' said Whitaker, exasperated. 'It just means that I'll have to write to your superior.'

'Oh, that'd be all right,' said Miss Tomkins, smiling maddeningly. 'Head Office can give it to you.'

Whitaker blew down his nose in annoyance. 'Come on, Billy,' he said, and turned and stumped out of the office, breathing angrily. Billy turned to accompany him and then looked at Miss Tomkins. 'I'm sure I've met you somewhere,' he said. 'What's your christian name?'

'Janet,' said Miss Tomkins, surprised into answering.

'Janet Tomkins,' said Billy thoughtfully. He leaned on the counter with one arm. 'Do you go to the disco on Mount Hill?'

'I should think not,' said Miss Tomkins, shaking her head so that all her floppy yellow curls bounced indignantly, 'I can't stand disco dancing.'

'Nor me,' said Billy. He smiled. 'I hate all that noise. I'm studying the flute in Salzburg, actually.'

Whitaker's head popped round the door. He looked puzzled.

'Do you like music?' said Billy, leaning on the counter with both arms, now, gazing at Miss Tomkins. Whitaker came back into the reception area and stood watching.

'Well, some,' said Miss Tomkins, thawing visibly. 'Country and Western—some Barbershop. Maybe that's where we've met?'

'No,' said Billy. 'Yet I'm sure I know you.'

'And this German you were enquiring about . . .?'

'Oh, just a guy I knew in Salzburg,' said Billy casually.

'What name?'

'I can't remember it. I think . . . it could be Toth. But I'm not sure.'

'Well,' said Miss Tomkins, smiling up at him, 'I suppose it

won't do any harm, seeing as you're connected. Have you a number I could contact you at?'

'Mr Whitaker gave you his card.'

'Oh, yes. And you are?'

'Just call me Billy,' said Billy.

Janet Tomkins giggled suddenly. 'That's sort of intimate,' she said.

Billy gave her a dazzling smile. 'Yes,' he said. 'Maybe we could go to a concert one night?'

'I might hold you to that. There's a Barbershop festival coming up.'

'Terrific,' said Billy.

'All right. I'll see what I can do.'

'Thanks—Janet.'

'Now you mention it,' said Janet Tomkins, looking Billy up and down. 'I'm sure we *have* met somewhere.'

'We'll work it out,' said Billy. 'I'll hear from you. Bye.' He turned from the counter and strolled out, ushering a somewhat bemused Whitaker ahead of him.

'That,' said Whitaker, outside in the car park, 'was the most nauseating display I have ever witnessed.'

Billy gave him a self-satisfied wink. 'Got results, though,' he said.

'I can always go through the usual channels,' said Whitaker. 'When had you met her before?'

'You're joking!'

'But she said...' protested Whitaker.

Billy shrugged. 'My fatal charm,' he said. 'Shall I drive?'

Whitaker handed him the keys and climbed into the passenger seat. 'Your fatal charm is going to be sorely tried at a Barbershop festival,' he said. As Billy started the car and drove out of the car park Whitaker began to sing 'Sweet Adeline'. Billy joined him and the car moved onto City Road to the quavering accompaniment of two voices united in trembling harmony.

When they had stopped laughing, Whitaker said, 'Why did you tell her you thought his name was Toth?'

'I don't know,' said Billy.

'Make you jump if that's who it turns out to be,' said Whitaker. 'Keep your eye on the road. And we are in a built up area—there is a speed limit, you know.'

When they had unpacked the car and put on the kettle, Whitaker went into his study and pressed the intercom that connected the house with the office.

'Yes?' came Miss Price's voice.

'Oh, Pricey, we're back,' said Whitaker. 'We're having a cup of tea. Would you like to join us?'

'I haven't time, Mr Whitaker,' said Miss Price. Even over the intercom she sounded tight-lipped. 'I'm filing.'

'Oh,' said Whitaker, in sepulchral tones. 'In that case I'd better get off the line.'

Miss Price sniffed. 'I'll come in a few moments,' she said. 'I'll just tell Rita to direct all calls through to the house phone.'

When Miss Price joined them for tea it was instantly apparent that the detested filing was not the sole cause of her tension. 'It's very good to have you back, she said, accepting a cup from Whitaker. 'I've been so worried.'

'No need,' said Whitaker, calmly, passing a plate of biscuits.

'But what do you expect?' said Miss Price. 'You both nearly got blown up. Vincent—we should go to the police.'

'And tell them what?' said Whitaker, settling into his fireside chair and stirring his tea. 'That we suspect some diabolical plot against Billy? They wouldn't believe us. And even if they did, what could they do? Keep Billy under constant surveillance?'

'Well it just seems absurd to go on as if nothing is happening,' said Miss Price. 'Eventually something...dreadful could occur.' She put her hand to he mouth. 'I'm sorry,' she said. 'I am trying to keep calm.'

'It's all right, Pricey,' said Billy.

'No, it isn't, Billy. You're saying that you think someone – heaven knows who – tried to kill you!'

'Not exactly,' said Billy, 'nothing's definite.'

At that moment, the telephone in the hall rang shrilly, making them all jump. Miss Price set her cup down on the table and started to rise.

'No, I'll go,' said Billy, getting up too.

'It's my job,' said Miss Price, making for the door. 'I'm best when I'm doing something.'

'Yes,' said Billy, remembering. 'Of course.' He sat down again. Miss Price went into the hall.

'She'll be all right,' said Whitaker. 'She's a bit worked up.'

'Maybe she's right to be,' said Billy.

Whitaker avoided his eye by paying great attention to his tea.

'Difficult to know what to do...' he admitted.

Miss Price came back into the sitting room. 'For you, Billy,' she said. 'Rita put it through from the office, though why they phoned the office number...'

'Who is it?' said Billy, getting up.

'A woman,' said Miss Price. 'Miss Tomkins?'

'Aha,' said Billy brightening. 'Janet.' He winked at Whitaker. 'That was quick.' He hurried out into the hall. Miss Price wandered over the window, and stood looking out.

'Sit down, Pricey,' said Whitaker gently.

'I can't,' said Miss Price. 'I'm frightened. The last time I felt like this you were in hospital.'

Whitaker watched her from his fireside chair. 'And you see how ill-founded that fear was,' he said. She turned to look at him, but she had her hand pressed over her mouth again. 'I'm here,' said Whitaker. Miss Price nodded and turned quickly to stare out of the window again.

In the hall, the telephone pinged as it was set down, but Billy did not immediately return to the room. Whitaker got up and went over to the door. He found Billy standing by the instrument, just looking at it. 'Well?' he said.

Billy grinned, not very convincingly. 'I'm caught,' he said lightly. 'There's a concert being given by the Bassingthorpe Shop Quintet next Friday. She wants me to go...'

'The name, Billy,' said Whitaker.

'The car was returned to the Beales Office at Newcastle Airport, last Friday evening.'

'The day of the accident,' said Whitaker.

'The man who hired it was in a hurry to catch a London flight,' said Billy, expressionlessly. 'He said he had a transfer connection to make.'

'His name, Billy?'

Billy gave him a weak smile. 'Jerri Toth,' he said.

'Driving licence number?' said Whitaker.

'I didn't think to ask.'

Miss Price appeared in the doorway behind Whitaker. 'Vincent?' she said.

'It's all right, Pricey,' said Whitaker, in his most genial voice. 'Nothing to worry about. Just Billy's fatal charm.'

'Oh don't be so stupid, Vincent!' said Miss Price. 'You make it worse if you won't tell me. What is it? What's happened?'

'The man who was seen in Seahouses,' said Billy, 'hired a car under the name of Jerri Toth.'

Miss Price looked at him, then turned on her heel and walked back into the living-room. Billy and Whitaker followed her. 'But if he was there,' she said, her voice sounding higher than usual, 'You're not safe anywhere, Billy.'

Billy shook his head. 'He must think I know something,' he said.

'Do you?' said Whitaker.

'Yes, I suppose I do,' said Billy. 'I know that Jerri is dead and that Kurt Gruber is alive.'

'But you've got nothing to do with *any* of this, Billy,' said Miss Price desperately.

'Yes, I have,' said Billy calmly. 'Ever since I started looking for my parents I've been walking into it. You see, I'm Jerri Toth's son.'

By the end of the week, Billy had made a number of practical decisions. He hitched a ride to Bamburgh, where his motorbike waited, then rode over to Seahouses and sought out Jim once more. He led him to the fishmonger's shed, opened the door and kicked gently at the hull of *The Amadeus*. 'Listen,' he said. 'Could you get her seaworthy again?'

'Yes,' said Jim. 'Easy. But why? I thought you said you were going back to Austria?'

'I still don't want her rotting away.'

'It'd cost you,' said Jim.

'I'll pay. And if you can get her seaworthy you can use her when I'm not here.'

'What for?'

'Use your imagination,' said Billy. 'Trips to the Farne Islands. Fishing trips.' He smiled. 'Might take you all the way to Berwick-on-Tweed!'

'You mean it?'

'I'd be glad of it.' He took a key out of his pocket and handed it to Jim. 'That locks this shed.'

Jim took the key. 'It would cost a fair bit,' he said, becoming wary and business-like.

'I've got your address,' said Billy. 'I have to go now. See you.' He crossed the road towards the motorbike which was balanced on its stand next to the sea wall.

'How much will you pay us?' Jim called after him.

'Much as I can afford,' said Billy without looking back.

'There's a going rate, you know.'

Billy put on his helmet and climbed on to the bike. He waved his hand once, kick-started the engine and drove off down the quiet street. Behind him, Jim's face broke into a broad grin. He squatted down beside the upturned hull and patted it affectionately, then began to examine the damaged timbers with meticulous attention.

Billy rode back to Newcastle where he had an appointment with Whitaker in the office. Appreciating Whitaker's attitude to business, he changed into a suit and presented himself at the office precisely on time. He was too nervous to sit, but stood by the window while Whitaker and Miss Price sat one on each side of the large desk and heard him out.

'... and so,' he wound up, 'I am making a formal application for money from the trust fund to finance my continued studies at the Zuckmayer Academy.'

'Very good, Billy,' said Whitaker admiringly. 'You'd be wonderful in a court of law.'

'Well?' said Billy.

'Tell me why you want to go back.'

'There are two reasons,' said Billy.

'Then tell us them both.'

'There's only one thing I can do about Kurt Gruber... or whoever it is. And that's find him. I've got to get him out in the open where I can see him. Otherwise—well, I'll never be able to relax again.'

'But when you've "got him in the open", then what?' said Miss Price.

'Then maybe the police will be able to help me,' said Billy.

'Vincent...' said Miss Price anxiously.

'It makes sense, Vincent,' said Billy. 'You must agree?'

'And the other reason?' said Whitaker.

'I miss the flute,' said Billy simply. 'I didn't realize how much.'

'Hm,' said Whitaker. 'Well, I don't think Alan and Marian would want you to miss that. But you'd better be very good by the time you leave the Academy because the money you're using now won't be there then.'

The intercom on his desk buzzed. Whitaker pressed the relevant button. 'Yes?' he said.

'There's a Miss Tomkins to speak to Mr Billy,' said the voice of the telephonist.

Billy shook his head urgently at Whitaker. 'I'm not here,' he hissed. 'I'm not in.'

'Put her through on my telephone, Rita,' said Whitaker, unperturbed.

'You rat, Vincent,' said Billy.

Whitaker lifted the receiver. 'Hallo?' he said. 'Yes of course. Just one moment.' He held out the receiver to Billy. 'For you,' he said. 'You're in for a very harmonious evening!'

Billy took the receiver from him with a look that would have stripped paint. 'Hallo?' he said. 'Oh great. How many tickets can you get?' He beamed into the receiver. 'Honestly? Well could you get an extra one for the old chap I was with the other day?' Miss Price turned her back on the desk, trying unsuccessfully to keep her face straight. 'Yes, I know,' Billy went on, 'but he's not bad really, and he doesn't get out much...'

'Billy!' said Whitaker in a hoarse angry whisper.

'That's great,' said Billy, '7.30 then. Give me the address...' He drew Whitaker's pen and telephone pad towards him and began to write.

'Pricey, you can go with him,' said Whitaker. 'It's out of the question for me, I'm a sick man.'

'Oh no, Mr Whitaker,' said Miss Price primly, 'I couldn't possibly leave mother.'

'We'll look forward to seeing you, then,' said Billy into the telephone. He replaced the receiver. 'Now you can't let me down, Vincent,' he said reprovingly. 'She's bringing a girlfriend for you. Her Aunty from Seaton Sluice!'

'A blind date!' said Miss Price. 'Do take care, Vincent. Some women can be very predatory.'

'Perfidious friends!' said Whitaker.

'And by the way,' said Miss Price, rising to her feet. 'Next time you go to Salzburg, I have every intention of accompanying you.'

'And your mother?' said Whitaker.

'Will have to take second place for once,' said Miss Price. She went to the office door, opened it, and then turned back and eyed Whitaker up and down. 'I should wear something casual for your evening,' she said. 'A solicitor's suit would look rather out of place in a barber's shop!'

She went out of the office, followed closely by Billy. Whitaker pounded on the arms of his chair with the flats of his hands.

'Damn and blast!' he muttered. He swung himself irritably from side to side in his chair and then, quite suddenly, he began to chuckle, and finally to laugh outright.

Chapter Nineteen

Circumstances allowed Billy a second chance. Karl Zuckmayer professed himself willing to re-admit him to the Academy as a fee-paying student. Whitaker, as trustee of Billy's money from the Newcastle house, agreed to release sufficient funds to enable him to pay these fees. Anna was happy to rent out her attic once more and he even managed to find himself a job so that he was able to meet his own living expenses. Yet, although Billy himself said nothing, Whitaker was well aware that going back to Salzburg would prove to be something of an ordeal; he therefore pronounced himself in need of a holiday. And, since Miss Price categorically refused to be left behind, the three of them flew to Salzburg together, nearly a year after Billy's first acceptance at the Zuckmayer Academy.

Billy started work immediately, in a job where he was encouraged to fit his working hours around classes and tutorials. He had found it purely by chance, through asking around, and he was grateful to his new employer for offering him work so readily, even though he was completely inexperienced and barely spoke any German. So now he waited at table in his old haunt, the Café Salz, which, it had turned out, was owned by the pleasant-faced, middle-aged man who had befriended him in the days when he had been a regular customer—Konrad Spetz.

He had only been at the café for two days when the young man came in. He was thin and dark, he looked tense, even rather unwell. He ordered a coffee in a low voice, and Billy went behind the counter to get it. As he put the full cup on the saucer he slopped a little on the counter. Hans, who had learned his English principally from American tourists, sighed and dabbed at it with a cloth. 'I hope you're a good flute player,' he said resignedly. 'Because you're sure a lousy waiter.'

Billy grinned. He carried the coffee over to the corner table and set it down carefully. Barely looking up, the young man mumbled, *'Ich suche Jerri Toth.'*

Billy froze. 'What did you say?'

The boy looked up at him with large dark eyes. 'Jerri Toth,' he said, more clearly.

Billy bent over the table. 'You speak English?' he whispered.

'A little.'

'My name is Billy Toth.'

'But that's not possible,' said the boy. 'I was told... an older man.' Abruptly he rose to his feet. *'Ich habe mich geirrt,'* he said and turned and ran for the door.

'Hey...' said Billy, but the boy was already through, the door swinging gently behind him.

Billy ran after him, almost bumping into Hans who was clearing another table, and shot out of the café into the narrow cobbled street beyond. To the left the street was empty, to the right there was only Konrad Spetz, walking with his slight limp towards the café.

'Did you see a boy pass you?' said Billy, as he drew level. 'Running?'

Spetz shook his head. 'I don't recall,' he said. 'Maybe.'

'Damn,' said Billy softly. They went back into the café together. The older man madc his way to his usual table, by the counter. 'You will join me?' he said.

Billy looked at his watch. 'I should have left five minutes ago,' he said. 'Well—for a moment, perhaps. I've got a coffee.' He collected the untouched coffee from the corner table and sat down with Spetz.

'Did Rockefeller pay you' said Hans, 'before he ran out?'

'No.'

'That's how people get rich,' said Hans.

'I'll pay,' said Billy.

Hans waved aside the offer. 'That's how people get poor,' he said.

'How is our genius, Hans?' said Spetz, using English for Billy's benefit. 'He makes a good waiter?'

'You want to be bankrupt,' said Hans, 'we'll be bankrupt. He doesn't take the money.'

Spetz laughed. 'Bring me a coffee with cream, Hans,' he said.

'Did you have a good trip?' said Billy. 'Hans mentioned that you've not been back long.'

'I come and I go,' said Spetz, amiably. 'Thank God I don't rely on this café for a living, with you as a waiter.' He reached across the table and patted Billy affectionately on the arm. 'Oh, now don't look like that,' he said. 'We can afford to give away a cup of coffee from time to time. Who was he? You know?'

'That's what's so odd,' said Billy. 'He said he was looking for Jerri Toth.'

'Who?' said Spetz, quite sharply for him.

'Jerri Toth,' said Billy. 'That was my father's name. But he's been dead... as long as I've been alive, really.'

'Oh, he got it wrong,' said Spetz, receiving his coffee and stirring it peaceably. 'He meant you. He'd heard about your virtuosity. He wanted you to put in a good word with the Maestro Zuckmayer!'

'So the minute he sees me he runs away?' said Billy.

'Why not?' said Spetz. 'That way he doesn't have to pay for his coffee!'

Billy looked at his watch again. 'I must go,' he said. 'I'm meeting my friends at the Tomaselli.'

'Another café?' said Spetz in mock horror. 'You have no loyalty.'

Billy laughed. 'Mr Whitaker wouldn't come here. He said I'd make him nervous.'

'Well, they will be happy at the Tomaselli,' said Spetz. 'It is, I have to admit it, the finest café in Salzburg!'

They were happy at the Tomaselli. It was too cool to sit out on the balcony so the tables and chairs had been cleared away, but Whitaker and Miss Price sat at a table on the top floor, just inside the balcony doors and wound up lunch with coffee and a cream cake each. Before starting on her cake, Miss Price rose to her feet and stood in the open balcony doors, directing her Instamatic camera towards the distant castle. As the shutter clicked, Whitaker said, rather crossly, 'That's the third one you've taken.'

'The other two may not come out,' said Miss Price mildly. 'I promised mother I'd bring back views of the city.'

'If you're going to take three of each,' said Whitaker, 'she may not be able to stand the excitement.'

'Come here a minute,' said Miss Price, gesturing for him to join her on the balcony. Whitaker sat firmly where he was. 'I refuse to be foreground interest,' he said.

'Oh no,' said Miss Price, 'I just wanted a frame for that statue down there.'

'A frame!'

Miss Price abandoned the idea, slipped the camera back into her bag and sat down at the table again. 'Isn't this bliss,' she said, picking up her cake fork.

'You are actually enjoying yourself,' said Whitaker, with a benign smile. 'You look quite different.'

'I'm a foreigner,' said Miss Price placidly. 'Foreigners always look different.'

'Dear Pricey!' said Whitaker.

Miss Price gave him a straight look. 'Do you *know* my christian name?' she said.

'Heavens!' said Whitaker. 'I expect I've got it down somewhere. It begins with an N.'

'B,' said Miss Price. 'It's on my office door.'

Whitaker nodded his head towards the stairs and Billy, who was just running up them.

'Saved!' said Miss Price.

Whitaker leaned forward across the small table. 'You are Barbara Price,' he said, quite quietly, 'and the day you came for your interview you were wearing a grey suit with a blue and white blouse.'

There was a slight pause. 'Well,' said Miss Price, confused, 'I usually wear grcy.'

Billy arrived at the table. 'I'm sorry I'm late,' he said, pulling up another chair.

Miss Price scooped at her cream cake. 'We're on holiday,' she said complacently.

'Now, what will you have?' said Whitaker to Billy.

'Nothing. I've been dealing with food all lunchtime.'

'But have you eaten?' said Miss Price.

'I've picked.' He looked at Whitaker. 'It's beginning again,' he said. 'A boy came in just now and said he was looking for Jerri Toth.'

'Oh no,' said Miss Price, setting down her fork and looking from one to the other. 'He said *Billy* Toth.'

'No, Pricey,' said Billy. 'He said Jerri. Then he ran off before I had a chance to ask what he wanted.'

'Vincent!' said Miss Price. 'Now we *must* go to the authorities.'

'And what are we supposed to say to your infallible

‘‘authorities’’,’ said Whitaker, snappishly. ‘That a young man asked for Jerri Toth? It’s like going up to an English bobby and saying ‘‘I’m looking for John Smith’’.’

‘So what do you suggest?’ said Miss Price. ‘That we wait until something terrible happens to Billy?’

‘It’s all right,’ said Billy, in his best soothing voice.

‘And you’re as bad,’ said Miss Price. ‘Really, I have enough to worry about without adding you to my list . . .’

At that moment Billy, who had been looking out across the balcony to the street beyond, saw a figure he recognized. ‘That’s him!’ he said suddenly, making them both jump. He pushed back his chair, ran through the café and clattered down the stairs. Miss Price and Whitaker got to their feet and hurried onto the balcony. As Billy appeared in the street below, Miss Price called down to him, ‘Where shall we see you?’

‘At Anna’s tonight,’ Billy called back. ‘Don’t worry. I just want to speak to him.’

They saw him run up to a thin young man who had been walking past the shop-front opposite, his head down and his hands in his pockets. He seemed to be contained in a world of his own and only stopped when Billy caught him by the arm. They spoke for a moment or two and then set off together in the general direction of the main bridge.

‘Do you suppose it’s all right?’ said Miss Price, as the two figures disappeared from view.

‘With Billy, you can never tell,’ said Whitaker.

They stood together on the balcony, in the bright but cool sunshine, and stared after him. ‘I wonder if he’ll ever be free of his past,’ said Miss Price, rather forlornly.

‘I thought he was,’ said Whitaker. ‘It keeps catching up with him.’

‘Dangerously?’

‘Not so far. Now don’t start fretting. Think of your mother—that always quietens you down.’

‘It may be a joke to you . . .’ said Miss Price, stung.

‘I was trying to make one,’ Whitaker confessed.

‘In very poor taste!’

‘I’m sorry Pricey.’

She looked at him for a moment, and then gave a long sigh. ‘Really anyone could think Billy was *my* child,’ she said. Then corrected herself, ‘young man.’

'You would have liked that?' She just looked at him. 'Oh, Pricey,' said Whitaker.

Miss Price seemed to give herself a mental shake. 'We'd better get up to the castle,' she said briskly. 'That was next on the itinerary.' She took a handkerchief out of her bag and wiped her nose surreptitiously.

'Don't I get a siesta in the afternoon?'

'Only in Italy,' said Miss Price. 'There's a cable car to the top.'

'How on earth do you know that?'

'Michelin,' said Miss Price. 'I'm a born tourist.' She wiped her nose one more time and put the handkerchief away. 'Though it's rather late in life to discover the fact. He will be all right, won't he?'

'Our worrying won't help,' said Whitaker. He reached out and took her arm and led her back to the table.

It was Billy's explanation that he was Jerri Toth's son that partially reassured the other boy. He gave his name as Stefan Kiesl and asked Billy to go with him to an hotel on the other side of the river where his mother, he said, was waiting. He took Billy to a small, rather mean room on the third floor of an unfashionable hotel in the newer part of town. The light from the narrow window, which shone dimly through a net curtain, showed two beds and, in one of them, a dark-haired woman, lying propped against the pillows from both. She turned her head as the two boys came in, and her white, tired face lifted with hope. Stefan went to her bedside and spoke to her, rapidly and softly, in German. Billy understood his own name but nothing more. When Stefan had finished, Frau Kiesl looked past him at Billy. 'I get tired,' she said apologetically in English. 'It is nothing.' She was not an old woman, probably no more than forty-five, but illness and anxiety seemed to have drained her face of all colour and all vitality. 'My family home is in Leipzig,' she said, as though this was the news Billy had been waiting to hear. 'You have been there?' He shook his head.

'You have taken the medicine I got for you?' said Stefan.

Frau Kiesl coughed then, as Stefan sat on the bed and reached for the bottle on the bedside cabinet, she pushed his hand impatiently away. 'It is not medicine I need,' she said. She motioned to Billy to come around the bed and sit on the chair at its other side. 'In Leipzig,' she said, 'are my home and my family. My sisters. My mother. We are apart from them, Stefan and I. I came to the West carrying Stefan in me, big in my womb. Where does he belong? There or here? Can you tell me?'

Billy's lack of response seemed to puzzle her. She looked at Stefan and said, *'Hast du ihn gefragt?'*

'She says—have I asked you,' said Stefan to Billy.

'What?' said Billy.

'I want for us to go back,' said Frau Kiesl urgently. 'To Leipzig. I want to see my mother and my sisters—and my father if he still lives. I want Stefan to see them.'

'But how can I help you?' said Billy. 'Surely you can just cross the frontier—go for a visit?' They stared at him. 'I don't understand,' said Billy. 'I'm sorry.'

'We were told to ask for you,' said Stefan. 'To go to the Café Salz and ask for you.'

Frau Kiesl looked at her son. *'Das ist nicht der Richtige,'* she said. *'Wer ist er?'*

'Er behauptet Jerri Toth's Sohn zu sein,' said Stefan.

Frau Kiesl frowned at Billy. 'You are the son of Jerri Toth?' she said. Billy nodded. 'You do not sound Hungarian.'

'My parents were Hungarian,' said Billy, 'but I was born in England. I was adopted when I was a baby. I was brought up by English people.'

'So,' said Frau Kiesl with a faint smile. 'Where do *you* belong?'

'Wherever I am, I suppose,' said Billy.

'A young answer,' said Frau Kiesl. 'I want to go home, where I grew up. That is where I belong. I want to see it once more, to smell the air and feel it on my face. I want to see my family.'

'But *I* can't help you,' said Billy. 'I'm sorry.'

'Yet you are the son of Jerri Toth,' said Stefan.

'My father is dead.'

'But I was told to ask for him...'

'Who told you?'

Stefan looked at his mother. Almost imperceptibly she nodded. 'In Hamburg,' he said, 'I met a man from Magdeburg. He told me he had come over the border with the Hungarian, Jerri Toth. He gave me the address of the Café Salz and said I was to ask the waiter.'

'How long ago was this?'

Stefan shrugged. 'Perhaps six months.'

'Why has it taken you so long?'

'We are not rich people,' said Frau Kiesl, suddenly angry. 'The

Hungarian, we were told, would require all the money we have got.' She watched Billy's expression. 'Yes, there are such people,' she said, 'who make a living out of suffering. The Hungarian, your father, he is such a one. All the money we have is very little, but even that took time to raise.'

'I just don't understand,' said Billy, his voice coming unevenly out of a tight throat. 'My father is dead. Why put yourselves through this? Why?'

'I am not well,' said Frau Kiesl. 'I will not last. Stefan is young to be alone. You understand?'

'Yes.'

'How could you?' said Frau Kiesl.

'Because I also was alone.'

'And now?'

'I have friends,' said Billy.

'But not family,' said Frau Kiesl. 'It is family that is important.'

'No,' said Billy, 'It's Stefan who is most important, to himself. It's taken me a long time to realize that, for myself. But it is true.'

Frau Kiesl coughed painfully. Stefan held the bedside glass for her to drink some water. 'I want Stefan to know his family and not be alone,' she said when she could speak again. She was near to tears. 'I want the barriers to fall and there to be no more divisions. What is faith that divides people and politics that builds barriers? We are all one people. We breathe, we live, and so soon we die. Why is our country divided?' She coughed again. 'For past deeds? What has Stefan to do with the past? He is now.' She looked at Stefan. 'To be an exile is to be only half alive,' she said. 'No one will help us. I will die in exile and you . . . it would be better if you had never been born.'

'No, Mother,' said Stefan gently. 'You cannot say that. My life is my own. I will make of it what I am able.' He looked across the bed at Billy. 'If you cannot help us, we must go now,' he said. 'She tires easily.'

'Where?' said Billy, standing.

'I must try again to find the Hungarian.'

'I'll come with you,' said Billy. 'I know someone who may be able to advise us. Come back with me to the Salz.'

'All right,' said Stefan, doubtfully. As he and Billy reached the door, he looked back at his mother. 'I won't be long,' he said.

'There are no birds,' said Frau Kiesl, ignoring him and staring across the room to the narrow window. 'I like to see them flying.'

At the Café Salz, Konrad Spetz listened carefully to the story that Stefan, with Billy's prompting, told him. At its end he said, 'But it is quite simple for people to visit their relatives in the Eastern sector. You write to them, get them to make an invitation... you pay a fee to the authorities... it is expensive, yes. But not as expensive as your wild scheme.'

Stefan shook his head. 'My mother is wanted by the authorities over there,' he said.

'Then my dear young friend,' said Spetz, 'I suggest most strongly that neither of you attempts to go there.'

Stefan spread his thin hands on the worn old table top and looked down at them. 'My mother is dying,' he said. 'She has leukaemia.'

'I am sorry,' said Spetz, gently. 'But you *must* forget these foolish plans. Write to your family in Leipzig. Perhaps it is not even impossible for them to visit you. Authorities are not always inhuman...'

'It is not just the people, it is the place,' said Stefan, desperately. 'It is the wish of a woman who is dying—who wants, I think, to die at home.'

'Keep your voice down,' said Spetz sternly. 'What you are discussing is a totally illegal act—the trafficking in human life. The penalties for such people are most severe.'

'He asked for my father by name,' said Billy angry now, but not with Spetz.

'Your father is dead,' said the older man firmly.

'But Kurt Gruber is not,' said Billy.

A moment's silence fell on the table. Then, 'I don't know this Kurt Gruber,' said Spetz.

'He is a man who trafficked, as you call it,' said Billy. 'I think Kurt Gruber had to disappear and so... he killed my father and took his identity...'

'Oh, Billy, Billy,' said Spetz, leaning back from the table and raising his hands in a despairing gesture. 'Stop this. You sound like a fairy tale. Now look—Hans is calling me to the telephone. I must go and so must you. Where are you staying, Herr Kiesl?'

'At the Hotel Stein.'

'Then go quickly to it,' said Spetz with kindly authority. 'Your mother, if she is as ill as you say, needs your nursing not your adventure story scheming. And you, Billy, have visitors. Surely you are expected to spend time some time with them?'

'I'll come and see you tomorrow,' said Billy helplessly, to Stefan. But Stefan only shrugged.

At Anna's that night there was a supper party. Gunter, Whitaker, Miss Price and Billy sat around her table, ate her excellent cooking and drank delicate Austrian wine. Even when the meal was finished, Gunter was still replenishing glasses.

'No more for Pricey,' said Whitaker reprovingly, as the bottle hovered over her glass.

'Yes, please, Gunter,' said Miss Price, pushing her glass a little nearer to the bottle's neck.

'You'll get tight,' said Whitaker.

'I'm already tight,' said Miss Price happily. 'You cannot slam the horse after the door has bolted.' She raised the glass.

'Slam the horse?' said Anna, puzzled.

Miss Price smiled at her vaguely. 'It's idiomatic,' she explained kindly.

Gunter finished his round of refills and sat down again. 'Yes,' he said, going back to the earlier conversation,'it is a sad story, Billy. But not so uncommon, you know. Many families are divided. Anna has most of her family in the Eastern sector of Berlin.'

'And you see them?' said Billy.

'Oh yes,' said Anna. 'It is quite possible to visit so long as you go through the proper channels. But your lady, Frau Kiesl,' she shook her head. 'If, as you say, she is wanted by the authorities over there, then it would be very dangerous for her to return. And yet I understand her. The call of your home is very strong. Particularly if you are denied it. People will...' She stopped herself. 'It is dangerous,' she said, 'and corrupt.'

'The corruption is,' said Miss Price, speaking most carefully, 'that people are denied their homes in the first place.'

'It goes back,' said Gunter quietly.

'But do we never forgive?' said Miss Price. 'Has man lost the capacity to...absolve?' She caught Whitaker's eye. 'You are quite right, Vincent,' she said, 'I am. But not "tight", that is quite the wrong word. I am "loose". I'm so sorry.'

Whitaker chuckled. *'In vino veritas,'* he said. Then he looked across the candles at Billy and his face became serious again. 'But I am sure that this is something that you should not be involved in,' he said.

'Of that I am absolutely certain,' said Gunter, quite vehemently. 'It is a highly dangerous topic. On both sides of the frontier the punishment for people who meddle in this way is extreme.'

'Yes, I know,' said Billy thoughtfully.

'No, you do *not* know,' said Gunter. 'What I am saying to you, Billy, is that you could end up in an Austrian prison—or a German one. Now forget all about Frau Kiesl and her son.'

'But they need help, Gunter,' said Billy.

'So do countless other people like them,' said Gunter. 'They are nothing to you.'

'If only we knew what Kurt Gruber looked like,' said Whitaker, twirling his wine glass meditatively.

'Vincent,' said Gunter. 'You encourage him!'

'Just natural curiosity,' said Whitaker. 'If we knew what he looked like, we'd know what we were looking *for*.'

'All right, that I agree,' said Gunter. 'But meanwhile it would be useless and stupid for Billy to get mixed up with the Kiesls.'

'They're so desperate, Gunter,' said Billy, almost pleadingly.

'But you cannot help them,' said Gunter, tapping on the table cloth with his forefinger for emphasis. 'No one can. Least of all Jerri Toth, whoever he may be. And even if they got to Leipzig, it is doubtful they could ever get back again.'

Billy nodded. He watched the candle flames as they bent gracefully in the slight draught from the door. 'Yet I think they'll go on looking until they find him . . . as you say "whoever he is".'

Two days later, Stefan stood with his mother at the side of a mountain road, several miles from Salzburg. A suitcase was by his feet. Frau Kiesl was warmly wrapped in a coat, a scarf around her head. She leaned heavily on her son's arm but her pale features were lightened by hope, as they had been so briefly two days before, when Stefan had brought Billy to her. The long straight road was entirely empty apart from a car which was parked on the opposite side to the Kiesls. In the car sat one man, Konrad Spetz, his face watchful, his eyes on the point where the road disappeared from view. The scene was very still, very quiet.

A car appeared on the road, at the point which Spetz had been watching. It was travelling fast, towards them. The Kiesl's did not look at this car, they looked instead across the road at the stationary car opposite. As the second car drew nearer, and its number plate became visible, Spetz looked for the first time at the

Kiesls and nodded, once. At the same moment, he put his car into gear and drove off, passing the oncoming car with no sign of recognition.

The second car reached the two waiting figures and stopped. Stefan spoke briefly to the driver and then opened the back door, pushed in the case, and stood back for his mother. Overhead, a flight of birds passed above the tree tops. Frau Kiesl looked up at them and smiled briefly. Then she got into the car, followed by Stefan. The door slammed and the car drove away, fast.

Chapter Twenty

Since it was impossible to imagine that a meeting with Mrs Dalgleish could ever be straightforward and ordinary, neither Whitaker nor Billy were unduly surprised when she suddenly summoned them both to London, saying that it was urgent that she should speak with them. By the time she contacted them she had already, with typically flamboyant generosity, made all the arrangements; booking a return flight from Salzburg for Billy, a first-class train ticket from Newcastle for Whitaker, and rooms in a smart hotel for both. In the state of bemused affection she induced in most people, they obediently made the necessary journeys, slept in their well-appointed bedrooms and woke to find a message inviting them to meet her at 11 a.m., beside the Albert Memorial.

As they approached the lush Victorian opulence of the monument, they saw the yellow Rolls-Royce, parked on the neatly trimmed grass in front of it and attended, this time, by two chauffeurs, one black and one white, both in immaculate uniforms.

'She can't park there!' said Whitaker, aghast.

The two chauffeurs were stooping one on either side of the car, polishing the headlights. There was no sign of Mrs Dalgleish. Billy and Whitaker walked up to the car. The polishing stopped and the two chauffeurs stood upright. ''Where is she?'' said Billy.

'What are your names?' said the black chauffeur curtly, in a strongly Glaswegian accent.

'I'm Vincent Whitaker and this is...'

'... Billy,' said Billy.

'Oh,' said the black chauffeur, unimpressed. 'Well I'm Number One and this is Number Two.'

'Where is Mrs Dalgleish?' said Whitaker.

'Ah,' said the white chauffeur, in a soft Highland burr, 'she'll have gone to the top of the steps. Have you met her before?'

'Yes,' said Whitaker.

'And you're a friend?'

'I hope so.'

The white chauffeur walked round to the front of the car, leaned on the bonnet and folded his arms. 'Only I've got a black belt in the Jiujitsu,' he said, 'And I'm very fond of Mrs Dalgleish.'

Whitaker blinked, then nodded and set off towards the steps of the Memorial. As Billy moved to follow him, the black chauffeur stepped forward and planted himself in his path. 'You after a job?' he said.

'No,' said Billy. 'We've come to see Mrs Dalgleish. She told us to meet her here.'

'Hm,' said the black chauffeur, 'Because if you're after a job you've come to the wrong shop. There's a waiting list.' He opened the driver's door, got in and sat behind the wheel. The white chauffeur opened the other door, got in and sat beside his colleague. Both doors slammed simultaneously and two faces, beneath two peaked caps, stared stonily out from behind the windscreen.

Billy shook his head to himself and ran after Whitaker. 'Two chauffeurs, now,' said Whitaker, *sotto voce,* 'And mine has a black belt in "the Jiujitsu".'

As they mounted the steps Mrs Dalgleish became visible, swathed in an ankle length white fur, leaning on the elaborate frieze around the base of the plinth. She was gazing across the road towards the Albert Hall.

'Mrs Dalgleish!' said Billy, going up to her.

She held out a hand to silence him. 'A moment,' she said. 'How many people does that hold?'

'The Albert Hall?' said Whitaker, catching up. 'Oh, a great many.'

'A great many,' said Mrs Dalgleish thoughtfully. 'And it would be possible to purchase all the tickets—at a reduction for a group?'

'I really couldn't say,' said Whitaker.

Mrs Dalgleish nodded her beautiful head. 'Yet I think it would be better to perform there and have *them* pay *me,'* she said. Her face became tragic. 'But...they never ask.' She tore her gaze from the concert hall and lavished a wide smile on them both. '*Dear* Mr Whitaker,' she said, 'it is too long since we have been seeing each other. You have married the typist?'

'The typist?' said Whitaker.

'I think she means Pricey,' said Billy with a grin.

'And Billy!' said Mrs Dalgleish, holding out her hands as if to frame his face. 'So tall—so young—such a good skin. I had forgotten that. Do *not* sunburn, it ages you. People always rush, rush, rush to the sun, the sun. They come back like...how is it you are having it?—pickled walnuts.' She smiled dreamily. 'Mr Dalgleish liked his pickles. He was a pickle baron. Now! Your hotel is comfortable? And the flight, Billy?'

'We must talk about all that, Mrs Dalgleish,' said Whitaker firmly. 'You cannot pay for us...'

Mrs Dalgleish held up a slim, black-gloved hand. 'I must, I must,' she said. 'But we will talk a great deal, this I promise. That is why I had to see you both. It is most important.' A tragic wave seemed to sweep over her. 'I *love* this place,' she said. Billy and Whitaker dutifully assumed expressions of respect and raised their eyes to the bronze figure of Albert beneath his Gothic canopy. 'She built it for her man,' said Mrs Dalgleish. 'I think that I will build a monument for poor Mr Dalgleish, and now I see it has already been done. I show you.' She pointed dramatically to the name *Albert* in the dedication. 'Mr Dalgleish was called Albert,' she said. 'I think of this as his memorial.' Abruptly she changed the subject again. 'I have much news for you,' she said. 'From Kurt Gruber.'

'You've heard from him?' said Billy.

'Oh yes, Billy, I have heard from him. I have seen him. He wants me to give you many messages.' She reached out and touched his cheek softly. 'We will go somewhere and picnic and it will be like being at Bumbrow,' she said. 'You remember?' She swept gracefully down the steps, towards the car, Billy and Whitaker following like a pair of acolytes.

The two chauffeurs had climbed out of the yellow Rolls-Royce and were in deep conversation with a stout middle-aged traffic warden. 'What is going on?' said Mrs Dalgleish, as she approached the scene.'Who is this person?'

'She's given us a ticket,' said the black chauffeur. 'For illegal parking.'

'A ticket?' said Mrs Dalgleish in a puzzled voice. 'We do not need the ticket.' She took it from him and handed it back to the warden. '*You* have it,' she said kindly.

'No,' said the traffic warden, accepting the ticket out of sheer surprise. 'It's for you.'

'How very sweet of you,' said Mrs Dalgleish. 'But this is my auto and I need no ticket. Goodbye.' She climbed into the back of the Rolls, Whitaker and Billy climbed in at the other side, and the two chauffeurs got into the front of the car in concert and now every door closed.

The traffic warden rapped on the window beside Mrs Dalgleish. Mrs Dalgleish smiled serenely at her and wound down the window. 'I'm sorry, madam,' said the traffic warden huffily, 'But you are in contravention of the Road Traffic Act and the parking laws of this City.'

'Yes, I'm sure we are,' said Mrs Dalgleish soothingly. 'But what harm have we done? I am from Hungary, you know. I was an opera singer there. I don't think we need worry about the little pieces of paper. Here,' she leaned down inside the car and then passed a bottle of champagne through the window and into the warden's gloved hands. 'Have this tonight, when you're cosy. But chill it first.'

'But I've made out the ticket now,' said the warden, her chin beginning to quiver with indignation. 'And besides, this is bribery.'

'You don't like champagne?' said Mrs Dalgleish. She reached out and grasped the bottle by the neck. 'I take it back,' she said, doing so. She narrowed her eyes. 'You have a ticket mentality,' she said, 'and that hat does not suit you.' She faced front again. 'Drive on, One,' she said. She looked at Billy, on the bucket seat opposite her. 'I never remember their names so I call them One and Two,' she explained. 'Such dear boys. So loyal, so strong. And such a good contrast, don't you think?' She returned her attention to the traffic warden. 'Goodbye,' she said with all her charm. 'So very pleased to have met you.' She lowered her voice confidentially, 'I think it is the yellow of the ribbon,' she said. 'Few can wear such a colour. Try the whole outfit in cream with a contrasting brown.' The engine purred into life and the car moved on its stately way, across the grass towards the road.

'You'll hear from us,' the traffic warden spluttered as the car drew away.

'Good,' called Mrs Dalgleish happily, through the still-open window. 'I love receiving letters. Goodbye!'

'You just see if you don't,' said the warden, venom now mingling with her fury.'You Rolls-Royce drivers are all the same. Parking on Hyde Park grass? Oh dear me, no!' The car was now well out of range and one or two passers-by had paused to enjoy her offended monologue. 'And you can all clear off,' she said, noticing them for the first time. 'Champagne! I *must* say!' She straightened her cap. 'Well, I don't like champagne, it's too gassy.' She waved an angry arm at the onlookers and stumped off through them, elbowing them aside. 'I feel quite shaken,' she fumed to herself as she marched back towards the road.

They drove to Chiswick House and settled themselves in the elegant grounds which, although open to the public, were virtually empty so early in the year. There they picnicked in Mrs Dalgleish's inimitable style. From the capacious boot of the Rolls the two chauffeurs produced a folding table and three chairs. They spread the table with an immaculate white cloth and set out plates, glasses, chilled champagne and an impressive banquet of cold food. 'We go on longer journeys now,' said Mrs Dalgleish to Whitaker, as One poured the champagne and handed round the glasses. 'I find it helpful to have a change of chauffeur. I don't like stopping, you see.' She raised her glass, 'We are returning to Scotland via Cornwall,' she said. *'Egészégére!'*

Whitaker and Billy raised their own glasses and echoed the toast.

'Now eat. Eat,' said Mrs Dalgleish. 'There is plenty more.'

Whitaker and Billy helped themselves from the table, which looked as though it might collapse under the weight of food if they did not relieve it of at least some of its burden.

'Thank you dear, dear boys,' said Mrs Dalgleish to the chauffeurs. 'You may leave us now.'

'You'll just holler if you want anything?' said One.

'Aye,' said Mrs Dalgleish. 'Dinna fesh yerself!' The two chauffeurs retired discreetly in the direction of the car. 'So sweet, so caring,' said Mrs Dalgleish, gazing after them. 'And, of course, they are on a very good screw.' She beamed. 'Time and a half with a daily rate for being away from home base.' Then she frowned. 'I never have understood it properly,' she said. At last she shrugged. 'But... I play the game and pay the wage. You have heard of the NUC?'

'NUC?' said Billy with his mouth full.

'The National Union of Chauffeurs,' said Mrs Dalgleish. 'I formed it. It seemed kind. In the old days I used to give them a bonus if I was satisfied... now I give them a "rate"... and do you know? It saves me money!' Her face clouded over. 'I talk too much,' she said. 'I am nervous, Billy. Kurt has been to see me. You must stop looking for him. I beseech you.' She reached out and touched his cheek. 'He knows you, Billy.'

'Yes,' said Billy, trying to sound light-hearted. 'He tries to kill me from time to time.'

'No, Billy,' said Mrs Dalgleish, utterly serious now. 'If he wanted that, you would be dead.'

'He blew up my boat...'

'Yes.'

Billy stared at her. 'You know?'

'He told me,' said Mrs Dalgleish. 'But it was only to warn you. To ask you to leave him alone.'

Billy pushed his plate away. 'I can't,' he said.

'No?' said Mrs Dalgleish, with sadness in her voice.

'I never knew my father,' said Billy. 'But I want him to be... just dead.'

Mrs Dalgleish shook her head. 'Leave Kurt,' she said. 'Forget Kurt. He doesn't want to hurt you.' Her voice took on a pleading note. 'He is your friend,' she said.

Billy frowned. 'Why did you say he knows me?' he said. 'Why do you say he's my friend?'

Mrs Dalgleish turned slightly away from him and sipped her champagne.

'It's someone *I* know?' said Billy.

There was a silence. The lawn where they sat, encircled by great trees, might have been a private garden.

'I promise you it isn't me,' said Whitaker at last.

'He killed Jerri Toth,' said Billy, trying unsuccessfully to make Mrs Dalgleish meet his eye.

'You did not know Jerri,' she said.

'He was my *father,'* said Billy. 'I'm only here because of him. He killed my mother. He killed them both.'

'He wants to make amends,' said Mrs Dalgleish softly.

'How can he possibly do that?'

The silence fell again.

'Just supposing I was him, Billy,' said Whitaker. 'Would that alter our relationship?'

'You're surely not advocating ignorance?' said Billy.

'No,' said Whitaker. 'Are you advocating revenge?'

'No. Justice.'

'Ah,' said Whitaker.

'Well surely you're in favour of that?'

'Of justice, yes,' said Whitaker. 'Of the penalty? I was never so sure.'

'He killed my parents!'

'Are you certain?' said Whitaker. 'How?'

'I don't know. But he knows.' Billy looked back at Mrs Dalgleish. 'Who is he?'

'A weak man,' said Mrs Dalgleish, 'who I thought was strong. But the weak ones are the dangerous ones, Billy.'

'Who is he?'

Mrs Dalgleish rose and walked a few paces away from the table, carrying her glass.

'Please, Mrs Dalgleish,' said Billy, with a note of desperation in his voice.

Without turning round, she held out the empty glass. 'Give me some more champagne,' she said.

Billy began to rise, but Whitaker stayed him with a gesture, picked up the bottle and took the champagne to Mrs Dalgleish. He refilled her glass. 'You haven't eaten anything,' he said. 'Come back to the table.'

'No,' she said, rather wistfully. 'Mr Dalgleish used to say "A sleekit woman is ma delight!" To be sleekit one must suffer.' She grasped his arm. 'He must stop searching for Kurt,' she said.

'Why won't you tell me who he is?' said Billy from the table, raising his voice so that it would cross the distance between them.

Mrs Dalgleish turned and looked back at him. 'Because if you knew,' she said, 'I'm afraid for what you might do to him.'

'You still care for him?'

She shook her head. 'No. I care for you, Billy.' She had not yet released Whitaker's arm. 'You understand?' she said to him.

'Yes,' said Whitaker.

'What did hanging do to the hangman, or the verdict of death to the innocent jury? I don't want that for Billy. Kurt is not worth that. I don't think you will ever hear from him again, Billy. Jerri Toth is finally dead. Kurt has told me so.'

'So what name is he living by now?' said Billy relentlessly.

'What's in a name?' said Mrs Dalgleish. She shivered within the white fur. 'Come, let us walk a little. Bring the champagne, Mr Whitaker. One can walk and sip, I am sure.' She raised her voice. 'Boys, don't clear the food,' she called. 'My guests may be hungry later.'

The two chauffeurs appeared from the trees and moved to the table, to mount guard over it, as Billy rose and took Whitaker's glass to him. Mrs Dalgleish drifted over towards the small lake. 'Poor ducks!' she said, gazing down at three Mallards who were paddling towards her in the hope of bread. 'To be always wet!'

'You're sad, I think,' said Whitaker.

'Yes. I am not good company. You must go soon.'

'We must,' said Whitaker. 'Billy returns to Salzburg tonight.'

'How goes his playing?'

'He's doing very well.'

Mrs Dalgleish moved nearer to Billy, who had been standing a little apart, deep in thought. She put her arm around his shoulders. 'Dear Billy,' she said. 'And the flat you are living at in Salzburg? It will be all right, now that the young lady is marrying her man?'

'Anna and Gunter?' said Billy. 'How did you know they were getting married?'

Mrs Dalgleish dropped her arm from his shoulders. 'Didn't you say?'

'I don't think so,' said Billy. 'I don't think I've mentioned them.'

'Then I expect it was Mr Whitaker,' said Mrs Dalgleish, turning again in the direction of the table. 'We should go back now.'

Billy looked at Whitaker.' 'Did you?' he said.

Whitaker thought for a moment. 'I might have,' he said. 'If you're not to miss your flight we should perhaps be moving.'

'I've got until tonight,' said Billy impatiently. 'I told you—I'm flying to Munich and travelling down with Gunter.'

As they moved back in the direction of the table, an old man came walking thrugh the trees towards them. Though his coat and hat were shabby and worn he was by no means a tramp and he had about him a certain style, a certain dignity. He doffed his hat to Mrs Dalgleish, with a discreet flourish, and said, ''Good day to you.'

Mrs Dalgleish inclined her head very slightly in his direction and then whispered to Whitaker, 'You know him?'

'I think he was speaking to you,' Whitaker whispered back.

Mrs Dalgleish pulled her lavish fur more closely about her and increased her pace. 'Then we must keep walking,' she said. 'It is not safe to be spoken to.'

But the old man replaced his hat and began to walk beside them. 'Forgive me,' he said. 'I thought you were...my mistake...' He turned as if to go.

'One moment, please,' said Mrs Dalgleish, standing still, Whitaker at her side and Billy behind her. 'Who did you think I was?'

'A very great artist, madam,' said the old man, with a slight but courtly bow.

'Who?' said Mrs Dalgleish breathlessly.

'I am an old man. I do not remember names.'

'Try. Please try.'

'What's in a name?' said Billy gently, attempting to draw her away.

'But he may be remembering me,' said Mrs Dalgleish. 'You understand? Me. As I was.'

'A singer...' said the old man, half to himself.

Mrs Dalgleish pressed her gloved hand to her mouth.

'...a very great singer,' said the old man. 'Of opera.' He peered into her face. 'It is you?'

'I think so,' said Mrs Dalgleish shyly. 'Lila Tzech. I was Lila Tzech.'

'I don't remember names,' said the old man. 'I'm sorry.'

'Where did you see me?'

'In Paris, madam. And here in London?'

'In Paris, yes,' said Mrs Dalgleish wonderingly. 'I never sang London.'

'If you are the one I am thinking of,' said the old man, 'you were the greatest.'

'Oh,' said Mrs Dalgleish, 'I am sure it is someone else.'

'And yet...' he smiled rather sadly at her '...I recognized you.'

'You *recognized* me,' she repeated. She reached out and linked her arm through his. 'Are you hungry?' She began to lead him to the picnic table.

Whitaker and Billy stood together and watched as the old man was ushered to a chair and Number One came forward to open some more champagne. 'Perhaps,' said Whitaker quietly, 'now is the time for us to withdraw.'

Mrs Dalgleish waved an arm for them to join her. 'Oh, Mr Whitaker,' she said, her face radiant, 'here is a gentleman who saw me perform. *Champagne, monsieur?'*

'Merci, Madame,' said the old gentleman, accepting the glass with pleasure.

'You did not see me singing in "La Bohème"?' said Mrs Dalgleish eagerly. 'I did not do "Bohème" in Paris. In Budapest . . . but never in Paris.'

'In Budapest . . .' said the old man slowly.

'Oh!' cried Mrs Dalgleish. 'You saw me sing in Budapest? Oh, you are so lucky. Two, dear, will you please drive Mr Whitaker and Billy wherever they want to go. I will remain here with my new friend.'

'Goodbye, then . . .' began Billy, but Whitaker shook his head at him. 'We'll see her again,' he said. Even as he spoke, Mrs Dalgleish rose to her feet, crossed the grass towards them and embraced them both. 'Goodbye, *dear* friends,' she said. 'You will forgive me? But it is so long since anybody knew me. I thought London a cold, unloving place. But it contained this dear, dear gentleman. One, give him some more champagne.' She returned to the table to offer cold Scotch salmon to her guest.

Whitaker and Billy followed Two to the yellow Rolls. He opened the door for them politely enough, but, as they climbed in, he said, 'Aye, that's right. Get a free ride out of her. That's what everyone does.'

'I beg your pardon?' said Whitaker.

'And I beg yours,' said Two, slamming the door on them and climbing into the driver's seat. 'It's just that I'm thinking she's a nice enough woman without everyone always sucking up to her for her money. That old git that's with her now . . . I doubt he's ever clapped eyes on her. Just out for what he can get.'

'But he is making her happy,' said Whitaker.

'Aye, but for how long?' said the chauffeur. He started the engine. 'Where to?'

'First to the hotel to collect our luggage, I suppose?' said Whitaker to Billy. Billy nodded. Whitaker gave the name of the hotel to the chauffeur, who put the car into gear and drove off. 'Why was she so anxious to see you anyway?' he said suspiciously.

'We're friends,' said Billy.

'Oh, aye? That's what the German chappy said when he called. If he was a friend why did she cry for twenty-four hours after he left?'

Billy looked quickly at Whitaker. 'What was his name?' he said nonchalantly to the back of Two's head.

'I don't know. Oh, wait, I did hear it, on account of him telephoning to someone abroad. You see what I mean? I think he just came to Scotland to use the phone. I remember he said the name of some sportsman... a swimmer... Spitz! That's it, Mark Spitz. It was a name like that.'

At the picnic table, Konrad Spetz sat in one of the folding chairs and Mrs Dalgleish in another. The old man stood beside Mrs Dalgleish, his brow furrowed, his hands clasping and unclasping. 'I am so... sorry,' he said. 'I was told... by this gentleman... that it was a little joke you would enjoy.'

'Oh, I did,' said Mrs Dalgleish too brightly, smiling too widely. 'See how I laughed. It has made my eyes to water and my make-upping to run. Thank you so much. You're sure you would not like more food?'

'Madam,' said the old man with quiet dignity, 'If I had heard you sing it would have been a great privilege. It is my regret that I never did.'

'Perhaps Madam would sing for you now?' said Spetz. 'She's been longing for an audience for years.'

Mrs Dalgleish waved her hand in a dismissing gesture. 'I have not the music,' she said, her voice hoarse with tears, her eyes swimming. 'Besides, the cold air has got into my throat.' She looked up at the old man apologetically. 'You understand?'

He nodded. Then he put his hand into the pocket of his coat and withdrew a five pound note. He placed in on the table in front of Spetz. 'Your money, sir,' he said. 'I am not part of your "little joke".'

'Go, then,' said Spetz, pocketing the money. 'I have business with this lady.'

'No, Kurt,' said Mrs Dalgleish. 'You have no business with me.

I have delivered your message as you requested. It is finished.'

'Goodbye, Madam,' said the old man, with his slight bow, his face showing obvious distress.

'Goodbye,' said Mrs Dalgleish graciously.

The old man walked slowly away. Spetz watched him go and then gave a helpless shrug. 'I wanted him to make you happy,' he said.

'When will you learn,' said Mrs Dalgleish, 'that falsehoods never make you happy? You cannot buy happiness, Kurt.'

'And . . . how was Billy?' said Spetz.

'What is Billy to you?'

He smiled suddenly. An engaging smile. 'The son I never had,' he said.

'Poor Kurt,' said Mrs Dalgleish. 'You are more unhappy than any of us.'

'He doesn't know who I am, does he?'

'How could he? You do not know yourself who you are.' She rose to her feet. 'I am not afraid of you any more,' she said. She laughed. 'Shall I tell you why? Because of that good old man. He paid you back, Kurt. It is as easy as that.' She looked down at him where he sat and said, politely but very firmly, 'I do not wish for your company. I thank you for it—and I return it.' She raised her voice. 'Arthur!'

The black chauffeur, Number One, moved towards them.

'It is Arthur, isn't it?'

'Yes, Madam.'

'The gentleman is leaving.' She turned and walked away from the two men. After a while the sound of the returning Rolls made her look round. Chauffeur Two parked the car and went to help One clear the picnic table. Billy and Whitaker climbed out of the car and hurried towards her. Of Spetz there was no sign.

'I know,' said Billy, as he reached her. 'I know who it is. I know he was here. You should have told me.'

Mrs Dalgleish looked at him for a long moment. Then she said, 'That old man had seen me perform. Isn't that wonderful? He had heard me sing.'

She linked arms with Whitaker, who gave her a benevolent smile. 'Do you think I should buy the Albert Hall, Mr Whitaker?' she said. 'Just for the night? I know it would cost a canny penny. But I'm sure Mr Dalgleish would want it.' She linked her other arm through Billy's. 'And Billy,' she said. 'You could perform. Your debut and my . . . farewell. William Toth and Lila Tzech.' She shook her head. 'No, I'm sorry. I think I'd better have first billing. Not for me, you understand, but for my public. They expect it. You don't mind?'

Billy smiled at her with real affection. 'No, of course not,' he said.

'You have so much time for top billing,' said Mrs Dalgleish.

'Konrad Spetz,' said Billy, more to himself than to either of them. 'Kurt Gruber is Konrad Spetz. It all fits.'

Mrs Dalgleish frowned. 'I do not know that name, Billy,' she said, then instantly drifted back into her dream world, drawing them unprotestingly with her. 'So much time in front of you, Billy,' she said. 'Oh! The life of an artist! It is beyond imagining! And that is who we are—*artists!*'

Chapter Twenty-One

Just over two weeks later, Whitaker and Miss Price flew to Salzburg to attend the wedding of Anna and Gunter. Anna met them at the airport, collecting them from the passenger lounge in an apologetic flurry. 'I'm late, I'm late, I'm so sorry,' she said, hugging each in turn and shepherding them out to her car. 'If the truth is told, I should have left the studio earlier. I must be the only bride in history who is more worried about the delivery date of a book than the actual wedding!'

'How's Billy?' said Whitaker, as they settled themselves in the car.

'All right,' said Anna. 'He left you a note.' She handed it over her shoulder to Whitaker who, despite Miss Price's protests, was in the back seat.

'What does he say?' said Miss Price.

'Very little,' said Whitaker.

'Typical!'

'Sorry not to be there to meet you,' Whitaker read aloud. 'I'll be back for the big day, and all explanations then. Love to Pricey.' He refolded the note. 'Hm!' he said.

'With Billy that could mean almost anything...' said Miss Price uneasily.

'Now don't worry,' said Anna, driving off. 'He's fine.'

'Where is he?' said Whitaker.

Anna laughed. 'He thinks I don't know, but I do. He's gone ski-ing.'

'Ski-ing!'

'Don't sound so scandalized, Vincent. It's a great temptation this time of the year. And he had no classes this weekend.'

'Ski-ing with whom?' said Whitaker.

'The man who got him the job at the café. You know? Herr Spetz.'

'The fool!' said Whitaker. 'Where?'

'I don't know,' said Anna. 'He didn't say. I only know he's with Herr Spetz because I saw them leave together. Does it matter?'

'I'm afraid it does,' said Whitaker quietly, 'yes.'

'Well, maybe Gunter will know,' said Anna. 'He's arriving from Munich this evening.'

Billy had received the invitation from Konrad Spetz with extraordinarily mixed feelings. Since hearing Hilde's story on the ramparts of the Hohensalzburg, Kurt Gruber had grown in his imagination from a misty and mysterious figure into an evil man, a dangerous man, a murderer whose next victim was likely to be Billy himself. Konrad Spetz, on the other hand, had, from the first meeting, shown himself to be a kindly humorous man who had become sufficiently fond of him to give him a job, encourage his music, and at last to take him on a ski-ing trip. Despite what he now knew, Billy found it almost impossible to fuse the two men into one in his mind. Part of him accepted the invitation in order to precipitate a confrontation with Kurt Gruber—but part of him accepted because he liked Konrad Spetz and felt at ease in his company.

Spetz owned the small ski resort, which was based on a pretty Austrian village where he had a home and, it turned out, a gentle Austrian wife called Magda. When he wasn't travelling on business, he said, he divided his time between his flat above the Café Salz and this peaceful place, which was never over-run with tourists, even at the height of the season.

He handed Billy over to his chief instructor, Anton, and settled himself at a table outside the café at the foot of the slopes, to watch, and to buy Billy a drink when he took a break from his efforts.

'Tops down,' he said cheerfully, raising his glass of beer.

'What!' said Billy.

Spetz laughed. 'Well it's no sillier than "bottoms up",' he said. He stretched himself luxuriously. 'Ah, I feel good today. Maybe I go up the slopes and show you what ski-ing really is.'

'Why not?' said Billy.

Spetz hit his lame leg. 'Because of this,' he said.

'Why are you lame?' said Billy. 'What happened?'

'An old war wound!'

'Which war?'

Spetz shook his head, smiling. 'It is not polite for the English and the Germans to speak of war,' he said. 'The war of life! You know, I was a very good ski-ier.'

'But now not at all?'

'Oh, sometimes. Sometimes. It is still possible.'

Billy downed his beer. 'I'd better get back to my class,' he said.

He was with the beginners. Anton was testing them out on the nursery slopes, discovering the abilities of each. Billy came down the slope last. He moved fast and gracefully and then swung to a neat stop in front of Anton, grinning with pleasure.

'You sure you never ski-ied before?' said Anton.

'I didn't say I hadn't.'

'You have?'

'A bit,' said Billy. 'But not for years.'

Anton looked at him unsmilingly. 'So,' he said, 'What you doing with the beginners? Trying to make me look foolish?'

'No,' said Billy, his grin fading. 'I didn't think I'd remember any of it, that's all.'

'So, OK, you remember,' said Anton. 'Tomorrow I take you up to the high slopes. See how you do there, clever one!'

'I'm not that good,' said Billy uncertainly.

Anton looked at him with an expression that bordered on dislike—then he turned his back, removed his skis and wandered over to join Spetz at his table. Billy shrugged to himself and set off up the nursery slopes once more. Anton glared after him until he was well out of range, then turned his frown on Spetz. 'What is he doing here?' he said. 'How much does he know?'

'I don't know,' said Spetz calmly.

'But you will find out?' said Anton.

'And then what? Kill him? Don't you think that would be a little like pointing the finger at me?'

Anton squinted up at the distant snow-covered slopes. 'Accidents are always happening in the mountains,' he said. 'Particularly to big-shot beginners who think they know all about ski-ing when they don't know a thing.'

'Poor Anton!' said Spetz. 'You're afraid of him. He's just a boy.'

Anton rapped on the wooden table with his knuckles. 'I like being free, Herr Spetz,' he said. 'One wrong word and I could end up in prison. Why did you invite him here?'

'I like him,' said Spetz, quite simply. 'And I like it here. Go back to work, Anton, no harm will come to you. Go.'

That evening, Billy stood in Konrad Spetz' living-room, his music propped on a borrowed stand in front of him, and played the flute. Spetz leaned against the mantlepiece, smoking a pipe and listening. When Billy had finished the piece, Spetz said, 'It does not bore you? Playing for me?'

'No,' said Billy. 'I have to practice anyway. This is the piece I'm going to play at the wedding.'

'Ah yes,' said Spetz. 'I remember, you told me.' He smiled. 'I hope they pay you well?'

Billy looked at him in some surprise. 'They're my friends,' he said.

The door opened and Magda came rather diffidently into the room. She had the gentle rounded good looks that were somehow typically Austrian and she dressed in the traditional dirndl and apron. *'Telefon für Dich,'* she said to her husband.

Spetz smiled at her and nodded. 'I am wanted on the telephone,' he said to Billy. 'I will not be long. Play for Magda.' He went out of the door, closing it behind him.

Magda moved over to sit by the fire. 'You play,' she said shyly. 'It is good.'

'I'm studying... in Salzburg,' said Billy.

'Ja, ja,' said Magda. 'Konrad tell me all the time about Billy. You will come often here?'

'I... don't know.'

'Yes? Why not? It would be good. My husband goes very often away. With you here—I think he is here more.'

'Have you been married long?' said Billy.

A very slight frown passed across her face. 'Why?'

'Just curious,' said Billy, embarrassed.

'You play now?' said Magda. She busied herself piling logs on to the fire, looking away from him and cutting off further conversation. Billy played the piece through again, aware that she stopped fussing with the logs and listened to him with evident pleasure. 'That is good,' she said when he had finished. She smiled rather wistfully at him. 'Yes, we are married a long time,' she said. 'So long you could be our son, I think. But we have no children. It is sadness.' She sighed. 'I used to think Konrad did not want the children—but perhaps that was only because we could not have them. I do not really know Konrad. Sometimes he goes away and I do not know when he is coming back. He has spoken to you of me?'

'Yes,' said Billy, too quickly, 'often.'

'No,' said Magda gently. 'I think not. I have lived always in this village you know. When Konrad first came here he was not well. His leg...'

What happened to his leg?'

'It broke. He did not have it joined properly.' She put her head on one side. 'You ask many questions.

'Do I?' said Billy awkwardly.

'All the time,' said Magda. 'I understand that. Konrad is all questions with no answers. What is your family name, Billy? I do not know it.'

'Toth,' said Billy, watching the expression that passed across her face. 'You're surprised?'

'No,' said Magda hastily. 'You play now.' She rose and began to walk towards the door. As she reached it, Konrad Spetz came in. 'I am going to bed now,' said Magda. 'Goodnight, Billy.'

'Goodnight, Frau Spetz.'

'Gute nacht, Liebling,' said Konrad as she passed him. He crossed to the fire again. 'She was talking to you,' he said to Billy. 'You are honoured. She does not talk much.' He stared thoughtfully into the fire. 'That was Hans on the phone,' he said. 'He tells me your friends were looking for you, at the café.' He turned away from the fire and looked very directly at Billy. 'You know, don't you?' he said.

'Know?' said Billy, playing for time.

'I think so,' said Spetz. 'It's odd. I knew it could come to this—and yet I can't begin it.' He spoke almost lightly. 'Can you?'

Billy felt himself stiffen all over. He felt as though he was standing awkwardly, not balanced right. 'You are Kurt Gruber...' he said nervously.

'Kurt Gruber is dead,' said the older man evenly.

'No! My parents are dead,' said Billy. 'You killed them, Kurt Gruber.'

'It was an accident,' said Kurt. 'You want to know?'

Billy felt the tears welling behind the eyes. 'That's why I've been looking for you for so long,' he said.

Kurt nodded. 'It would have been better to have left the past—for all of us,' he said. 'You were a happy English schoolboy. Why ever change it?'

'I didn't have any choice. My "happy English parents" died.'

'I understand. And you wanted...'

'To know about my real parents.'

Kurt leaned forward and tapped out his pipe in the grate, very slowly. 'Tania and Jerri,' he said thoughtfully. 'Nice couple. Rather ordinary, really. Like so many ordinary people, living in an extraordinary world.'

Billy chucked the flute down on to the sofa behind him. 'You killed them!' he said. Anger, pain, and relief that the awful moment he had sought was here at last were making his voice sound strangled and hoarse.

'What are you going to do with me, Billy?' said Kurt, his voice as calm and friendly as it had been from the beginning. 'Turn me over to the police?' He got up and went to the dresser behind his chair and began to refill his pipe from a tin of tobacco. 'They should be here soon. Your friends will go for them. It shouldn't be difficult to find out where Herr Spetz of the Café Salz has gone to.'

'You tried to kill *me.*'

'No. I wanted only to warn you.'

'You killed your mother,' said Billy, suddenly desperate to arouse some emotion in the other man. He succeeded up to a point. 'No!' said Kurt sharply. Then, more softly, 'Perhaps I am guilty. But she took her own life.'

'And Hilde, you killed Hilde,' said Billy. 'She was going to tell me. She sent me a letter. She said you knew everything. You *killed her.*'

Kurt lit his pipe, in silence. 'Yes, I did kill Hilde,' he said at length. 'I had to.'

'Had to!' said Billy. 'To protect yourself.'

'And Magda,' said Kurt. He moved back to the fireside and leaned on the mantlepiece. Billy watched him, listened to him, with a sickening sense of unreality. Even now, the pleasant face of Spetz refused to turn into the evil face he had imagined for Kurt Gruber. 'I think the saddest thing I know,' said Kurt, 'is to love someone and for them not to believe it. That's me with Magda. I came to this village after...after the Toths' accident. It was useful for me that Kurt Gruber became officially dead and I could take the name Konrad Spetz. He was a man I was helping to escape from East Germany.' He shrugged. 'He died on the journey. I didn't at once mean to take Jerri Toth's identity. Originally I just had it in reserve. It is useful sometimes to be several people, you know. I came to Austria because I could not see my mother, or my wife Hilde. To them I was dead. And here, Billy, I met Magda. I fell in love. I started to use Jerri Toth's name for my other activities. It really did seem like a new beginning. But! We get careless. Hilde and I walked slap into each other in the Domplatz.' He shook his head and chuckled slightly to himself. 'We came, shall we say, to an arrangement. She got a lot of money out of me, over the years. The last thing she wanted was for it to stop. The last thing I wanted was to lose Magda. Everything was fine—until you arrived. You were a great complication, Billy. You made each of us face up to the realities. I wonder if my mother's suicide is not some of your doing? Hm?'

Billy said nothing.

'Hilde was my youth,' said Spetz. 'Magda—my maturity. When I knew what mattered. How often, I wonder, does maturity come too late?'

'Why did you want people to think Kurt Gruber was dead?' said Billy, subdued.

'What a very naive question,' said Kurt. 'He was a marked man, you could say. A little incident with a border guard which the guard, unfortunately, did not survive. The police were hounding me. Then one night in 1963 I drove through a barrier on the frontier—bullets screaming—your mother at my side and Jerri Toth hiding behind the back seat. It had all gone wrong. Tania's father had died before we could get him out, and then when we came to cross the border the guards moved more quickly than I had hoped. So. I leaped clear and BOOM!' He made a slightly apologetic face. 'The car was always booby-trapped for emergencies,' he said. 'There were two bodies in the wreck. One of them had to be Kurt Gruber.' He waited for a reaction from Billy but got none. 'How much does your friend, the old man, know?' he said.

Billy hesitated. 'As much as I do,' he said.

'Pity,' said Kurt. Then unexpectedly he raised his voice. 'Come in, Magda,' he said. 'You must be cold in that passage.'

Magda ran in through the partly open door. Tears were streaming down her face. She stopped just short of her husband and looked up at him. 'How perfect,' he said sadly, 'That you should hear it through Jerri Toth's son—Jerri Toth who gave me the freedom to start again. I did love you, you know. All the time.'

Rapid footsteps approached the door and Anton burst into the room. He caught Kurt by the arm and spoke excitedly to him in German. After a moment, Magda joined in the conversation. Billy, unable to understand, could only watch Anton's nervous, angry gestures, Magda's obvious distress, and Kurt's apparently unshakeable calm. At last Kurt turned to him. 'Hans has given this address,' he said in English. 'He was never the strongest of characters. I am afraid, Billy, you are going to have to buy me some time. At first light you must come up the mountain with Anton and me.'

'Ah!' said Anton, a grim pleasure coming to his face. 'Now we find out how good you are on skis!'

In the chill of the early morning, Whitaker, Miss Price and Anna stood together at the bottom of the chair lift at Herr Spetz' modest ski resort. They were looking up at the apparently empty white mountainside, their eyes narrowed against the glare of the snow. Beyond them, and nearer to the telephone which connected the foot of the chair lift with the small restaurant at its top, several uniformed Austrian police conferred discreetly with a senior officer.

'What are the police *doing*?' said Miss Price.

'I don't know,' said Whitaker crossly. Then he looked at her, standing beside him in her woolly coat and fur hat, staring fearfully up at the shining white slopes. He put his arm round her. 'At least he's alive,' he said gently.

'How do we know?'

'They can see him through their binoculars,' said Whitaker. 'You want to look?'

'No,' said Miss Price. 'I want it all to be over. Where's

Gunter?'

'I don't know,' said Anna, standing at her other side. 'He went off with two or three of the police.' She took Miss Price's arm. 'Pricey, come and sit down.

'No, no,' said Miss Price, shrugging herself free like a frightened child. 'I'd rather be here.'

At that moment one of the policemen called out, 'Herr Whitaker!'

'That's me,' Whitaker called back, walking hurriedly but carefully over the snow towards him. While Miss Price and Anna watched, the policeman handed the telephone receiver to Whitaker and a brief conversation followed. After a few moments, Whitaker rejoined them.

'Vincent?' said Miss Price. 'What was all that?'

'It was Billy,' said Whitaker. 'The police wanted me to identify his voice over the telephone. He's all right and he says they mean him no harm. They're . . . holding him hostage, I suppose.'

'But there's nowhere they can go,' said Miss Price. 'They have to come down here.'

'Not necessarily,' said Anna. She had raised her own binoculars to her eyes and was scanning the mountainside. 'They could go over the tops. There'll be skis up there.' Suddenly she raised the binoculars higher. 'There are people, right up above them,' she said. 'It's Gunter . . . I think. And the Alpine police.'

Whitaker frowned. 'He did mention there was a way over from the ski lift in the next valley,' he said. Miss Price turned her back on the scene, not knowing whether she wanted to watch or not.

The small restaurant at the top of the ski lift was closed, but there was a certain amount of activity outside it. Kurt and Anton and, under their instructions, Billy, were all fixing skis and preparing to move away.

'We make for that dip, there,' said Anton, pointing. 'Then follow down into the low crevasse. From there the going is a bit rough until we reach the tree line. Meyerhoff will have a car waiting for us in the next valley. We can make it, easy!'

'And then what?' said Billy angrily. 'Just keep running?'

'Don't worry,' said Anton, sarcastically. 'We have spent our lives disappearing. It's what we are best at!' He cast a somewhat hostile glance at Billy, then set off diagonally across the snow.

'So, Billy,' said Kurt, making a last adjustment to a ski and standing upright. 'We must part. You see? I am not going to harm you.' An expression of great sadness passed briefly across his face. 'You are the son I always wanted,' he said. 'And if I really was Jerri Toth...'

'But you're not,' said Billy. 'You never could be. You can't borrow people like... things!'

'Very interesting, Billy,' said Kurt, 'But I'm afraid I must go.'

'I won't let you,' said Billy desperately. He flung himself at Kurt, as if to knock him down, but Kurt caught him easily, tipped him off balance, and threw him down into the snow. 'You crazy?' he said angrily. 'You are out of your depth, Billy...'

'Maybe,' said Billy, struggling to his feet. 'But I've got to stop you because if I don't...'

Far off across the snow a cry of 'Kurt!' came from Anton. They both looked towards his figure, tiny in the distance. He was pointing up the mountainside, then he turned and ski-ied off at speed. Billy and Kurt looked where he had been pointing and saw four skiers coming down the mountain towards them.

'Damn!' said Kurt.

'... because if I don't,' said Billy, 'I'll never be free of you. Jerri will never be free of you.'

'Jerri is dead, you fool,' said Kurt. Despite the approaching line of ski-ers he seemed almost reluctant to end the confrontation.

'Then let him *be*,' said Billy.

'I must go,' said Kurt. He pulled his snow goggles down over his eyes. 'No doubt one day we'll meet again.' He turned and began to ski rapidly away, in the wake of Anton.

'No!' said Billy. 'It must end here!'

Behind him the leading ski-er called out, in Gunter's voice, 'Billy! Billy! Hold back.'

Billy paused for just long enough to shout, 'They've got a car waiting in the next valley.' He ignored Gunter's cry of 'Leave him to us,' and pushed off in pursuit of Kurt, who had swerved away and was making for a lower crest than Anton.

Behind him, the Alpine police divided—two following Anton, who was now out of sight, and one accompanying Gunter in Billy's tracks.

Kurt had vanished and Billy lost all sense of fear in his need to catch up with him, to stop him, to wind up the gathering tension of so many, many months. He shot over a great crest of snow—and only just managed to stop. For ahead of him a series of rough outcrops of rock led straight to a sharply inclined, near perpendicular rockfall. As he slewed to a stop, only feet from the edge, Billy saw Kurt—he had gone over, but had managed to throw himself back against the rock. Now he hung by his hands, unable to get a sufficient grip to pull himself up. Hastily, Billy got rid of his skis and crawled to the edge of the drop. 'Kurt!' he said.

'No, Billy, get back,' said Kurt.

Billy lay down on his stomach and stretched out an arm. 'I can't reach you,' he said hopelessly.

Kurt's face, white and tense as it was, became puzzled. 'You want to?' he said.

Billy edged himself painfully nearer to the lip of the drop. He reached his arm lower and managed to catch Kurt's hand. 'Why, Billy?' said the older man. 'Be free of me...'

Their hands linked and locked together—but Kurt's other hand was already slipping and his weight was too much for the precarious hold he had on the icy rock and on Billy. His hand slid out of Billy's and he fell. Billy, trying desperately to retain his grip on the hand as it pulled free of his almost fell too, but Gunter had arrived on the scene behind him and caught him just as his own weight threatened to drag him down also. Gunter pulled him upright and led him away from the brink. 'It's all right,' he was saying, 'it's all right. You're safe now.'

'Kurt!' shouted Billy. The cry echoed down the great rockfall and came back to them, broken up by the mountain—and unanswered.

Gunter and Billy rode down in the chair lift, side by side. Billy's face was white and he did not speak. Gunter watched him, but did not interrupt his thoughts. Billy was not seeing the mountains, or the other chairs which lurched down the slope ahead of them. He was seeing a border post on a misty night. A car racing for the barrier, crashing through it, splinters flying high. Border guards leaping clear, recovering, firing. The car door opening and a man's figure half-falling, half-jumping out. Rolling. The car speeding ahead. Guards pursuing. The lone man crouching into the undergrowth, unseen. The booby-trapped car skidding, slewing sideways, exploding into an orange flower of flame, crashing head-on into a wall. Border guards approaching. The car burning vividly against the grey night. The hidden man, well back from the road, watching. Then, still crouching low, limping away, unnoticed.

The chair lift reached the ground and Gunter caught at Billy's arm. Together they slipped off the chair and ducked aside as it passed on its way. Billy's eyes came back into focus. He saw mountains, white calm mountains against clear blue sky. He saw Anna run to Gunter and put her arms around his neck. He saw Whitaker, walking towards him across the tightly packed snow, Miss Price just behind him.

Whitaker stopped. 'Dear boy!' he said. His voice sounded odd. Then he stepped forward and embraced Billy. 'Don't *ever* do a thing like that again.'

'I promise,' said Billy.

Whitaker released him. 'Did you . . . find what you were looking for?'

Billy nodded. He could not speak. Miss Price moved forward, tearful with relief. Billy put his arms round her.

'No more searching?' said Whitaker.

'It's over,' said Billy. Whitaker was standing at his side, one hand on his shoulder. Miss Price was on the other side, watching his face. 'All over,' said Billy.